THE BIG BAD WOLFE FAMILY

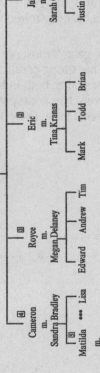

Cameron Wolfe, Sr. m. Matilda "Maddy" Simmons

[4] Cameron
m.
Sandra Bradley

[5] Matilda *** **Lisa**
m.
David Macdonough

[3] Royce
m.
Megan Delaney

Edward Andrew Tim

[2] Eric
m.
Tina Kranas

Mark Todd Brian

[1] Jake
m.
Sarah Cummings

Justin Jeffrey

*** indicates twins

1 – WOLFE WAITING
2 – WOLFE WATCHING } BIG, BAD WOLFE: Ready to Wed? On sale December 1999
3 – WOLFE WANTING
4 – WOLFE WEDDING } BIG, BAD WOLFE: At the Altar! On sale February 2000
5 – WOLFE WINTER

JOAN HOHL

was born, raised and still lives in southwestern Pennsylvania. The winner of numerous awards, including the Romance Writers of America Golden Medallion Award and two *Romantic Times Magazine* Reviewer's Choice Awards, Ms. Hohl has penned over forty novels and boasts over five million copies of her books in print!

As one of the romance genre's most popular authors, she is well-known for her strong conflicts, dramatic style and her heady sensuality, both in her historical and contemporary novels. Her widespread appeal proves that she is indeed a master storyteller.

JOAN HOHL

BIG, BAD WOLFE: AT THE ALTAR!

Silhouette Books

Published by Silhouette Books

America's Publisher of Contemporary Romance

If you purchased this book without a cover you should be aware that this book is stolen property. It was reported as "unsold and destroyed" to the publisher, and neither the author nor the publisher has received any payment for this "stripped book."

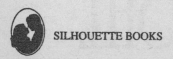 SILHOUETTE BOOKS

ISBN 0-373-21703-X

by Request

BIG, BAD WOLFE: AT THE ALTAR!

Copyright © 2000 by Harlequin Books S.A.

The publisher acknowledges the copyright holders of the individual works as follows:

WOLFE WANTING
Copyright © 1994 by Joan Hohl

WOLFE WEDDING
Copyright © 1996 by Joan Hohl

All rights reserved. Except for use in any review, the reproduction or utilization of this work in whole or in part in any form by any electronic, mechanical or other means, now known or hereafter invented, including xerography, photocopying and recording, or in any information storage or retrieval system, is forbidden without the written permission of the editorial office, Silhouette Books, 300 East 42nd Street, New York, NY 10017 U.S.A.

All characters in this book have no existence outside the imagination of the author and have no relation whatsoever to anyone bearing the same name or names. They are not even distantly inspired by any individual known or unknown to the author, and all incidents are pure invention.

This edition published by arrangement with Harlequin Books S.A.

® and TM are trademarks of Harlequin Books S.A., used under license. Trademarks indicated with ® are registered in the United States Patent and Trademark Office, the Canadian Trade Marks Office and in other countries.

Visit us at www.romance.net

Printed in U.S.A.

CONTENTS

Dear Reader,

Hello. I'm back with another volume of my BIG, BAD WOLFE series.

If you'll recall, the first volume contained the stories about the youngest and second youngest of the four Wolfe brothers, Jake and Eric, and their respective ladies, Sarah and Tina. This volume, subtitled *At the Altar!*, is comprised of the third and fourth books, *Wolfe Wanting* and *Wolfe Wedding*.

In *Wolfe Wanting,* you'll meet the second oldest Wolfe brother, Royce, a Pennsylvania State Police officer, stationed in the Pocono Mountain region, and Megan, the beautiful illustrator in danger from a stalker. But it's Royce who is in real danger of losing his heart to Megan.

In *Wolfe Wedding,* you'll meet the oldest and toughest of the Wolfe brothers, Cameron. He's an FBI agent in Denver, and soon meets Sandra, a cool, beautiful lawyer, threatened by the irate ex-husband of a former client. Things heat up between them in a remote mountain cabin.

I hope you enjoy reading about the Wolfe brothers as much as I enjoyed giving them life.

Best,

WOLFE WANTING

One

She was a mess.

Royce Wolfe clenched his teeth and gave another yank on the driver's-side door of the mangled sports car. A grunt of satisfaction vibrated his throat as the door popped open. The interior light flashed on. Pushing the door back, he stepped into the opening.

The woman was slumped over the steering wheel, her face concealed by a mass of long, dark red hair. A frown of annoyed disapproval tugged at his brows and lips.

She was not wearing the seat belt.

Royce shook his head and reached inside, grimacing at the faint but unmistakable scent of alcohol. Booze and rain-slick roads were a deadly combination.

Brushing the long tresses aside, he pressed his fingertips to her throat. The pulse was rapid, but strong.

The deflated air bag, now draped limply over the wheel, had very likely saved her life.

The woman moaned, and her eyelashes fluttered.

"It's all right," Royce said, giving her shoulder a comforting pat. "Help's on the way," he assured her, catching the sound of sirens in the distance, swiftly approaching from opposite directions.

"Wha-what hap—?" The woman blinked, then squeezed her eyes shut, in obvious pain.

"You went off the road," Royce said, answering her unfinished question. "Crashed into the guardrail."

And you were going like hell. Royce kept the disgusted observation to himself. The information would go into his report, but right now, she had enough to contend with.

A drop of water fell from the wide brim of his hat and splashed onto her pale cheek. The woman flinched. Royce pulled back, away from the opening. Cold rain pattered on his hat and slicker.

March. Where was spring?

Royce shivered, and shifted his bleak gaze, first back the way he had come, then toward town. The wail of the sirens was louder, closer, as the vehicles converged, lights flashing atop the ambulance and police car.

Well, at least it isn't snow, he thought, shooting a glance at the woman as the vehicles came to a screeching stop—the ambulance facing him, opposite the sports car, the other vehicle, Pennsylvania State Police emblazoned on its side, directly behind his own car.

"She's alive," Royce said to the paramedic who jumped from the driver's side.

"What you got here, Sergeant?" the police officer asked, loping up to Royce.

"Hi, Evans," Royce said, acknowledging him. "Female, all alone," he said, sending a spray of rainwater flying with a jerk of his head toward the car. "Shot out of Pine Tree Drive, back there." Water ran in a narrow stream from the brim of his hat as he inclined his head to indicate the side road, less than a quarter of a mile back. "Cut right in front of me, doing at least seventy. She lost it almost at once. I had no sooner taken off after her in pursuit when she plowed into the rail."

"Drinking?" Evans asked, stepping closer to the sports car to give it the once-over.

"I caught a whiff of alcohol." Royce shrugged. "But I don't know if it was above the legal level." He raised his voice to the two paramedics working to ease the woman from the car. "You guys come across a purse?"

"Yeah," the man who had entered the vehicle

from the passenger side replied. "Just found it." He handed it to the man outside, who passed it to Royce.

"Thanks," he muttered. "Can you tell if she's going to be all right?"

"Can't see anything major from here," the paramedic said. "Won't know for sure until we get her out of here and back to the hospital."

"Need the jaws?" Royce asked, referring to the jawlike apparatus used to pry mangled metal apart, commonly called the Jaws of Life.

"Naw," he said. "She's regaining consciousness, and if she can move to help, there's enough room for her to slide out from between the wheel and the seat." The man ran a quick glance over the front of the car. "But I'm certain you're gonna need a wrecker for this heap."

"Yeah." Royce shared the man's opinion.

"I'll call for one, and get some flares set up," Evans offered, turning away. He took two steps, then turned back, a frown drawing his brows together. "Didn't you go off duty at eleven, Sergeant?"

"Supposed to," Royce answered. "I stayed to finish some paperwork, left the barracks around eleven-thirty. I was on my way home when this lady cut out of the road in front of me." While he was speaking, he kept an eye on the paramedics, monitoring their progress as they transferred the woman from the car to a gurney, then to the rear of the ambulance.

"How's she doing?" he asked.

"Okay," one of the men answered. "She managed to slide out, but she's lost consciousness again."

A gust of wind blew rain under the wide brim of his hat and into his face. Royce shivered.

"Why don't you go on home now?" Evans suggested. "I'll ask for assistance when I call for a wrecker, then I'll go on in to the hospital."

The rear ambulance door thunked shut. Royce started for his car, shaking his head. "Night like this, we need every man on the roads." He opened the door, shucked out of his slicker, then slid behind the wheel. It felt good to get out of the stiff coat and the pouring rain. "You wait here for the wrecker," he said, tossing the woman's purse and his hat onto the passenger's seat. "I'll follow the ambulance into town. I live only a couple of blocks away from the hospital. I'll go home after I've talked to the woman, and I'll file a report in the morning."

"Whatever you say, Sergeant." Evans sketched a salute of thanks for being spared the chore of the extra paperwork, then strode to his car.

Royce tailed the ambulance into the small town of Conifer, Pennsylvania, and pulled alongside the covered, brightly lit entrance to Conifer General

Hospital's emergency unit, where the ambulance had parked.

Having been alerted to expect an accident victim, a nurse and two orderlies were awaiting their arrival. Since Royce's assistance was obviously not required, he took a few minutes to fish the woman's wallet from her purse before stepping out of the car. Flipping it open, he read the information on her driver's license.

The first thing that caught his eye was her picture. It was not great, yet even with the inferior quality of the photograph, she was clearly not unattractive. Then his eyes shifted to her name.

Megan Delaney. Nice name, Royce thought absently, his eyes moving up the laminated card, past the issue date, to the medical restrictions. Must wear corrective lenses. Hmm... There had been no sign of glasses when he brushed her hair away from her face. Had they flown off on impact, or was she wearing contact lenses? Check it out.

His eyes moved again, skimming over the expiration date, classes, endorsements and driver ID number, and came to rest on birth date.

The woman was twenty-seven years and three months old—eight years his junior.

Old enough to know better than to drink and drive, Royce thought, especially on a rain-slick road.

His eyes skipped over the top line of information, and settled on one tiny section. Blue eyes. Big surprise, for a redhead he reflected, closing the wallet.

Royce glanced up at the sound of the automatic entrance doors swishing open. With the nurse leading the way, the orderlies were pushing the gurney into the building. Gripping the purse, he stepped out of the car, gave a casual wave to the paramedics and followed the group inside.

"Hey, Sarge!" a fresh-faced young nurse called out cheekily from behind the desk just inside the doors. "Don't tell me you've given up the desk job to go back on road duty again!"

"Okay, I won't tell you that," Royce drawled, flashing a teasing grin at her. "You want to hit the release?" he said, inclining his head toward the second set of automatic doors, which for safety reasons were activated by buttons accessible only to hospital personnel.

"Sure."

The doors parted, and with a murmured thank-you, Royce stepped through the opening.

"*Are* you back on highway duty?" the nurse called after him.

Royce paused in the opening, keeping the doors apart. "No," he answered. "I was on my way home when this woman crashed into the guardrail. And, since I was coming into town anyway..." He shrugged.

"Gotcha." The nurse turned her attention to a man who came limping up to the desk, but slyly observed, "By the way, Sarge, I must tell you that your red handbag definitely clashes with your uniform."

Responding to her teasing comment with a dry look, Royce continued past the doors, which closed behind him, and to the doorway of a long room containing a row of curtained cubicles. The orderlies were pushing the now-empty gurney from the last cubicle.

"Hi, Sarge," one of the men said as Royce passed by on his way to the cubicle. "Haven't seen you in here for a while. Where have you been hiding out?"

"Behind a desk," Royce answered. "Where it's dry and warm. No mangled bodies. No blood. No gore."

"Nice work if you can get it," the other man said, grinning. As he pushed the gurney through the doorway, he called over his shoulder, "I just love your purse."

"Yeah." Royce didn't return the grin or respond to the good-natured gibe as he normally would have. This little jaunt to the hospital stirred too many unpleasant memories, strongly reminding him of his reasons for having accepted the desk job when it was offered to him six months ago.

Royce was a good cop. If pressed, he would have had to admit, without exaggeration or conceit, that he was a damn good cop. But, with over ten years with the state police, investigating robberies, working on drug busts and patrolling the highways, he had had his fill of trips to the hospital with torn, bleeding and sometimes dead bodies.

The day would come when, restless and tired of pushing papers, Royce would request a transfer back to highway patrol. But until that day arrived, he'd just as soon avoid the distinctive scents of disinfectant and medicine.

Royce wrinkled his nose at the assault on his senses by the familiar smell, and shoved the curtain aside.

"Doc Louis not here, Jill?" he asked the nurse, a middle-aged woman who had been on duty in Emergency for as long as he had been on duty in the Conifer district. She was standing by the gurney where the woman lay, taking her pulse.

The nurse frowned, concentrating on the pulse count. "Busy down the line," she said, gently laying the woman's arm by her side. "He's stitching a head wound."

"Accident?"

"No." Jill gave him a tired smile, and a shrug of resignation. "Knife fight in a barroom. As you can see, we're pretty busy, and stretched mighty thin. Dr. Hawk's splinting a finger—a slightly inebriated teenager slammed a car door on it." She sighed. "Just the usual Friday-night fun and games."

"Yeah." Royce grimaced.

The nurse frowned. "What are you doing here? I thought you were riding a desk now."

"I am." Royce suppressed his growing impatience; he was getting pretty tired of answering the same question. "I just happened to be close by when the lady decided to test the strength of the guardrail." He shifted his eyes to the ashen-faced woman. "She all right?"

"Looks like all surface injuries. A few cuts, abrasions, bruises—a lot of bruises—but..." She lifted her shoulders in another shrug. "I'm sure the doctor will want X rays after a more thorough examination."

Royce nodded.

The woman on the gurney moaned.

Jill gave her a sharp-eyed look. "She's coming around. If you'll stay here with her, make sure she doesn't roll off the gurney—" she moved past him "—I'll go see if I can take over for one of the doctors."

"Will do," Royce agreed. "Don't stop for a coffee break along the way...okay?"

She grinned at him. "Not even if I bring you a cup on the house?"

"No, thanks." He grimaced. "I've tasted what that machine passes off as coffee."

"It grows on you," she said, laughing, as she pushed aside the curtain.

"That's what I'm afraid of," he drawled, smiling at her retreating back.

A low moan sounded next to Royce, wiping the smile from his face. Turning, he placed her purse at the bottom end of the gurney, then moved closer to the other end to gaze down at the fragile-looking woman.

She moaned again. Then her eyelashes fluttered and lifted, and he found himself staring into incredibly lovely, if presently clouded, sapphire blue eyes.

The license photo did her a terrible disservice, Royce realized absently. Even with the nasty bruises marring the right side of her face, Megan Delaney was not merely attractive, she was flat-out, traffic-stopping gorgeous.

Facial bruises? Royce frowned, and took a closer look. Why hadn't the air bag protected her from—

She moaned again, louder this time, scattering his thoughts, demanding his full attention.

The clouds of confusion in her eyes were dissipating, and she moved, restlessly, in obvious pain.

Following the nurse's request, Royce stepped closer, until his thigh pressed against the gurney. Bending over her, he placed his right arm on the other side of the gurney to prevent her rolling off, onto the floor.

"It's all—" he began, but that was as far as he got in his attempt to reassure her, because she screamed, drowning the sound of his voice.

"Get away from me!"

Royce started, shocked by the sheer terror evidenced by Megan Delaney's shrill voice and fear-widened eyes. Her hands flew up defensively, and she began striking at his face. One of her fingernails, broken and jagged-edged, caught his skin, scratching his cheek from the corner of his right eye to his jaw.

"What the hell?" he exclaimed, jerking backward and grabbing her wrists to keep her hands still.

She continued to scream, struggling wildly against his hold. "Get away! Don't touch me!"

"What in the world is going on in here, Sergeant Wolfe?" The voice was sharp, authoritative, and definitely female. Recognizing it, Royce sighed with relief.

"Damned if I know, Dr. Hawk," he answered, shooting a baffled look at her as she came to a stop beside him. "She took one look at me and started screeching like a banshee." He winced as Megan Delaney let out another piercing cry. "Maybe you can do something with her." Releasing Megan's wrists, he moved aside to give the doctor access to the patient.

"Get him away!" Megan sobbed, clutching at the doctor's white lab coat. "Please, get him away!"

Dr. Hawk gave him a quick glance of appeal. "If you'd wait in the corridor?"

"Sure," Royce said, relieved to comply. Turning smartly, he strode from the cubicle, then from the room.

Shaken by the experience, by the injured woman's strange reaction to his attempt to help her, Royce stood in the corridor, unmindful of the usual Friday-night bustle and activity going on around him.

"What happened to your face?"

The startled-sounding question jerked Royce into awareness. He glanced around to meet Jill's surprise-widened eyes. "That woman in there attacked me," he said, his voice revealing his sense of amazement.

"Why?" Jill looked as baffled as he felt.

"Damned if I know." Royce shook his head, trying to collect his thoughts. "She opened her eyes, took one look at me, and began carrying on like a demented person, screaming and hitting me. Her nails scraped my face."

"I'll say," Jill observed, leaning toward him for a closer look at his face. "It's open. Come with me and—"

Royce cut her off, dismissing the scratch with a flicking hand movement. "It's nothing."

"It's open," Jill repeated in a no-nonsense tone. "It needs cleaning and an antiseptic." She drew a breath and leveled a hard stare at him. "Now come with me." It was not a request; it was a direct order.

Pivoting, Jill marched down the corridor with the erect bearing of a field marshal, obviously confident that Royce would meekly follow.

And he did. A smile quirked his lips as he trailed in the nurse's wake. Here he was, a sergeant in the Pennsylvania State Police, six feet five inches of trained law-enforcement officer, docilely obeying the dictates of a nurse who stood no more than five feet four inches in her rubber-soled shoes.

But she was a head nurse, Royce recalled, suppressing an impulse to chuckle. Besides, Jill had always reminded him of his mother. Not in appearance, for there was no physical resemblance between the two women, but in manner—kinda bossy, but gentle and caring.

Jill led the way into a small room at the end of the corridor, and indicated the examining table in the center of the floor.

"Have a seat," she said, turning to a cabinet placed close by, along one wall.

Sitting down on the very edge of the table, Royce watched with amusement as she collected cotton swabs, sterile packets of gauze, a plastic bottle of antiseptic and a small tube of antibiotic ointment.

"All that paraphernalia for a little scratch?" he asked in a teasing drawl.

Jill threw him a dry look. "Do I tell you how to conduct the business of law enforcement?"

"Point taken," he conceded, turning his head to allow her better access to his cheek.

Royce winced at the sting of whatever it was Jill swabbed on the cut to clean it.

"Big tough guy," she murmured, laughter woven inside her chiding tone.

"Don't push your luck, Jill." The warning was empty, and she knew it.

Jill laughed aloud. "What are you going to do if I push my luck?" she asked, smearing the ointment along the length of the scratch. "Throw me in the slammer?"

Royce grunted, but didn't answer; his bluff had been called. In truth, Jill's remark was straight on target. Royce had something of a reputation for being tough, simply because he *was* tough. But never, ever, did he assume the role of tough cop with women, even felons. It was not in his nature. Royce treated women, all women, with respect...even the ones who didn't deserve it.

"The ointment should do it," Jill said, breaking into his thoughts. "I think we can dispense with the bandage." She turned away to return the ointment to the cabinet.

"Thanks." Royce raised a hand to his cheek.

"Don't touch it!" Jill ordered, heaving an impatient sigh. "I just cleaned it, for goodness' sake. And now you want to put your dirty hands all over it."

Royce grinned at her. He couldn't help it. Jill

was the only female he knew who said "for goodness' sake" in that particular tone of exasperation. However, he did hastily pull his hand away from his face.

"Men." Jill shook her head as she returned to stand in front of him, preventing him from rising from the table. "So, *Sergeant* Wolfe," she said, with a heavy emphasis on the title, "what did you do in there to earn yourself that scratch?" She jerked her head to indicate the other room. "Did you start grilling that poor woman before she was fully conscious or something?"

"Of course not." Royce's sharp reply let her know he resented the charge. "I tried to reassure her that everything would be fine, but the minute I started to speak, she went nuclear on me." He shook his head in bewilderment. "I mean, she went off like a bomb, screaming and striking out at my face. Hell, I didn't know what to do with her, so I caught hold of her wrists. Fortunately, that's when Doc Hawk came into the room and rescued me."

Jill frowned. "Strange."

"Strange?" Royce mirrored her reflection. "Try *weird.* This has never happened to me before." He shrugged. "After ten years on the force, I've seen enough accident victims to understand shock and trauma. But damned if I've ever seen anyone fight against someone trying to help them."

"Neither have I," Jill said sympathetically.

"But she seems to have quieted down now." She smiled. "Dr. Hawk is very good at calming agitated patients."

"Yeah, I know. She's great." Royce moved restlessly.

Understanding his silent message, Jill stepped away from in front of him and headed for the door. "I think I'll go check out the situation."

"I'll go with you." Royce smiled and held up his hands placatingly when she shot him a narrow-eyed look. "Only as far as the corridor, I swear."

"Okay, let's go." She marched from the room.

Laughing to himself, Royce again trailed in her wake.

He cooled his heels for twenty-odd minutes, passing the time with the hospital personnel as they wandered by. At regular intervals, Royce sent sharp glances toward the door of the cubicled room, his impatience growing as he waited for some word from either the doctor or Jill. He was tired, and it was now past one-thirty in the morning.

Royce wanted to go home to bed. Leaning against the corridor wall, out of the way of the back-and-forth traffic, he yawned, stole another look at his watch, and contemplated storming into the room and the cubicle where the victim was confined. He was pushing away from the wall, determined to at least call Jill from the room, when the doctor came through the doorway, carrying the patient's chart and purse.

"I'm sorry to keep you waiting so long." Dr. Hawk offered him a tired smile. "But, when I explain, I'm certain you will understand the reason, Royce." Her use of his first name said much about the working friendship they had established.

"Problems, Virginia?" Royce arched his gold-tipped brows. "You sound troubled."

"She was attacked," she said, getting right to the point. "Before the crash."

"What?" Royce went rigid. "Was she—"

"No, she wasn't violated," she answered, before he had finished asking. "She managed to get away from the man. That's why her seat belt wasn't fastened." A grim smile curved her usually soft mouth. "She was thinking, rather wildly, about flight, not driver safety."

"And that's why she went wild with me."

"Yes. She opened her eyes, saw a large man looming over her, and..."

"Thought she was right back in the situation," Royce said, completing the explanation for her.

"Precisely."

"Bastard," he muttered.

"My sentiments exactly." Virginia Hawk expelled a deep sigh. "She is still in shock, traumatized."

Royce gave her a shrewd look. "Are you trying to tell me I can't question her?"

"You got it, Sarge," she said. "She is in no condition to be questioned. From my examination, I feel quite positive that her injuries are all external, but I'm having X rays done to confirm my opinion."

"So, if your diagnosis is confirmed, I'll talk to her afterward," he said. "I'll wait."

"No." She shook her head. "If my diagnosis is confirmed, I'm going to sedate her."

"My report, Virginia," he reminded her gently. "You know the rules."

She smiled. "I also know who is in charge here," she reminded him, just as gently. "Royce, that young woman has been through enough for one night. She needs rest, escape. Your report can wait until morning." Her tone was coaxing now. "Can't it?"

Royce was always a sucker for a soft, feminine entreaty. He gave in gracefully. "Yeah, okay."

"You've got a kind heart, Sergeant Wolfe," she said. "I told my husband so from the first day I met you." Her eyes teased him. "You're almost as nice as he is."

"Almost as tough, too," Royce drawled, recalling the tall Westerner she was married to.

Virginia Hawk laughed. "I'd say it's a toss-up." She ran a professional glance over him. "Right now, you appear ready to cave. Go home to bed, Royce. Come back in the morning. I'll prepare her for you."

"Okay." Royce looked at the woman's purse. "But first, I'd better check for next of kin, see if there's anybody—a husband, relatives—I should contact."

"I asked. She said no."

"She has no one?"

"Oh, she has family. Her parents retired, five, six months ago. They're on a cruise they planned and saved years for." Virginia sighed. "She doesn't want them notified."

"No husband, boyfriend?"

"Boyfriend?" She arched her fine blond brows.

"Okay, man friend, significant other." He shrugged. "Whatever happens to be current."

"Apparently not." Her lips curved into a taunting smile. "But it wouldn't matter if there were. She said she didn't want anyone notified. End of story, Royce."

His lips twitched. "You know what, Doc?"

"What?"

"You're even tougher than either your husband or I—and maybe even my superior officer."

Dr. Hawk laughed delightedly. "Bank on it."

"Good night, Doctor." Laughing with her, Royce turned and started for the automatic doors. Then memory stirred, and he stopped, keeping the doors open. "By the way, I think she's wearing contact lenses."

"She was." Virginia grinned. "I found them."

"Good, I'm outta here." He took a step, then

paused again. "But I'll be back bright and early," he called over his shoulder. "And if anybody tries to prevent me from seeing her, you're going to see *real* tough. And you can take *that* to the bank."

Two

She was waiting for him.

Megan was sitting straight up in bed, her legs folded beneath her, her fingers picking at the lightweight white hospital blanket draped over her knees.

Dr. Hawk had said the Pennsylvania State Police sergeant would very likely be paying her a visit early this morning. That had been when the doctor was making her regular rounds, about seven-thirty or so. It was now nearing nine. Breakfast was over—the nurse's aide had been in to remove the tray from the room thirty minutes ago.

So, where was he? Megan asked herself, unconsciously gnawing on her lower lip. Where was this law officer Dr. Hawk had told her about, the one who bore the mark of Megan Delaney on his cheek?

A shudder ripped through Megan's slender body. Lord! Had she really struck...scratched the face of a policeman?

She must have, for not for a second could she convince herself that the doctor would have said she had, if in fact she had not.

Tears blurred Megan's vision. Absently raising a hand, she brushed the warm, salty moisture from her eyes with impatient fingers. She never cried... well, hardly ever.

But then, she never struck, hit or scratched people, either, Megan reminded herself. At least not until now.

But there were extenuating circumstances, Megan thought defensively. She hadn't been in her right and normal mind at the time, and she had had excellent reason for striking out at the man...or at least at the man she believed him to be at that particular moment.

But where was he?

Megan was not stupid. She realized that she would very likely not be too stable—emotionally, psychologically—for an extended period. Scars would remain, perhaps indefinitely.

It was not a pleasant prospect to contemplate.

On the other hand, unless she kept her mind occupied, it could slip into a reflective mode, recalling—

No! Megan slammed a mental door on that train of thought. She would need to explain the circumstances to the state cop, relive that choking terror.

Where was *he?*

Megan just wanted it all over with, the horror, humiliation and degradation of the memory. And she wanted nothing more than to crawl into a hole and hide.

She was trembling—no, shaking—with nerves and trepidation when he walked into the room fifteen minutes later.

Megan knew him immediately. She did not, of course, recognize him, as one would a friend or acquaintance. He was not in uniform. His attire was casual—jeans, a striped cotton shirt, a tweed sports coat. Fairly new, and rather expensive-looking, leather slip-ons encased his feet. Actually, he looked somewhat like a construction worker on his day off.

But Megan knew exactly who he was at first sight.

He did not stride into the room, fueled by self-importance. In truth, though, he did radiate an aura of importance and intimidation.

He was tall. Lord, was he tall! He was blond, not yellow blond, but golden blond, a shade that would likely be called sun-kissed brown, she supposed. His shoulders and chest were broad, flatly muscular; his waist and hips were narrow, his legs straight, long-boned. And he was good-looking... too good-looking. The comparison of a classic Greek statue sprang to mind; Megan dismissed it at once. No statue she had ever gazed upon in awe, up close or on film, looked that good, that attractive, nearly perfect.

All of which should not have mattered to Megan in the least at that particular point in time, but somehow did.

"Miss Delaney?"

Even his voice was golden, smooth and rich as warm amber velvet. The sound of it set Megan's teeth on edge. She swallowed, quickly, swallowed again, failed to work up enough moisture even to allow speech, then replied with a curt nod.

He was prepared, which told her a lot about him.

"Sergeant Wolfe, Pennsylvania State Police." He raised his hand, palm out, displaying his identification as he moved nearer to the bed for her to examine it up close.

Megan wanted to feel pressured, put-upon, persecuted, but she couldn't. She wanted to scream a demand to be left alone. But she couldn't do that, either. She looked at his face, at the long red scratch from his eye to his jaw, and felt sick inside—even sicker than she already felt.

"I...I, er...I'm sorry." Megan felt a hot sting behind her eyelids, and lowered her gaze. Damn!

She would not cry. She would not let this man, any man, bear witness to her weakness.

"Sorry?" He frowned. "For what?"

The hot sting vanished from her eyes. Her head snapped up. Her eyes narrowed. Was this a trick? What could possibly be his purpose for playing this "For what" game? He knew full well what she was sorry for.

"Your face," she said, unaware that her voice had lost a small corner of its frailty. "I've marked you, however unintentionally, and I'm sorry."

"Oh, that?" He moved the hand he still held aloft near to his face, and drew his index finger the length of the scratch. "It's surface. I'm not branded for life." Then he smiled, and damned if his smile wasn't golden brown, as well.

How could she think of startlingly white teeth as golden brown? Megan chided herself, staring in near-mesmerized fascination at him. And yet it was. His smile lit up not only his face, but the entire room, like a burst of pure golden sunlight through a dark and angry cloud.

Megan didn't like it. She didn't trust it. But there wasn't a thing she could do about it. She had run her car, her beautiful new car, into a guardrail. And this…this golden-haired, golden-smiled one-up-on-a-Greek-god was the law. He was in charge here. Although he hadn't yet given so much as a hint of flaunting his authority, he was in a position to do so.

Just get it over with.

The cry rang inside Megan's head, its echo creating an ache to fill the void of its passing. Suddenly, she needed to weep, she needed to sleep, she needed to be left alone. Distracted, agitated, she lifted a hand to rub her temple.

"Pain?"

Megan wasn't quite sure which startled her more, the sharp concern in his voice, or the sudden sound of his ID folder snapping shut. Before she could gather her senses enough to answer, he was moving to the door.

"I'll get a nurse."

"No!" She flung out her hand—as if she could reach him, all the way near the door, from her bed. "I'm all right. It's just a dull headache."

He turned back to run an encompassing look over her pale face, his startling blue eyes probing the depths of her equally blue, though now lackluster, eyes.

"You sure?" One toasty eyebrow climbed up and under the silky lock of hair that had fallen onto his forehead.

"Positive." Megan sighed, and nodded. "Please, have a seat." She indicated the chair placed to one side of the bed. "I'd like to get this over with."

"Well…" He brushed at the errant lock of hair as he slowly returned to her bedside. "If you're sure you don't need anything for pain?'' The brow inched upward again.

"I'm sure,'' she answered, suppressing yet another sigh. "It'll pass.''

"All things do.''

Strangely convinced that his murmured reply was not merely the voicing of conventional comfort, but a genuine and heartfelt belief, Megan watched him lower his considerable length into the average-size chair.

He should have appeared funny, folded into the small seat, and yet he didn't. He looked... comfortable.

"In your own words, Miss Delaney,'' he said, offering her a gentle smile. "And in your own time.'' He glanced at his watch. "I'm in no hurry.''

Megan felt inordinately grateful for his compassion and understanding. She dreaded the coming purge, the dredging up of details, the accompanying resurgence of fear.

"I...I...''

"Start at the very beginning,'' he inserted, his voice soft with encouragement.

"Thank you, Sergeant, I—'' She broke off when he raised a hand in the familiar "halt'' gesture.

"Let's make this as easy as possible. Considering the circumstances, I think we can dispense with the *sergeant* and *sir* stuff. Okay?'' Both toasty brows peaked.

"Yes, but what *should* I call you?"

"My name's Royce," he said. "Royce Wolfe."

Royce Wolfe. Megan tested the name silently, deciding at once that she liked it. "Okay, Royce," she agreed, "but on one condition. And that is that you call me Megan."

"Deal." His teeth flashed in a disarming smile. Withdrawing a notebook and pen from his jacket pocket, he settled into the chair. "Whenever you're ready…Megan."

"I have one question."

"Shoot."

"Well, you said I should start at the beginning," she said, frowning. "Where? Of the evening, of the atta—" The very word stuck in her throat.

Megan drew a breath before trying another attempt; Royce was faster.

"You can start from the day of your birth," he suggested, quite seriously. "If that's easier for you."

"My birth?" Megan frowned again. "Why, I was born right here, in Conifer. I grew up here, lived here until I went away to college." The frown line smoothed at the realization that starting from the very beginning *was* easier.

"That was probably before I was assigned to duty here," Royce reasoned aloud. "What college did you attend?"

"Kutztown State, now University." She smiled. "It offered a great fine-arts program."

"You're an artist?" He sounded impressed.

"No." Oddly, Megan hated having to disillusion him. "It didn't take long to discover that I wasn't good enough for that. I'm an illustrator."

Royce was quick to correct her. "Illustrators are artists. Norman Rockwell was an illustrator, and so was the first of the painting Wyeths...."

"Well, yes, of course, but..." Megan broke off to frown at him. How had they strayed from the point, and what difference did it make, anyway? "Does it matter?"

"Not really." Royce grinned at her. "But you are a lot less nervous than when I came in."

Megan smiled. She couldn't help smiling. "Yes, I am. Thank you."

"You're welcome." His voice was low, honeyed, encouraging. "Ready to continue?"

"Yes. Where was I?"

"You didn't return to Conifer after college," he said, prompting her.

"Oh, right." Megan shrugged. "I had decided that to succeed, I would have to go where the action was—that being New York City, naturally."

"Naturally," he concurred in a drawl.

"I was right, you know."

"I don't doubt it." Royce appeared extremely relaxed in the small chair. "I personally wouldn't like to live there," he added. "But I don't doubt that you were right."

Megan sighed—damned if he hadn't hit the nail directly on the head.

"After all this time, I finally discovered that I personally don't like living there, either," she confessed. "That's why I jumped at the excuse to come home for a while."

"You've lost me," Royce said, in obvious confusion. "Jumped at what excuse?"

"To house-sit for my parents while they're away." She smiled, and explained, "My parents left three weeks ago on a world cruise. They'll be gone a year."

"A whole year!"

"Yes. Wild, huh?"

"It sounds great." Royce chuckled. "I wish I could talk my mother into something like that."

"Your mother's alone?" Megan asked, interested, but still conscious of playing for time, keeping the moment of truth at bay for a little longer.

"Yeah." Royce exhaled. "We lost my dad almost two years ago." He looked pensive for a moment, and then he mused aloud, "Maybe I'll talk to my brothers about all of us chipping in on a cruise vacation for Mom, if only for a week or two."

"I always wanted a brother." Megan's voice held a note of wistful yearning. "How many do you have?"

"Three," he said, laughing. "And we were a handful for my mother. Still are, at times."

"Sounds like fun." Megan sighed in soft, unconscious longing. "If I had a brother, he would..." Her voice faded, and she stared into space through eyes tight and hot, yearning for a brother, her father, someone to be there for her, hold her, protect her, tell her she was safe.

There was a moment of stillness. Then a blur of movement on the bed near her hip caught her eye. Blinking, Megan lowered her gaze and focused on the broad male hand resting, palm up, on the mattress. Without thought or consideration, she slid her palm onto his. His fingers flexed and closed around hers, swallowing her hand within the comforting protection of his.

A sense of sheer masculine strength enveloped Megan. Not a threatening, intimidating strength, but an unstated, soothing I'm-here-for-you strength, the strength she needed now, when her own had been so thoroughly, horribly decimated.

Megan blinked again, touched, and grateful for the gentle offering from this gentle giant. Unaware of her own flicker of power, she gripped his hand, hard, hanging on for sanity's sake to the solid anchor, seeking a measure of stability in her suddenly unstable world.

"It may be easier to get it over with."

Royce's soft advice echoed, joined forces with her own earlier silent demand.

"Yes." Megan's voice was little more than a breathless whisper. "I have friends who own a getaway place in the mountains," she began, steadily enough. "They called me up yesterday, said they had come in for the weekend, and invited me to meet them for dinner at the French Chalet. You know where that is?" She met his eyes; they were fixed on her face.

"Yes." Royce nodded. "In the mountains, along that side road you shot out of onto the highway in front of me."

"Did I?" Megan swallowed. "I...I never saw you."

"I know...now." His smile was faint, but encouraging. "Please, go on."

"We had a great reunion, and a lovely dinner." She paused, and then rushed on. "I had two glasses of wine, but that's all, only the two small glasses."

"Easy." His tone soothed. "I got the results of your blood-alcohol test."

Megan released the breath she'd been holding, relieved to know that at least she wouldn't be facing a drunk-driving citation in addition to yesterday's experience.

"Continue," he said gently.

"After dinner, my friends decided to stay for the music, do a little dancing. I...I was tired, and said I'd pass on the entertainment. I left...and..." Megan shut her eyes as memory swirled, filling her mind with a replayed image. "The parking lot was already filled when I'd arrived, and I had to park way in the back, at the edge of the forest," she explained in a reedy whisper. "But when I left, the lot had emptied out. My car was the only one back there."

Megan hesitated, drawing in short, panting breaths. With her inner eyes, she could see the lot, see her car, see herself hurrying to the car, unlocking it, sliding behind the wheel, inserting the key in the ignition even as she tugged on the door to pull it shut.

"I was closing the car door when…suddenly it was yanked wide open again…jerking my arm…pulling me down and sideways, nearly out of the car." Her breathing was now shallow, quick, and the words were tumbling out of her parched throat.

"Then there was a large shape looming into the opening. A hairy-backed hand grabbed my shoulder…shoved me down…and back inside." She was trembling, uncontrollably, and she was unaware of her fingernails digging into the flesh of the hand clasping hers. "My face…the side of my face scraped the steering wheel as I was pushed down…down…"

Reliving the horror, Megan didn't hear the door to her room open, didn't notice the figure of Dr. Hawk standing just inside the door, quiet, watchful, poised to go into action should she deem her patient in need of her attention.

"He was all over me!" she cried in a terrified croak. "The hand that had grabbed my shoulder moved down to clutch at my breast! His...his other hand..." She was gasping now, barely able to articulate. "He shoved that hand between my legs!"

"I'm here. You're safe."

Soft. Rock-steady. Royce's voice penetrated the ballooning fog of panic permeating Megan's mind. The fog retreated. Her entire body shaking from reactive tremors, she clung desperately to his hand and purged the poison from her system.

"Somehow I managed to work one of my legs up, between his. I...I...*rammed* my knee into his groin! He cried out, 'you bitch!' and hit me, in the face... Then he pulled back...just enough so that I could raise my leg farther. I worked my foot up to his belly. And then...and then, I pushed again, as hard as I could. He...he fell back, onto the macadam."

"Go on."

"I—I—" Megan choked, coughed, sniffed, swiped her free hand over cheeks wet from tears she was unaware of having shed. "I...don't remember, exactly. I turned the key as I struggled up, behind the wheel. I drove away from there...from *him*...with the door wide open. I don't know when or where I thought to pull it shut. All I knew, all I could think, was that I had to get away!"

Megan heard wrenching sobs, and didn't even know they came from her tight, aching throat.

"I don't remember hitting the guardrail!" She

blinked, stared, and found sanctuary in the com-
passion-filled blue eyes staring back at her.

"I don't re— I don't re—"

"It's over," he inserted in a low, calming voice.
"It doesn't matter. Let it go."

"Yes. Yes." Megan's chin dropped onto her
chest, and she began to cry, not harsh, wracking
sobs, but a quiet weeping of utter exhaustion.

They let her cry, the state cop and the doctor,
let her weep the catharsis of healing tears.

Megan fell asleep with her hand still gripping
his.

Three

Damn, she was tall!

Megan Delaney was being released from the hospital this morning. Royce had offered to drive her home.

He felt a tingling thrill of pleasure as he stared at the woman standing next to the hospital bed—a thrill of pleasure that contained a hint of attraction. Being so tall himself, Royce did appreciate height in a woman, but there was more entailed here, something beyond mere appreciation, something Royce didn't want to examine or even acknowledge.

The very fact that he was taking pleasure from such a simple thing as a woman's height startled

Royce. What did Megan's height have to do with anything? he asked himself, frowning in consternation. And the other underlying sensation...that didn't bear thinking about.

Dismissing his reaction and the unmentionable accompanying sensation as unimportant, Royce focused on Megan Delaney. Yes, she was tall, and she was unquestionably attractive, but at the moment every inch of her slender form was taut, visibly tense.

Royce repressed the sigh that rose to tighten his throat. Megan had gone through an extremely nasty experience, and it showed.

Royce recalled that, during her stuttered and disjointed recitation, he had been shaken by a startling conflict in the emotions tearing at his senses and sensibilities. His intellect had been outraged by the disclosure of the details of the attack on Megan. Assailed by fury, he had had to impose restraint on an overriding urge to jump up and dash from the room to search out, find and personally destroy the bastard who had terrorized her.

At one and the same time, his emotions had responded in an unprecedented way to a sudden and strong sense of attraction at the touch of her hand clinging to his.

Though Royce had pushed aside the unusual sensation then, as he did now, the memory lingered, a wisp of flotsam tossed about by an overwhelming wave of compassion.

Royce felt a deep, almost compulsive need to help her, in some way to ease the frightening mental and emotional aftereffects he knew she was suffering.

Frustration ate away at Royce like acid; Megan looked so damn vulnerable.

But how to help? The question had nagged at Royce for more than twenty-four hours. What could he do? He was a trained law-enforcement officer, but that certainly did not qualify him to deal with in-depth mental or emotional problems.

The only options that presented themselves to Royce seemed puny weapons of combat in relation to the magnitude of the inner battle tormenting Megan.

He could extend his hand for grasping. He could volunteer as a shield of law between her and the world at large. He could offer his strength as protection.

Puny, indeed, but...wait, Royce thought with sudden inspiration. The old adage of laughter being the best medicine had recently gained new, stronger credence. He had heard of physicians using it to treat a multitude of ills.

Maybe it would help, Royce mused. Surely, if doctors were employing it, it couldn't hurt.

Unnoticed as yet by the two women in the room, Royce stood silent, his eyes inventorying the look of Megan, comparing her beauty to the different yet equal beauty of the other woman, Dr. Virginia Hawk.

In point of fact, there really was no comparison, except that they were both beautiful women.

Whereas Megan had a mass of long, unruly-looking, fiery red hair, Virginia was a cool-looking blonde. And where Virginia was average in size, and maturely, enticingly curvaceous, Megan was tall, willowy, long-legged…and, in Royce's instant assessment, she looked more the model than the artist. Funny, he had never before been attracted to the lean, angular type.

But the attraction was certainly felt now, banished to the fringes of his awareness, but there just the same.

Royce didn't like it, but there wasn't a damn thing he could do about it.

"Oh, Sergeant, I didn't hear you come in."

Virginia Hawk's soft voice gently snared Royce's distracted attention.

"I just arrived a moment ago," he said, strolling into the room with a self-imposed casual air.

"Oh, good morning." Megan glanced around at the sound of his voice, revealing the bruised side of her face to his gaze. "I'm just about ready to go."

"No hurry. Take your time." Royce had difficulty keeping his voice steady, concealing the feelings bombarding him. The sight of the discolored bruises marring her lovely face reactivated conflicting feelings of burning anger and drenching tenderness. "Is there anything I can do to help?"

"No." Megan began to shake her head, but halted the movement at once, wincing in pain. "I just have to slip into my shoes, and we can leave."

"Okay." Royce shifted his gaze to the doctor. "Paperwork all cleared up?"

"Yes." Virginia smiled and nodded her head. "Megan is fine," she said, letting him know she had seen and understood his reaction to the other woman's appearance. "She has agreed to come in to my office next week for a follow-up visit, but it will simply be a checkup. I expect no adverse effects." Virginia hesitated, then added a qualification. "at least, no lasting physical effects."

Royce gave a brief, sharp nod of understanding. He had seen enough rape and attempted-rape cases to know that the major ramifications were primarily psychological in nature—and devastating in effect.

"I'm fine...really." Megan gave the doctor a bright, reassuring smile—too bright to be genuine, or reassuring. "But I promise I'll keep my appointment."

"Good, then get out of here," Virginia ordered, starting for the door. "I've got work to do."

A near-palpable tension entered the room the moment the doctor exited, leaving Royce and Megan alone together. In that instant, the average-size room seemed to shrink, becoming too small to contain both occupants.

Megan fidgeted with her blazer, which matched the stylish calf-length skirt she had worn to dinner with her friends. The skirt was now wrinkled and creased from her struggle with her unknown attacker.

"I...I want to get out of here," she said, in a harsh, wobbly voice. "I need a bath... desperately."

Royce understood that, as well. He knew, from experience, from talking with others who had gone through the same degrading horror Megan had suffered, the resultant feelings of being dirty, unclean, tainted.

"Then let's get moving." He didn't offer to help her as she shrugged into the blazer; he knew better. The last thing Megan wanted at this moment was to be touched, however impersonally, by a man, any man. Her grasping his hand yesterday had been an unconscious, instinctive reaction to reliving the fear-inducing incident. But that was then. This morning, she was fully conscious, aware and wary.

Megan preceded him from the room, the lithe gracefulness of her movements evident even through the tension tightening her tall form.

Royce felt his breath catch in his throat at the sight of the brave front Megan maintained. Admiration swelled inside him for her fierce display of independence, her attitude of calm and composure, despite the fine tremor quivering on her soft lips, in her slim fingers.

Wanting to help her, if only in a show of unstated support, Royce strode to her side, adjusting his long stride to hers, a silent buffer, there if she needed him.

Megan didn't say anything, but she slid a sidelong glance at him, a faint smile of comprehension and gratitude flickering briefly over her lips.

Dammit! Royce railed as her smile died a quick death, killed by the persistent tremor. And damn that bastard attacker to the deepest regions of hell.

"Which way?"

Royce blinked and glanced around, surprised to see that they were on the sidewalk outside the main entrance to the hospital, even more surprised by the realization that he had no actual recollection of traversing the corridors from point A to point B. All he could recall was moving beside her, ready, willing, to scoop her into his arms and run with her, should Megan give any sign of faltering, unable to continue on.

Pull it together, Wolfe, he advised himself, before you make an absolute jackass out of yourself. Megan gave every appearance of being the last woman in the world to lose control to the degree of needing to be bodily carried anywhere.

"Er...over there." He gestured vaguely toward the opposite curb. "The Pontiac Bonneville across the street."

"Nice car. I like that shimmery dark green color," Megan said, crossing the sidewalk. "Is it new?" She glanced right, then left, along the empty street before starting across.

"I've had it a couple of months." Royce shrugged. "It was new, but last year's model."

"Mine was brand-new." She heaved a sigh. "I had to wait for the exact shade of red I wanted. It was delivered to the dealer just three weeks ago."

"Too bad," he murmured in genuine sympathy.

Megan flicked a sidelong look at him. "The damage was extensive, wasn't it?"

"Yes," Royce said, knowing it was pointless to be less than truthful. "I checked with the mechanic at the garage yesterday afternoon. It's totaled, a write-off. The entire front end crumpled. We couldn't lift any fingerprints, because the door had wrinkled. I'm sorry."

"Why?" Though her shoulders slumped, Megan gave him a tired smile. "You didn't do it, I did."

Since there really was no argument against her assertion, Royce didn't bother attempting one. "You're alive," he said, offering her a compassionate smile as he unlocked and held open the passenger side door for her. Then, in silence, he circled around to the driver's side.

"Buckle up," he said without thinking, as he slid behind the steering wheel.

"I usually do." Megan's tone bordered on sarcasm. "I only ever forget when I'm in trauma."

"Happens a lot, does it?" Royce tried a teasing note, in hopes of defusing with a touch of humor the sudden tension humming inside the confines of the car.

Megan carefully connected the belt before slanting a wry look at him. "Trauma? Or—?

"Trauma," he quickly inserted, along with a grin.

She was quiet a moment, her expression pensive as she studied his eyes, his grin. Then, just as Royce could feel his face falling as flat as his obviously ill-timed levity, his mind frantically groping for something, anything to say, she gave him a weak smile in return.

"Yes," she said. "I suffer bouts of panic-inspired trauma with the approach of each and every assignment deadline."

"Ah…" he murmured, relieved that his earlier idea of applied laughter hadn't completely bombed, although in truth Megan wasn't laughing, she was just putting forth an effort to respond. "You're one of those artistic types who work close to the edge."

"Hardly artistic." Megan actually did manage a parody of laughter. "Truth be told, I'm one of those lazy types who screw around until the last minute, then pressure themselves into blind panic."

Royce found her candor refreshing, and amusing. He laughed with her. "A procrastinator, are you?"

"In spades." Megan's shoulders rippled in a half shrug, conveying a slight lessening of tension. "Always was." A smile of reminiscence tugged at her soft lips. "I always put off doing my homework, and every other chore, until I was threatened with dire consequences, like being grounded or having my allowance withheld. Drove my parents nuts, since they both are self-starters."

Encouraged by the easing of the tautness in her body and her stark expression, Royce said the first thing to come into his mind, in hopes of keeping her distracted.

"You could be describing my youngest brother," he said, chuckling. "When he was a kid, Jake had a positive talent for goofing off, and driving our parents nuts."

"Jake." Megan repeated the name, testing the sound of it. "I like the name. It sounds solid, somehow, not at all the name of a first-class goof-off."

"Oh, he's not anymore." Royce inserted the key and fired the engine. Then, since his distracting ploy appeared to be working, he quickly continued, "Jake goofed off for more than his share of years, but he's finally settled down, and settled in." He checked for oncoming traffic before pulling smoothly away from the curb.

"In what way?" Megan had turned sideways in

her seat to look at him, and she sounded genuinely interested in hearing about the trials and tribulations the Wolfe clan had endured through the maturing period of the youngest of the brood.

Royce was only too happy to oblige. Anything to keep her mind occupied, away from the memory of her ordeal. "After kicking around the country for a lot of years, Jake came home, attended the police academy, then took a job with the hometown police force." Drawing the car to a halt at a stop sign, he turned to smile at her. "Mom tells me that Jake has turned out to be a damn good cop. As good as all the others in the family."

Megan arched delicate auburn eyebrows. "There's more than you and Jake? Cops, I mean."

Royce laughed as he set the car in motion again. "A bunch...or at least there were. Following the law is a family tradition, dating back over a hundred years. Even as we speak, there are four—count 'em, four—Wolfe men working in law enforcement."

"All of you?" She blinked in astonishment.

"Yeah. A real hoot, huh?"

"And a holler," she drawled. "Turn right at the next intersection."

"I know." Royce slanted a wry glance at her. "I'm a cop, remember? I know the district."

"I'm impressed."

"I seriously doubt it."

Megan laughed, a free-floating sound that lifted

Royce's spirits. The fact that she looked both relaxed and comfortable in the plush seat was an
added bonus.

"What branch of law enforcement are the other
two Wolfe men in?" She flashed Royce a quick
grin. "Wolfe men...conjures up images of hairy
faces and hands, and sudden claws, and long, ululating cries to the full moon."

Royce nearly lost it. Gripping the wheel, he
choked back a roar of laughter, and shook his head
in helpless amusement. Megan Delaney was prov-
ing to be a real trip. Her display of humor after the
ordeal she had been through spoke volumes about
her inner strength.

Royce liked what he heard; and he liked her.
The liking enhanced the attraction he felt for her.
That, he didn't particularly appreciate; Royce
wasn't heavily into frustration, emotional or otherwise.

He frowned.

"You've forgotten?"

"What?" Royce shot a scowling look at her.

"What branch of law enforcement your brothers
are in?" she said, scowling back at him.

"Oh." Royce offered a sheepish smile; she returned it with a dry look. "Well, Eric—he's the
third son—followed our father into the Philadelphia police force. He's currently undercover with
the narcotics division. And big brother Cameron is
a special agent for the FBI."

Megan frowned in concentration. "That means that Cameron's the oldest, right?"

"Right. The Lone Wolfe."

"That's his code name?"

"Nah." Royce laughed. "That's the moniker his friends and fellow agents hung on him a couple or so years ago."

"Self-contained, is he?" she asked. "All of an individual piece?"

"Yeah." Royce rewarded her with an admiring glance. "That's very good...apt."

"Here's the driveway," Megan said, taking evident pleasure from his compliment. She indicated the drive with a fluttery hand motion. "It's a sharp turn."

"No kidding, Dick Tracy," he muttered, flicking a glance into the rearview mirror before hanging a hard right.

She gave him a puzzled look. "What?"

"Nothing." Royce shrugged, and flashed another grin at her. "Mumbling to myself."

"Uh-huh," she responded, again as dry as dust.

Located a little way beyond the limits of Conifer, the split-level house of natural stone and wood was set like a gem into the tree-dotted landscape, secluded yet not isolated from several surrounding properties.

"Pretty," he observed, bringing the car to a stop in front of the house.

"Yes," Megan softly agreed. "When my parents had it constructed twenty-five years ago, it was the only house in the area. They've picked up a few neighbors since then."

"So I see." Royce set the hand brake. "Close, but not too close. How big is the lot?"

"Two and a half acres." Megan smiled, and reached for the door release. "Which equates to a whole lot of mowing for my father." She shoved the door open and slid her legs out, then hesitated on the edge of the bucket seat. "Er...would you like a cup of coffee?"

"Sure," Royce said at once, picking up on the sudden note of uncertainty in her voice. The story was written plain as day on her face. She was trying hard to conceal it, but the tension was back, riddling her taut form, terrorizing her mind, making her fear entering the house alone.

"I'd offer you lunch..." she said, stepping from the car and waiting for him to join her before heading for the front door. "But I can't recall what I have in the house to eat." She gave a shaky-sounding laugh. "Strange, I've only been away two nights, and yet it seems so much longer."

"Stuff happens," Royce murmured.

"Yeah." Megan sighed; her fingers trembled as she fumbled the key into the lock. "Mind-bending stuff."

"It'll fade." His voice held just the right note of authority...Royce hoped.

"When?" For all the demand in her tone, a

tremor of fear and uncertainty filtered through, delivering a blow to his emotions. Flinging the door open, she strode inside, then whirled to confront him as he followed her into the small flagstone foyer. "A month? A year? Ten years?"

"Stay calm, Megan," he said, soothingly, softly, hurting for her, and for himself, for not having met her before a brainless, violence-prone jerk messed up her mind.

"Calm. Yes." She took a deep breath. Tried a smile. Missed it. Sank her teeth into her lower lip. Shook her head. "Oh, hell!" Blinking furiously against the sudden brightness in her eyes, she spun around and dashed away, down a short hallway, heading toward the rear of the house. "I'll…I'll make the coffee."

Wanting to go to her, to comfort her, yet knowing he should not, Royce stood in the middle of the foyer, controlling himself, while giving her time to gather her own control.

Silently counting off the seconds, he glanced around, taking inventory of his surroundings.

To his right, along the hallway, were two closed doors. Bedrooms? Royce wondered, shrugging. To his left, the hallway was open, railed with intricate wrought iron. Three half-moon-shaped flagstone steps descended into a spacious living room, brightly illuminated by the sunlight pouring through two oversize picture windows, one facing the front of the house, one facing the side.

The living room was open-ended, flowing into the dining room. The decor was country, in primary colors—forest, bark brown and Williamsburg blue. The furniture was high-backed, with plump cushions, a mute invitation to rest and relaxation.

Royce liked it; it reminded him of home.

Three minutes had elapsed, by his silent figuring. Drawing a breath, he struck out, trailing in Megan's wake.

She was standing at the kitchen counter, staring fixedly at the water trickling through the grounds basket into the glass pot of an automatic coffee-maker.

"Okay now?" Royce kept his voice low, unobtrusive.

Megan exhaled a ragged-sounding sigh. "Yes... but..." She turned to ricochet a glance off him. "I..." She gulped in a breath. "I suppose it's silly, but I must have a shower," she said, rushing on, "and I'm afraid of being here, in the house, alone." She lifted fear-darkened eyes to his. "Would you mind very much having your coffee alone? Staying until I'm finished?"

Royce felt her imploring look to the depths of his heart and mind. "Not at all," he said, in a soft, yet reassuring voice. "I don't start work till three."

"Thank you." Megan lowered her gaze, swallowed, then glanced up at him once more. "The coffee's almost done. Help yourself. There're cups in the cabinet." She walked toward him, a silent plea in her eyes for him to step aside so that she wouldn't have to brush against him as she passed.

"I'll find them." Royce stepped aside, giving her space. "I promise not to drink it all."

"Thank you." A fleeting smile touched her lips. "I, uh, may be awhile. If you get hungry, feel free to rummage in the cabinets and fridge for sustenance."

"Okay, thanks. Can I get something for you?"

Megan hesitated, hovering in the doorway, obviously anxious to escape, yet also obviously appreciative of his offer of help. "I'm not really hungry right now. Maybe later. But thanks, anyway," she said. Then she scurried through the doorway and back along the hall to the first door inside the entrance.

Royce watched her until the door closed behind her. There came the faint but definite sound of the lock clicking into place. Heaving a sigh, he turned to glance around the room.

He liked the kitchen even more than the living room, but then, that wasn't too surprising—Royce was a kitchen person. And this particular kitchen held definite appeal.

Done in earth tones of terra-cotta and sage, with bright splashes of pumpkin and honey-brown, the room was warm and homey. A large, solid-looking round table was placed in front of a wide window overlooking the side yard. Four armed captain's chairs circled the table.

Finding a cup in the cabinet above the coffee-maker, Royce filled it with the steaming brew and carried it to the table. He found milk in the double-door refrigerator, sniffed it, then tipped a quick dollop into his coffee.

Then, sliding a chair away from the table, he settled into the curved, padded seat, stretched out his legs and sipped at the hot liquid, prepared to wait as long as it took for Megan to decide she was once again clean.

Royce's stomach grumbled a demand for sustenance on his third trip from the table to the coffeepot. He sent a brooding look through the doorway and along the hall. The bedroom door Megan had disappeared behind remained shut. He switched his gaze to the refrigerator, and his expression grew contemplative.

Should he or shouldn't he?

Why not? He *had* been invited to browse.

Pulling the double doors apart, Royce took stock of the freezer section. Vegetables, microwave dinners, individually wrapped and labeled packages of meat.

He shook his head. Too heavy for lunch.

Closing the door, he turned his attention to the contents of the other, bigger side. The wire shelves contained much more promising fare. There were cartons of milk, both whole and low-fat. Other cartons of juices—tomato, orange and grapefruit. Bottles of springwater bearing a French label. On the shelf below were packets of luncheon meats and sliced white American cheese, jars of pickles, olives, mustard, mayonnaise, ketchup and horseradish.

Things were looking up.

Royce bent to peer at the lower shelf. Not quite as interesting. The covered containers bore the definite appearance of leftovers.

Forget that.

There were two drawers beneath the bottom shelf. Royce slid out the first one. Now we're getting somewhere, he thought, identifying lettuce, tomatoes, celery, and a dark green bunch of parsley. He removed all but the last, leaving the dark green bunch all on its lonesome.

Depositing the veggies on the table, he returned to the fridge to investigate the bottom drawer. Oranges, grapefruit, kiwi fruit, seedless green grapes, and a small basket of fresh California strawberries. Yum, yum....

Royce found an assortment of bottled salad dressings on a narrow shelf on the door and a small can of white tuna in one of the cabinets above the countertop.

He was in business.

Twenty-odd minutes later, Royce stepped back from the counter to admire the results of his industrious labor. A smug smile of satisfaction played over his lips as he shifted his gaze from the large wooden bowl piled high with crisp salad sprinkled with pieces of white tuna to a smaller glass bowl, colorful with its tossed assortment of fresh fruits.

Okay. What now? Frowning, Royce shot another look the length of the hallway; the bedroom door remained shut.

Beginning to wonder if he should go rap on the door, if only to make sure Megan hadn't drowned herself, he sighed and began opening cabinet doors again, searching out dishes and glassware to set the table for two—just in case Megan's appetite was awakened by his offering.

When the table was ready, Royce hunted up the ground coffee and started a fresh pot of coffee. He was staring at the liquid trickling from the basket into the pot in the exact same manner Megan had been earlier, when her quiet voice broke through his concerned reverie.

"You have been busy, haven't you?"

Relief shuddered through Royce. Controlling his expression, he slowly turned around.

The sight of her ripped the breath from his throat.

Megan was standing in the doorway, looking beautiful enough to stop rush-hour traffic. And yet her choice of attire could only be called casual in the extreme.

Soft-looking faded jeans embraced her slender hips and long legs. Crumpled pink satin ballerina slippers encased her narrow feet. An oversize baggy sweatshirt emblazoned with the words Kutztown State concealed her breasts.

Her face looked fresh-scrubbed, pale, devoid of artifice; not so much as a hint of blush, lip gloss or eye shadow had been applied to enhance her colorless skin.

In sharp and blazing contrast, her long mane of fiery hair gave the appearance of a living flame, framing her face and tumbling in springy spiral curls around her shoulders and halfway down her back.

Stunned, Royce could barely breathe, never mind speak. Still, he gave it a shot.

"Uh, I, uh, yeah…" He moved his hand in an absent way, indicating the table. "I made lunch."

"I see." Megan's somber gaze followed his hand. "Everything looks good, appetizing."

Inordinately pleased by her mild approval, Royce moved his shoulders in a dismissive shrug. "It's only tossed salad and mixed fruit."

"But you took the time and trouble to do it…for me." She swallowed with visible difficulty. "I…I…" She broke off to swallow again. "Thank you, Royce. You're a nice man." A tiny, faintly bitter smile feathered her lips. "And right now I'm inclined to believe there aren't an awful lot of nice men littering the ground."

What could he say? Royce asked himself. How could he refute her new, hard-earned belief? She had suffered the debasement of a man attempting to force himself on her. In his opinion, she was justified in her need to withdraw, to wrap herself within the folds of a cloak of detachment from all things male.

"Ah, Megan..." he murmured, heaving a defeated sounding sigh. "Trite as I know it is, there is, nevertheless, truth to the saying that it will pass in time."

"Oh, God! I hope so!" she said in a soft, fervent cry. "Because I hate the fragile, helpless, frightened way I'm feeling now!"

Resisting an urgent impulse to go to her, pull her into the safe, protective haven of his arms, Royce moved in stiff-legged strides to the table.

"Come, eat something," he implored her, sliding a chair away from the table invitingly. "Things always look better on a full stomach than on an empty one."

Megan arched one auburn eyebrow. "You're just full of homespun wisdom, aren't you?" she chided.

"That's me, your friendly old philosopher." He made a low, sweeping bow, trying to lighten the atmosphere. "Won't you join me for lunch?"

"I'm really not hungry," Megan said, taking a cautious step toward him.

"Then how about joining me while I have lunch?" Royce pleaded, plaintively, pathetically. "Like most bachelors, I eat alone most of the time. It gets...lonely."

His tone, combined with the sorrowful expression he pulled, drew a small but real smile from her. Heaving an exaggerated sigh, she crossed the room to accept the chair he still held in readiness for her.

"You're a fraud, Sergeant," she said accusingly, slipping onto the chair, being careful not to touch him. "A sham," she continued, with less strain, when he moved to the chair opposite her. "You're not a big bad Wolfe at all."

The response that sprang into his mind was triggered by a remark Megan had made earlier, while they were still in the car, discussing his family. Without thinking, he allowed it to flow softly from his lips.

"Don't bet on it, Megan. Wanna hear my ululating full-moon howl?"

Four

Laughter erupted from Megan's throat. She couldn't help it. Even feeling shaky, vulnerable to the point of fragility, she just could not contain a burst of appreciative laughter.

Royce slanted a sly, assessing look at her.

He had done it on purpose, Megan suddenly realized. Royce had deliberately tossed the wry remark at her. The look of him, the light dancing in the depths of his incredibly blue eyes, told her all she needed to know for now about the man seated, lounging in a deceptive pose of laziness, opposite her. He had wanted to alleviate her feelings of anxiety and strain, ease the tension tearing at her, by making her laugh.

What a thoroughly decent man.

The evaluation of him startled Megan, considering her rather low opinion of the male species in general at this particular time.

But this man was different, she mused, absently helping herself to a good-size portion of salad.

Her eyes flickered upward to his face, then quickly away again as another equally startling thought popped into her head. Royce was not only different from that hulking, grunting beast who had attacked her, Royce was different from any other man she had ever met.

The difference was unrelated to looks; even though Royce was one very good-looking man. Megan knew many good-looking, even downright handsome, men. And it had little to do with his size, which was considerable, imposing.

No, Megan mused, raising her salad fork to her mouth. The difference lay in the man himself, his personality, the innate decent character traits slowly being revealed to her. Royce Wolfe was a good man, a good person who genuinely cared about people. Megan would unhesitatingly have wagered her last dollar on it.

Having someone care about the ordeal she had been through, the resulting trauma she now had to deal with, consoled Megan more than she would have believed possible. The knotted feeling in her stomach relaxed, simply because he was there, caring, lending a sense of security.

He was staring at her. Though she kept her gaze lowered to the luncheon plate, and the salad she had begun eating without conscious intent, Megan could sense, feel, Royce's pensive and probing stare upon her.

What was he watching for, waiting for?

Was Royce expecting her to crumple into a heap and wail like a lost or injured child?

Megan swallowed down a small piece of lettuce that had caught, then stuck, in her throat.

She very easily could let loose and cry like an abandoned child, simply because that was precisely what she longed to do. More than wail, though, she wanted to scream at the top of her voice, rant and rave, rail against the vagaries of a fate that had placed her in that particular parking lot at that particular time.

Megan took another bite of salad and chewed determinedly. She didn't taste the delicate flavor of the tuna, the crispness of the vegetables, or the creaminess of the ranch dressing.

What good would screaming and ranting do her, anyway? Would it change her situation? Would it wipe from her memory the choking fear she had felt, the fear that still curled around the edges of her mind? Would it return her to the confident, carefree frame of mind she had enjoyed, taken for granted before the attack?

No. No. No.

Nothing would ever be the same. *She* would

never be the same. Megan knew it, and she resented the knowledge.

She had done nothing, nothing, to encourage an attack. How dare that hulking bastard, how dare any person take it into his maggoty mind to make a victim of her or any other human being?

"Megan?"

Megan shuddered at the softly intrusive sound of Royce's voice. A great deal of effort was required on her part to keep from snarling in response.

"What?"

"Hey, c'mon, calm down," Royce said, raising his hands in a sign of surrender. "I'm friendly, remember?"

"Sorry." Megan sighed, and gave him a faint smile. "I was all caught up in my thoughts."

"Bad, huh?"

"Yeah."

"Yeah," he echoed, exhaling harshly. "I want to tell you to put it out of your mind, but I know that's one whole hell of a lot easier said than done."

"Yes, it is." Her smile took on a self-deprecating slant. "It's at times like this that we realize how very trite we tend to be when offering our unsolicited advice to others." Megan sighed again. "I'm afraid that I'm as guilty of doing so as everyone else. Sad, isn't it?"

"Don't go down."

Megan blinked. "I beg your pardon?"

"You're in a downward spiral," Royce explained, his glittering eyes piercing hers. "I can hear it in your voice, see it in your face. I've witnessed it before, that mental lure into depression. Fight it, Megan."

Megan glanced away from him, his intensity. She blinked again, this time not in confusion, but against a hot rush of moisture to her eyes. "As I believe you mentioned," she murmured, "it's easier said than done."

"But it can be done." His voice was hard, adamant. "Get help if necessary, from Dr. Hawk, or your pastor, if you have one, or maybe a close friend, but fight, fight with every atom of resistance you possess. *Don't let him win.*"

The very strength of his voice, of his command, drew her gaze back to his sternly set features, and then to the hand he had extended across the table to her, palm up, in exactly the same way he had in the hospital.

Get help. Fight. His command spun through her head, sparking corollary, comforting thoughts.

With the simple act of offering her his hand, Royce was silently offering his help, offering his strength, offering to fight with her, beside her.

Megan's throat closed around an emotional lump.

Had she judged Royce Wolfe decent? she thought, reaching for his proffered hand. *Decent* seemed much too mild a term to apply in defining the man.

Megan's palm slid onto his; it was warm, not smooth, as she might have expected of the hand of a desk jockey, but rough, calloused, the hand of a man familiar with hard physical work. It was oddly reassuring, the rough feel of that hand.

Megan swallowed to relieve the tightness, and when that didn't work, she cleared her throat of the tear-congealed emotional lump.

"I..." She cast a quick glance at him, and was nearly undone by the look of tenderness that had eased the stern set of his features. "Thank you."

"Hey, you're welcome." Royce's voice was low, soothing, and held a hint of entreaty. "How 'bout some fruit?"

Fruit? Megan frowned and looked at her plate. It was empty. When had she eaten the last of her salad? She shook her head to clear the cobwebs of confusion, cast another look at him, and once again had to smile.

"Okay, Sergeant Perceptive," she agreed on a sigh, "let's have some fruit."

Royce grinned, and the room appeared to brighten considerably. "Awright..." he said, releasing her hand, then shoving his chair back and springing to his feet. "You dish up the fruit, and I'll pour the coffee."

The house was quiet, too quiet, after Royce left to go to work. At loose ends, Megan wandered from room to room, glancing at everything, each carefully selected piece of furniture, each accent piece her mother had purchased after days, sometimes weeks, of shopping for just the right colors, the perfect decorative items. Since her mother's taste was excellent, the decor was both aesthetically appealing and comfortable.

The beauty and ambience were lost on Megan in her present frame of mind. Although she looked, she did not see the warmth, the welcome. All she saw was the emptiness.

She was alone.

It scared her sick.

Fight.

The echoing sound of Royce's voice rang so clear in Megan's mind, she jumped and whirled around, expecting to see him standing in the doorway, his right hand extended in an unstated offer of help.

He wasn't there.

But the subconscious memory echo had served its purpose. Megan's vision cleared. She was home. She was safe. And she would be damned if she'd allow herself to tumble into that downward spiral into depression Royce had warned her against.

Squaring her shoulders, Megan strode from the living room to her bedroom, and straight to the work area, in a corner between two oversize windows. She trailed her hand along the edge of her drafting table set at an angle to the large desk beneath one window. Glancing aside, she stared into the black screen of her computer, on which she created graphic designs for certain assignments.

But Megan was not using the computer for her current assignment. She was working in the medium of her first love, illustrative painting, with real paints and real brushes and the very real odors that went with it.

Megan respected the computer, and its mind-boggling capabilities, and so she gave it a quick nod of recognition. It was then that she noticed the tiny red light on the answering machine next to the telephone on the corner of the desk. She rewound the tape and pressed the play button. The first message was from the friend she had dined with Friday night.

"Hi, Meg, it's Julie, as if you didn't know." Julie's tinkling laughter brought a sad smile to Megan's lips. "It's Saturday morning, 10:35," she went on, "and I suppose you're off shopping or something."

Or something, Megan thought, suppressing a shudder spawned by the memory of her emotional display while relating the events of her ordeal to Royce in the hospital Saturday morning.

"...wonderful seeing you again..." Julie was going on, recapturing Megan's attention. "Cliff and I have really missed your company and smiling face since you moved back here, but we do understand how you might feel safer here than living alone in New York.''

Safer! Megan groaned. The machine beeped and Julie's voice was cut off. Seconds later, the beep sounded again, and Julie was back, laughter in her voice.

"It's me again. Meg, I'm gonna have to run. Clifford is bugging me to get moving. We're off on a hike into the hills— How lucky can one woman get? If I don't get a chance to talk to you before we leave tomorrow, I'll give you a buzz one day next week. See ya.''

"See ya,'' Megan murmured, envisioning her friend's dear pixie face, her smiling eyes. "And please be careful, both of you. There's danger in those hills,'' she went on in a choked whisper, as a hulking form intruded on her vision.

Caught up once again in the memory of that violent man, that terrifying experience, Megan began to shiver. Tears welled up to sting her eyes and clog her throat. A moan of protest was torn from the depths of her chest, and she shook her head to dispel the vision, the memory.

"Royce.'' Megan was unaware of whimpering his name aloud, of crying out for his stabilizing presence, the physical strength of his hand, the psychological strength of his being.

He was not there to rescue her. The answering machine responded in his stead. It beeped, then played another message, this one from her current employer—and onetime would-be lover—Jefferson Clarke, Jr. Though Megan had never been able to respond on an emotional level to Jeff, he had continued to utilize her professional talents, and they had developed an abiding friendship.

Jefferson held the title of associate publisher with Clarke and Clarke, Inc., father-and-son publishers of a quarterly magazine with a chic and savvy format, geared for the young—and not-so-young—up-and-coming executive.

"Megan, I'm waiting for the illustrations that were supposed to be on my desk last week," he said, not unkindly. "Can I look for them anytime soon?"

The sound of Jeff's chiding voice broke through the haze of remembered fear gripping Megan. She smiled faintly and sniffed as the machine issued a double beep, indicating the end of her messages. Raising her hand, she swiped the film of tears from her eyes before erasing the tape and resetting the machine.

Should she give Jeff a call, explain the situation, and the subsequent psychological and emotional effects? Megan mused, drawing in deep, shuddering breaths. Knowing Jeff, she felt certain that he would react to her ordeal with both compassion and understanding, and very likely offer her a deadline extension, possibly even the option of scrapping the project. In all likelihood, Jeff might go so far as offering to come to Conifer to be with her for a while, to give her moral support.

But she *had* moral support, right here in Conifer.

Of course, the thought conjured up an image of Royce, and the image sparked an attendant vision, demanding a comparison between the two men.

Megan frowned as she mentally examined the pictures filling her mind. In truth, there really was no comparison.

Jefferson Clarke was a bit taller than average, a tad taller than Megan herself. He had a dark olive complexion, dark eyes and hair. His build was slender, elegant, a living, breathing reflection of the conventional concept of the aristocrat. In other words, Jeff was the complete opposite of the very tall, muscular, sun-kissed, earthy Royce Wolfe.

It wasn't until that instant that Megan realized that she preferred earthy to aristocratic.

Preferred? Megan's frown deepened. The connotations inherent in the word gave her pause. At the moment, under her present circumstances, her preference in regard to men should have been the absolute last thing to spring to her mind.

Yet, there it was, nudged to the forefront of her consciousness by the persistent image of Royce's visage confronting her, stirring a flicker of feminine interest to life inside her.

A shiver skipped down Megan's spine, a shiver born more from excitement than from fear.

Ridiculous. Megan moved her head in another

hard shake, dislodging the visions of both men. Then a faint smile of gratitude curved her lips as the thought occurred that, in point of fact, the two images had superseded that of her frightening attacker—and all because of a phone message.

Sending a silent but heartfelt thanks to Jefferson Clarke for saving her from herself, from surrendering to fear, she turned away from the desk to stare lovingly at the work in progress attached to her table.

Megan had worked on numerous projects for Clarke and Clarke since going free-lance. She enjoyed working with the Clarkes, father and son, and the bright, energetic and imaginative employees of the company, and she hoped to continue working with them in the future.

But she wouldn't have a prayer of seeing her hopes realized if she cringed in a corner. She had an assignment to complete, and she was already over deadline, as Jeff had pointedly reminded her via her answering machine.

Ever since she first took a colored pencil to drawing paper at the age of five, Megan had been able to lose herself in her imagination, and the creations it conjured up. Her lips compressed into a thin line of determination to fight backsliding with her strongest weapon, Megan slid onto the stool in front of the table.

It was time for all good little illustrators to cut

through the emotional crap and get down to business.

It was a long workday, and it was only a little more than half over.

Royce shot a glance at the office wall clock and suppressed a sigh. The hands stood at 8:37.

It had been dark outside for several hours now. How was Megan handling the nighttime hours?

The thought directed his gaze to the phone. Royce lifted his hand, then let it drop to the desktop again.

He wanted to call Megan, hear her voice assuring him that she was all right.

Of course she was all right, he chided himself, closing the folder on the desk in front of him. He slid the folder into the out basket and reached into the in basket for another one. He opened the folder and frowned at the top sheet of paper. The information contained on the page merged into wavy lines of seeming gibberish.

Frustrated, impatient, unsettled, Royce pushed the file aside and sat back in his chair, one foot tapping a rhythmic tattoo on the tile floor.

At the rate he was moving, he mused, he'd be lucky to get halfway through the stack in the in basket by quitting time.

And it was not his style. Royce had a reputation for dedication to detail, and for completing his work duties ahead of schedule. His fellow officers loved ribbing him about being a workaholic cop.

Royce didn't mind the flak, because he knew it was just that, good-natured flak. Besides, in all honesty, he knew there was more than a little truth to their claim. He *was* something of a workaholic. He was also a good cop.

But, at that precise moment, Royce felt anything but either. He felt helpless and ineffectual.

Yet, like it or not, there wasn't a whole lot Royce could do about the situation. He had already talked to the officer investigating the attack on Megan. And Stew Javorsky had sounded as frustrated as Royce felt.

"Sorry, Sarge, but there's not much to report," Stew had said, his expression woeful. "Nobody saw anything. Nobody heard anything. There have been no other reports or complaints of similar occurrences." He'd heaved a sigh. "And there isn't even a heck of a lot to go on. I mean, the description—'large, hulking and rough-voiced'—isn't exactly...exact."

"I know." Royce had moved his wide shoulders in a helpless shrug. "I'm hoping Miss Delaney will recall more details of the man's appearance when the initial shock and trauma wear off."

"Wouldn't hurt," Stew had agreed dryly. "Meanwhile, I'll keep you informed if anything should turn up."

Royce had thanked Stew, then tried to bury his frustration and impatience in his work.

That had been hours ago, and his diversionary ploy had produced only minor results.

Should he just go ahead and call her?

Royce scowled as he mulled over the question, unwilling to admit, even to himself, that there was an aching need expanding inside him just to hear the sound of her voice. Yet, whether or not he was willing to admit to it, the attraction to Megan that he had initially experienced had been gaining strength and momentum ever since she grasped his hand and hung on as if for dear life, yesterday morning in the hospital.

But the really telling incident had happened several hours ago, when Megan had once again placed her hand in his.

Royce had been hard-pressed to keep from jolting in reaction to the feel of her soft palm gliding onto his. A confusing and unfamiliar tingling sensation of applied heat had flashed from his palm to the outer reaches of his body.

Concealing his reaction from Megan had taxed every ounce of control Royce possessed.

Both shocked and baffled by the intensity of the excitement dancing along his nerve endings from their connecting palms, Royce had been forced to grit his teeth to squash an urgent impulse to caress the back of her hand, test the texture of her soft skin with his long fingers.

Against all reason, against all decency, Royce wanted Megan.

It was stupid.

It was reprehensible.

It was there, the wanting, burning in the core of his body, the depths of his mind.

Damn his soul, his maleness, his physical responses.

Although Royce had continued to damn anything and everything he could think of about himself, as a man, as a person, his feelings had not changed one iota.

He wanted Megan.

There was only one thing Royce wanted more than to be with Megan: He wanted her safe.

Without conscious direction, his hand again moved toward the phone. Stopping himself short, Royce drew his hand back and laid it flat on the desktop.

She was all right. Of course she was all right. He'd have heard if she wasn't. Hadn't he made a point of having her promise to call the barracks, call him, if there were any incidents, or anything at all, regardless how seemingly unimportant, out of the ordinary?

He had. Before leaving her, Royce had insisted Megan make that promise to him.

And since Megan hadn't called, he had to assume she was perfectly fine, secure in the safety of her parents' home.

Employing an old phrase his mother had chided her sons with whenever they appeared to be getting overanxious about anything, Royce called himself a worrywart, opened the folder in front of him and told himself to get with the program.

Nevertheless, before focusing his full attention on his work, Royce made an anxiety-easing promise to himself.

He shot another glance at the wall clock and stifled a curse of impatience.

Now the hands stood at 8:57. He had two and a half hours to get through before he could leave, but then he'd be out of there, intent on carrying out his promise.

When his shift was over, and before going home, Royce had decided, he'd make a swing by Megan's place...just to check out the situation for his own satisfaction.

Five

Megan started awake at the jarring sound of the doorbell. Disoriented, she glanced around, heart pounding, nerves jangling, adrenaline surging through her bloodstream. The bell sounded again, and she jolted upright, out of the chair.

Who—? Megan shuddered as an image of a large, hulking, rough-voiced man filled her mind.

She was alone in the house, and it was late. How late? Megan shot a look at the gleaming sunburst clock on the wall above the fireplace mantel.

The clock read 12:05.

The bell pealed once more, followed by the un-mistakable sound of the doorknob being turned.

Megan froze. Dear heaven! Was it him? she

thought frantically. Was it that awful man, trying to get at her to finish what he had started Friday night?

Panic crawled into her stomach, making her feel physically sick, weak-kneed, terrified.

But wait! Think.

The attacker didn't know her name...did he? Megan frowned in concentration. Into her mind stole the faint echo of his voice, nasty-sounding, at first calling a generic "lady," then, as she struggled, fought him, snarling a guttural command: "Be still, you crazy bitch."

No, Megan reasoned, he probably didn't know her name. Therefore, he couldn't very likely know where she lived, she thought, exhaling a whooshing sigh of relief that caught in her throat when another summons trilled from the doorbell.

Panic flared anew, causing a flutter inside her chest, but a faint voice inside her mind called for deeper thought.

Obeying the order from her subconscious, Megan drew in deep, calming breaths, and applied her mind to more reasoned, rational contemplation, backtracking, then following the trail of her earlier actions.

Losing track of the passage of time, Megan had labored over her worktable until after nine, and wouldn't have quit then if not for a nagging and painful cramping in her lower back. Weariness had slammed into her when she slid from the stool and stepped away from the table.

Rubbing the base of her spine, Megan had stood still for a moment, gathering the dregs of her strength. A rumble of hunger from her empty stomach had finally propelled her from her bedroom on rubbery legs.

Leaving the lights burning in her bedroom, Megan had turned on the lights in each successive room she entered. In the kitchen, she'd fixed a quick meal consisting of a sandwich and a glass of skim milk.

It was while she methodically chewed the tasteless sandwich that Megan had been swamped by an overwhelming need to talk to her mother. She'd rushed to the wall phone, and been reaching for the receiver before she remembered that her mother, her parents, were halfway around the world, on a ship on the high seas, midway between ports of call.

The realization that she could not bolster her flagging spirits with the comforting sound of her mother's voice had drained the last of Megan's meager supply of energy.

Forgetting the remains of her slapped-together supper, and again leaving the bright overhead kitchen light on, she'd wandered into the living room, flicking on the swag light above the dining room table, the wall sconces, and then every table and floor lamp in the living room.

After securely closing the drapes over the wide living room windows, Megan had sunk into her father's favorite, deeply cushioned recliner and shut her eyes...just to rest for a few minutes.

She had been lost to the world within seconds.

That had been over two hours ago. Now, the last foggy wisps of sleep banished from her mind, Megan stood, taut and wary, her brain working at near full capacity.

Except for the draped windows in the living room, the house was ablaze with lights, indicating to any and all friends, neighbors and passersby that somebody was not only at home, but awake and aware.

Yet how many friends, neighbors or passersby came visiting after twelve o'clock at night?

Megan went stiff as a board as the doorbell trilled again, hard, quick, as if from the impatient stab of a finger stiffened by anger.

Get a grip, Megan told herself, fighting for all she was worth against paralyzing terror. Even if the attacker had somehow gotten her name and address, would a potential rapist announce himself by ringing the doorbell?

Not hardly, Megan chided herself bracingly, exhaling another whooshing breath of relief.

The bell rang yet again, immediately followed by a rapping tattoo against the wood-encased steel panel and a low-pitched, sharply concerned call.

"Megan, are you in there? Are you all right?"

Royce!

As his name exploded inside her mind, Megan was off and running to the door.

"I'm here!" she answered, raising her voice in case he had turned away. "Don't leave!" she cried, mentally cursing as she fumbled with the security lock.

"I had no intention—" the lock clicked, and she swung open the door "—of leaving."

Sergeant Royce Wolfe did not look like a very happy man. In point of fact, decked out in his smart state police uniform, he looked intimidating as hell.

Megan thought he was the best-looking thing she had seen in…well, in forever.

"You having a party or something?" Royce asked in a terse, clipped voice.

"A party?" Megan blinked. "Of course not! Why in the world would you think that?"

"You want an immediate answer," he fairly growled, "or may I come in out of the rain?"

"Oh! It's raining again." Megan backed away from the doorway. "I didn't know. Come on in."

"Thanks." Royce stepped past her into the flagged foyer, and only then did she notice the damp patches on the shoulders of his uniform jacket. "It's more a heavy mist than a rainfall," he said, raising his hand to remove his stiff-brimmed hat. "But the temperature's dropping, and it's beginning to freeze on the ground.'' He passed the hat to her.

"Don't you have a slicker or something for protection?'' Megan asked, watching as he unfastened the buttons on his jacket. ''And I thought you guys were issued plastic thingies to cover your hats.'' She ran her hand over the stiff, damp brim.

"Thingies?'' The light of anger in Royce's glittering blue eyes gave way to a gleam of amusement.

"You know what I mean,'' she retorted, reaching for the jacket as he shrugged out of it.

"Yeah, I know what you mean.'' Royce surrendered the jacket to her, along with a smile. ''The *thingie* is in its bag, which is in the car, on the seat, beneath the slicker.''

"Oh.'' Megan stood there, holding his jacket and staring at him in bewildered admiration.

In the gray police-issue shirt and pants, Royce was a sight to behold. Of course, Megan mused, bemused, at least in his case, the smart-looking dark gray uniform did not make the man. Quite the contrary. With his so-tall, muscularly trim physique and his sharp-featured, sun-kissed good looks, Royce most decidedly made the uniform.

He'd said something.

"Huh?'' Megan shook herself out of distraction and into awareness.

"I asked if you were feeling all right.''

"Yes, fine,'' she said. ''Why do you ask?''

"Because you're staring at me," he answered, frowning. "And you've got a strange look on your face."

"Oh." Upset with herself for becoming distracted by his masculine appeal, Megan raked a hand through her already tousled hair, and searched her mind for an intelligent response. "Really?" was all she could come up with, which sounded pretty lame, even to her own ears.

"Yes, really," Royce replied. "Something bothering you? Something about me, I mean?"

"Oh, no," she told him, giving a sharp shake of her head to reinforce her falsehood. "I had dozed off on the recliner in the living room, you see," she babbled. "The doorbell startled me, and I guess I'm still not quite awake yet."

"Uh-huh," he murmured, eyeing her speculatively. Then, his voice taking on a note of understanding, he asked, "You afraid to go to bed?"

"Afraid?" Megan repeated, bristling at the mere suggestion of a lack of inner fortitude…even if it did happen to be true. "Why would you think that I'm afraid?"

"Elementary, my dear Megan," Royce said, dryly paraphrasing a famous fictional detective. "Your falling asleep on a chair in the living room with every light burning in the house would naturally lead one to deduce that you are afraid of placing yourself in the vulnerable position of being in a bed in a dark house."

All the fight went out of Megan, and her rigidly held shoulders slumped in defeat. "Okay," she admitted tiredly. "I was afraid to go to bed." She looked past him, as if seeing the night beyond the closed front door. "It's pitch-black, and I don't know who might be skulking about out there."

"But I *do* know," he said. "There isn't a soul skulking about out there."

"How do you know?" Megan asked, without pausing to think or reflect.

"I looked." His lips tilted into a chiding smile. "I peeked behind every tree and bush."

"I should have known," Megan confessed, giving him an apologetic smile in return. "You are exceptionally thorough in your work, aren't you?"

"Exceptionally," Royce agreed, without so much as a shadow of underlying conceit. "Besides," he went on, shrugging, "I asked the local municipal patrolman to keep a sharp eye on the place while making his sweep of the area."

"Thank you, Royce," Megan said, in quiet recognition of his dedication beyond the call. "I appreciate your concern for my safety."

"Enough to offer me a hot drink?" he asked, arching his burnished brows over eyes beginning to sparkle with inner laughter. "It's cold work beating the bushes and peering behind trees, especially when said bushes and trees are coated with a fine film of ice." His mouth quirked in an invitation for her to share his amusement. "Bites the fingers, you know."

As had happened before, Megan succumbed to his whimsical appeal to her sense of humor. Though her gurgle of laughter was faint, it was genuine, unforced.

"Coffee or tea?" she asked, turning to hang up his jacket in the foyer closet.

"Tea sounds genteel, and more suited to the midnight hour, but I'd prefer coffee," Royce said. "If you don't mind?"

"Whichever," Megan replied, shrugging to show her unconcern and pivoting to lead the way into the kitchen.

She had no sooner crossed the threshold than her glance settled on the half-eaten sandwich and barely touched glass of milk she had left forgotten on the table.

"I'll just clear away my supper things," she muttered, crossing the room and sweeping the plate and the glass from the table. "Then I'll start the coffee."

"That was your supper?"

Megan winced at the note of censure in Royce's voice. "I wasn't very hungry," she said defensively, moving to the sink. Dumping the milk and the remains of the sandwich, she rinsed the plate and glass, then turned to the coffeemaker.

"Besides nourishment, you need to feed your nerves, Megan," Royce said, sauntering across the room to stand beside her. "Or else you're going to come unglued."

A retort telling him to mind his own business sprang to her lips, but Megan held it in check, recalling the emptiness she had experienced on rising from her stool at the worktable, the weakness of needing to hear her mother's voice, the panic that had gripped her at the jarring ring of the doorbell.

"You're right, I know," she admitted, carefully spooning coffee grounds into the lined basket. "But I never fuss with meals to begin with, and tonight…well…"

"You were more than usually alone?"

"Yes," she said in a grateful murmur, no longer surprised by the depths of his understanding and insight.

"Well, you're no longer alone," Royce said, plucking the water-filled glass pot from her trembling fingers and tipping it over the grate on top of the coffeemaker. "And I'm always hungry." He angled his head to grin at her. "What do you say— should we raid the refrigerator?"

"I'm afraid there's not much to raid. I was planning on doing my grocery shopping on…" Megan's voice faded. She swallowed, then went on gamely, "Saturday morning."

"How about in here?" Royce asked, going to the end wall cabinet. "Any canned goodies, soup and such?"

"Sure," Megan answered, giving him permission to look with a wave of her hand. "Help your-self."

In the end, what Royce helped himself to was a can of luncheon meat, which he sliced and fried in one pan, six eggs, which he beat and scrambled up in another pan, and four pieces of slightly stale bread, which he put Megan in charge of toasting and buttering.

Megan surprised herself by polishing off two pieces of the meat, a quarter portion of the egg mixture, and a slice of toast, liberally buttered and slathered with strawberry preserves. But she passed on the coffee, sipping a small glass of orange juice instead.

The bits of conversation they exchanged during their meal were general and innocuous, light-years removed from the root cause of their association. After they finished eating and clearing the table, and as if they had known each other for years, Royce jotted down items on a scrap of notepaper, Megan calling out to him as she took stock of the end cabinet and the refrigerator, deciding what she needed to pick up at the supermarket.

It was nearing two-thirty in the morning by the time Royce made his way to the front door. Reluctant to see him go, Megan retrieved his jacket from the hall closet and watched, sad-eyed, as he shrugged into it.

"You're okay now?" Royce asked, settling his

hat low on his forehead before reaching for the doorknob.

"Yes." Megan dredged up a smile for him. "I feel much better, thank you."

"No thanks necessary, unless it's from me."

Megan frowned. "For what?"

"For our late-night indulgence, or whatever you might call it—a late supper, an early breakfast...." He grinned.

Megan experienced an unfamiliar, unwanted, but definite spark of response of a sensual nature. Dismissing it as absurd, under the circumstances, she returned his grin with a faint, remote and cool smile.

Royce looked baffled for an instant. Then, with a barely discernible shrug, he turned the doorknob and swung open the door. A blast of frigid air swept into the foyer.

"Whoa!" he muttered, stepping outside. "It's cold as a witch's..." He caught himself up short, shrugged again, then went on. "It's damn cold out here." He took another step, wobbled, then straightened. "Like a sheet of glass, too."

"Be careful," Megan called, hovering behind the protection afforded by the door. "And drive carefully."

"I will," Royce promised. "Go inside and shut the door," he ordered. "I want to hear that lock click into place."

"But..."

"Go, Megan, I'm freezing!"

"All right," she snapped, stepping around the door to glare at him. "But call me when you get home," she tacked on.

"Me-gan," Royce groaned. "I'll be all right."

"I want to know you aren't wrapped around a tree somewhere," she insisted. "Will you call?"

"Okay, okay, I'll call." He heaved a sigh. "Now, will you get the hell inside?"

"I'm going," she grumbled, moving back behind the door. "Good night, Sergeant."

"Good night, Megan," Royce responded in a tone of rapidly dwindling patience. "Lock the door."

"Sorehead!" Megan shut the door with a bang, then bullied the lock into place.

Royce's bark of laughter reached her, even filtered through the wood-encased steel door.

As had happened before—was it once, twice?—Megan could not deny the chuckle that escaped through her smiling lips. And it was the tug on her lips, the very sound of her soft laughter, that brought home to her the realization of how beneficial his unexpected visit had been to her.

By his very presence, his easy manner, his everything-under-control attitude, Royce had effectively chased the fears, real and imagined, from her rattled mind.

Decent? Megan mused, absently drifting from room to room, extinguishing lights as she went.

Royce Wolfe was a lot more than a decent individual; he was the genuine article, a *man,* in every true sense of the word.

Returning to her bedroom, Megan began undressing. Distracted by her thoughts, she was unconscious of the wide, uncovered windows flanking her desk and worktable, the late-winter darkness beyond the panes.

Stripped to the buff, she gathered up her discarded clothing, grabbed a clean oversize navy-blue nightshirt emblazoned with white lettering spelling out Penn State Nitney Lions, and made for the bathroom and a quick, hot shower.

Still contemplating the man who had so recently departed for his own place, and whose call she was expecting momentarily, Megan reentered the bedroom, clad in the nightshirt and a liberal application of face and body lotion.

What facets did he possess that, to her way of thinking, made Royce the living, breathing embodiment of her personal ideal of what a man should be?

Megan mulled over the question as she plied a brush to her shower dampened, tangled mass of long auburn hair.

Appealing surface attractions aside—great bone structure, riveting crystal-blue eyes, a mouth both firm and sensuous, set in a well-shaped head crowned by a vibrant shock of sun-tipped golden brown hair and sitting atop a tall, muscularly trim, fantastic body—Royce Wolfe possessed inner qualities that, in her opinion, surpassed mere appearance, however handsome and sexy-looking he was.

In the short time Megan had known him—had it really only been two days?—Royce had displayed to her a wide and deep range of personality traits.

While Royce was blatantly male, strong, self-confident, determined, even a tad arrogant, he was also understanding, concerned, caring and sensitive...to the point that he had opted for a desk job when the growing routine slaughter of the highway scene, the investigations into cases involving robbery, rape, murder and mayhem had gotten to him.

The very fact that Royce had not only identified and faced his occupational dilemma, but acted to remove himself from the crux of the problem, while maintaining a position within the profession he so obviously loved, told Megan a lot about the man, as a man.

A sobering thought struck. Megan's hand stilled, the brush midway along a silky strand of red hair. The very fact that she was mentally evaluating the man told Megan a lot about her own feelings.

She was interested in the man.

Interested? a taunting inner voice chided.

Try intrigued.

Try excited.

Try...

All right! Megan thought, silencing the inner voice with the acknowledgment.

Royce interests, intrigues and excites me, but—

The phone rang.

Royce!

Dropping the brush to the dressertop, Megan ran for the console on the corner of the desk. She snatched up the receiver in the middle of the second ring.

"Hello?"

Silence.

Megan frowned. Definitely not Royce. But then who? A chill crawled along her spine.

"Hello, who's calling?" she demanded, despairing at the note of incipient panic she heard in her voice.

Nothing.

A large, hulking image filled her mind, terrorizing her senses, stealing her common sense. Reacting to instinct, Megan slammed down the receiver, then stood frozen, staring at the instrument, as if afraid it would leap from the cradle and lunge for her constricted throat.

It rang again.

Oh, my god, oh, my god, oh, my god! A low, keening wail broke from Megan's throat. No. No. Please, no.

A second ring, and then a third.

Not breathing, afraid to think, Megan extended a shaking hand and grabbed the receiver.

"Who is this?" she cried. "Why are you doing this to—"

"What the hell?" Royce exclaimed into her ear. "Megan! What's going on?"

"Oh, Royce! Oh, Royce!" Megan's voice was little more than a sobbing gasp. "I...I just had a phone call...but nobody spoke. It was him. I know it was *him!*"

"Megan, listen to me," Royce commanded her in a calm, stern tone of voice. "Don't fly apart. I'm on my way. I'll be there in a few minutes. Keep it together, honey. I'm coming."

He disconnected. The dial tone buzzed in Megan's ear. Gripping the receiver, she stood, repeating his promise over and over to herself.

I'm on my way. I'll be there in a few minutes. Keep it together, honey. I'm coming.

Honey?

A chill of a different nature scurried down Megan's spine. Surely it had been nothing more than a spur-of-the-moment expression. Royce certainly hadn't meant it as an endearment—had he?

Megan swallowed, and felt a spark of something in her stomach.

Honey?

The beeping noise from the phone penetrated the speculative thoughts distracting her mind.

"If you want to make a call—" the tinny voice of the recording grated against her ears, and patience "—hang up and dial again."

"Take a flying leap," Megan muttered, sighing in relief when the instrument went silent.

Clutching the now-dead receiver to her chest, Megan kept it together as best she could until, at last, after what seemed like hours, but in actuality couldn't have been more than ten minutes, she heard the blessed sound of crunching tires and squealing brakes from Royce's car in the driveway.

The telephone receiver landed on the carpeted floor with a dull thud. Megan didn't hear it—she was already dashing from the room to the foyer and the front door.

"Megan!" Royce yelled, rapping his knuckles hard against the door. "Are you all right?"

Unaware that she was sobbing, Megan fumbled with the lock with trembling fingers. Cursing, she finally released the lock, pulled the door open, and literally flung her shaking body against the reassuringly solid wall of Royce's chest.

Six

Royce's arms automatically closed around Megan's shivering body. Holding her tightly to him, he stepped into the foyer and nudged the door shut with a backward tap of his heel.

She was even taller than he had first decided; her nuzzling face fit neatly into the curve of his neck.

The broken sound of her uneven, hiccuping breaths impelled him to tighten his arms protectively, drawing her pliant form more closely to his alert-tautened body.

Royce immediately knew he had made a mistake. The feel of Megan's soft curves pressed against him caused an instantaneous reactive response.

He was at once hard and hurting.

Fortunately, Megan appeared to be too upset to notice the pressure against her abdomen.

Silently cursing the inconvenient and inappropriate, if normal and natural, reaction of his flesh and senses, Royce exerted iron-willed control over his gathering response and murmured words of comfort and reassurance.

"It's all right, Megan. I'm here," he said, loosening his arms to clasp her shoulders and move her back a step, away from physical contact with him. "I'm not going to let anything or anybody hurt you."

"But…but suppose it was *him?*" Megan cried, raising a hand to swipe at her wet cheeks. "That…that hulking, horrible man?" she went on, voice rising.

"Calm down, calm down," Royce said in a soothing voice, flexing his fingers gently in her soft flesh, attempting to instill his strength in her. "You told me you had never seen the man before, and that he hadn't called you by your name. Didn't you?"

Megan gulped and nodded. "Yes."

"Well then, I'd say that chances are it was a wrong number, probably dialed by a person with an unsteady finger, or someone who raised one glass too many."

"Do you honestly think so?" she asked, in a small voice so filled with hope it tore at his heart.

"Yes, I do." Royce infused adamant conviction into his voice. "It happens." He shrugged. "It's happened to me. Sometimes you hear a slurred voice, demanding to speak to someone you've never heard of, but more often the offender just hangs up, like the inconsiderate drunk he probably is."

"Yes." Megan gave a quick nod. "I've had a few calls like that at my place in New York."

Royce could see her fighting to suppress the panic that had threatened to overtake her. He could also see the enticing peaks of her breasts, and the sweet curves of her hips and tush, barely concealed by the soft cotton nightshirt. Beneath the midthigh hem of the shirt, her long, shapely legs were exposed for his joyful examination.

Royce dragged his gaze away from her body, back to her pale cheeks and fright-widened eyes. Megan looked exhausted, in need of a lot of hours of solid sleep. Dark shadows pooled in the hollows under her eyes. Weariness tugged her tempting lips into a drooping curve.

He smothered a sigh, and managed a smile.

"Why don't you go to bed?"

"Bed?" Megan's eyes grew wider still, and she shook her head rapidly back and forth. "No. I can't... No!"

"Megan, honey, c'mon," Royce said, smoothing his palms down her arms. "I'll give the area a good once-over, make sure there are no intruders lurking about, before I leave.''

"Leave!" Megan yelped, bringing her hands up to grasp his shirt and inadvertently digging her nails into his chest. "You're going to leave? You can't leave! What if the phone rings again?'' Though she had asked, she didn't wait for an answer, but rattled on, "I couldn't sleep, not now, not if you leave. I just know I'd sit staring at the phone until morning.''

Feeling the stab of her nails in his skin, all the way down to the burgeoning heat of his desire, Royce heaved another, deeper sigh.

"Okay, okay...." He surrendered, purely in self-defense. "I'll stay, but—"

"Oh, Royce, thank you." Megan eased her nails from his skin to smooth her palms over the front of his shirt—unconsciously, he felt sure. "I know it's a dreadful imposition, but I'll sit up with you. Uh, are you hungry, thirsty? I can..."

"No, we just ate, remember?" he said, interrupting her. "And you will not sit up with me. *You're* going to bed." Letting his hands fall away from the allure of her soft arms, he motioned toward the darkened living room. "I'll stretch out on the recliner in there."

A frown tugged at Megan's brow as she shifted her gaze from him to the recliner, then back to him, sweeping a glance down the length of his body.

"You can't rest in that chair," she protested. "It's not nearly big enough for you."

Since she wasn't telling him anything he didn't already know, Royce merely shrugged. "What would you suggest?" he asked, rather dryly. "The sofa?"

"Uh, no...." Megan shook her head. "If anything, the sofa's even smaller than the chair."

"Right." Royce nodded. "So?"

"There's the guest room." Megan indicated the second door along the hallway with a flick of her hand.

"I don't think so." Royce shook his head. "I don't want to get too comfortable."

She bit her lip, and gave him a helpless look.

"Uh-huh." Royce returned her look with one of his own—not helpless, but knowing. "I'll stretch out on the chair."

"Oh, Royce..." she began, in a low tone of contrition. "I'm sorry, but—"

He cut her off, gently. "Not to worry. I've managed to catch some zees in worse positions." He laughed easily. "Believe it or not, I actually dozed off standing up on a train some years back." His smile grew into a grin at the skeptical look she gave him. "No kidding. Fortunately, I jerked awake when the train pulled in at my station, or, who knows, like that guy in the song, I mighta been the man who never returned."

Megan laughed, and though the sound was

weak, Royce considered it a good indicator of her easing tension. Acting on it, he again clasped her arms and turned her around to face her bedroom doorway. Then he gave her a light nudge to get her moving.

"Go, Megan," he ordered. "Get some rest."

"But—" she again began in protest, tossing a concerned look over her shoulder at him.

"No buts. Cut me a break, please. I'm tired, too." He yawned elaborately, if indelicately, to prove his assertion. "Get going."

She sighed, but gave in. "Okay." She took two hesitant steps, then, spinning to face him, insisted, "But I know I won't be able to sleep."

Royce simply smiled at her.

"I mean it."

"All right, just go rest your eyes for a while."

The fight went out of her, yet it was still only with evident reluctance that Megan went into her room. Moments later, she opened the door a crack and thrust her arm out, extending the extra comforter she'd obviously just thought to give him.

"You'll need this," she said, calling him back up the three steps to the hallway. "The house is chilly now."

"Thank you," he murmured, relieving her of the lightweight down cover. "Now go to bed."

"Good night," she whispered, peering around the door at him. "But I still say I won't sleep."

"Well then, you rest, and I'll sleep." Royce offered her a wry smile. "Wake me if you need me, okay?"

"Yes."

Her shadowed eyes brought a tightness to his throat and a pang to his chest. Royce heaved a breath and swallowed in a futile attempt to relieve both. Giving up, he smiled again and turned toward the steps into the living room.

"Good night, honey."

Honey.

Megan lay curled up in the center of her bed, beneath the down comforter, repeating his casually voiced endearment over and over inside her tired mind.

And deep inside her weary body a flicker of warmth ignited in response to the mental echo.

Honey.

It meant nothing, of course, Megan told herself sleepily, uncertain whether the thought was in connection to the endearment, or the unfurling sensation of warm arousal she felt.

She shifted position to dislodge the feeling; the warmth merely intensified.

Ridiculous, Megan told herself. She was suffering mild trauma and shock. She could not be responding sensually to such an offhand, probably unconscious, endearment.

Could she?

The inner warmth spread, causing a tingling along the inside of her thighs, and at their apex.

Megan shifted position again, only this time her movements were sinuous, languorous. She frowned and moved her head against the pillow in a fruitless bid to deny the proof of her body's sensual response to the physical attraction presented to her by Royce Wolfe.

Royce. The thought of his name created his image; the image drew the tingling sensation from the lower regions of her body to her breasts, her shoulders, her arms, and then to her fingertips. Megan could feel again the solid strength of his flatly muscled chest beneath her fingers, her palms. Her breath grew shallow, her nipples grew taut, the tingling in her thighs grew into a stinging heat of need.

Startled by the sheer intensity of her physical response, Megan coiled her arms around her waist and held on to herself, afraid to move, afraid to think, afraid to face the truth of her own feminine desires.

It simply could not be, Megan told herself. Especially not after what she had so recently endured at the hands of a crude and violent man!

But Royce Wolfe was not a crude and violent man, her exhausted brain reminded her. By his actions, his caring, Royce had revealed himself, his character. She herself had labeled Royce a thoroughly decent man.

Decent.

Nice.

Attractive.

The warm flow inside brought another adjective from Megan's weakening consciousness.

Sexy.

Megan tightened her arms around her slender form, as if instinctively holding herself together.

Honey.

The echo of his voice whispered through her mind, as sweetly as the endearment itself.

But he didn't mean anything by it.

Did he?

Fortunately for Megan, the inner warmth wasn't the only response flowing throughout her body. The languor had crept through her system, to invade her mind, as well. Her eyelids grew heavy. She yawned. Her eyes closed.

Within moments, Megan was drifting, free of the disturbing questions. Lost to the world, she was blithely unaware that not once had she so much as given a thought to the fear of the ringing phone breaking the quiet of the night.

For Royce, ensconced in a chair, his legs and arms dangling from footrests and armrests, it was a very long night. But not only due to the inadequate length of the recliner. His mental discomfort added to his physical unease.

Damned inconvenient time for his libido to go

into overdrive, Royce reflected, squirming for the umpteenth time within the close confines of the chair.

Inconvenient, but—considering the circumstances of his recent personal history—not by any means earth-shattering, or even unpredictable, for that matter.

It had been some long months since he had been with a woman…more like a year. Thanks to the crushing effects of being ignominiously dumped by a woman he'd been dangerously close to falling in love with, Royce had spent the previous eleven months cooling his heels, and his libido, so far as the opposite sex was concerned.

But the fact that his celibacy had been self-imposed had little bearing on the current issue. From all indications, his inclination toward abstinence had run its course. Now, thanks to another woman, a tall, willowy redhead, Royce was again back among the ranks of the randy.

Thinking of Megan sent a tongue of fiery desire licking through Royce. He smothered a groan and squirmed again, grunting when his hip made hard contact with the arm of the chair.

Chill out, Wolfe, Royce advised himself disgustedly. Stop acting like a teenager in the throes of a massive hormone explosion, for pity's sa— Royce's thoughts scattered at the sudden sound at the window.

It was the wind, wasn't it? At once wide awake,

alert and tense, Royce focused his attention on every slight noise from outside, and slowly, carefully retracted the recliner's footrest and eased his long frame from the chair.

Moving silently on stockinged feet, Royce crossed to the wide window. Hesitating, he listened, straining to hear any sound not produced by nature.

There was only the low moan of the wind, brushing the windows, sighing through the branches of bare limbs and fir trees and small ornamental bushes.

Raising one hand, Royce nudged the edge of the drapery panel aside and peered through the pane. There was only the night, and the pale moonlight glittering on the thin layer of ice sheening the ground.

Damn, would spring never come?

Heaving a sigh, Royce let the drapery panel fall back against its counterpart, then padded into the dining room to inspect the windows there. Nothing. From the dining room, he drifted into the kitchen to repeat the drill, then into the kitchen and the laundry room, and on into the central bathroom. He then went into the remaining two bedrooms, one of which was obviously the master suite used by Megan's parents, the other the guest room Megan had mentioned.

Royce stood for a moment, staring longingly at

the single bed. Then, heaving a sigh, he returned to the living room.

Suppressing another sigh, Royce settled once more into the recliner, deciding that, if nothing else, the exercise had been a diversion, an escape from his wayward thoughts about Megan, and his physical response to her allure.

All of which, of course, brought the thoughts and feelings rushing right back.

Damn, Royce groaned in silent misery. It was going to be a *really* long night.

Diffused sunlight filtered between the horizontal mini-blinds brightening the room, waking Megan.

For a moment, she lay still, frowning with the effort of bringing recall to her sleep-fuzzy mind. Then memory kicked in, surging back with a flood of the incidents of the night: the phone call, her near-panic, Royce.

Royce!

Tossing back the comforter, Megan leapt out of bed and, not bothering to take the time to look for her robe, ran to the door, flung it wide, and dashed into the drapery-shrouded living room. At the bottom of the three steps, she came to an abrupt halt, her eyes widening in fascination and admiration.

Royce stood in the center of the room, arms raised over his head, belly sucked in, his long muscles rippling as he stretched the cramps and kinks from his body.

Throwing his head back, he opened his mouth wide in a huge, noisy yawn. That, combined with his pose, and his shock of tawny hair, reminded Megan so much of a big, morning-hungry lion, she couldn't stifle the giggle that burst from her throat.

Lowering and turning his head to face her, Royce gave her a quizzical look. "Something funny?"

"No." Megan clapped a hand over her mouth to smother another giggle, then spread her fingers to continue through them, "I, uh… You just struck me as looking like a big, disgruntled cat, stretching and growling."

"I wasn't growling, I was yawning." Royce silently padded across the room to her. A slow, feral, devastatingly effective smile curved his attractive mouth. "If I growl, honey, you'll know it."

There it was again, the careless endearment, so casually tossed out, so potent in impact.

Megan's breath caught, and she fought against revealing the confusion and mixed emotions she was experiencing. She smiled. It quivered, then stuck to her dry lips.

"Uh, do you growl often?" she asked, for want of something, anything, to say.

His smile grew into a Wolfe-ish grin. "Now and again," he drawled. "At my men, when I'm seriously pi—ah, ticked off." His voice lowered to a near-purr. "And occasionally, but altogether differently, when I'm caught up in the throes of passion.''

A bolt of sensation, crackling like heat lightning, shot through Megan. Suddenly, her lips were not only dry, they felt hot. Her breasts felt heavy. Her body felt...empty.

Royce said something; she shook her head.

''What?''

His lips twitched. ''I asked if you ever growled while in the throes of passion?''

How had she gotten into this discussion? Megan wondered wildly, raking her mind for a coherent reply.

''Uh, no....'' Well, she had raked for coherent, not brilliant, or even intelligent.

''Pity,'' Royce murmured.

''Pity?'' Megan frowned. ''Why?''

''Oh, just an off-the-wall opinion of mine.'' His blue eyes were bright, teasing.

She was almost afraid to ask, but of course she had to. ''Which is?''

''That unless you've reached the point of growling, you haven't truly plumbed the depths, or tested the fire, of the throes of passion.''

Megan couldn't believe she was having this conversation with any man, let alone a man she hardly knew. And she was still in her nightshirt, to boot! She couldn't decide whether she wanted to laugh or run back into her bedroom.

Not the bedroom!

Resisting an impulse to tug at the hem of her nightshirt, she opted to laugh.

Royce laughed with her. "I warned you that my opinion was off-the-wall."

"I'm beginning to think that *you're* off-the-wall," Megan said, only half teasingly. "Or that you think I might be."

"No, I don't think that, honey." Royce's tone was now deadly serious. "I'm beginning to think you're rather special."

Honey. Rather special. Megan felt a distinct melting sensation inside. Fighting the feeling, and the attraction of the man who had caused it, Megan withdrew behind a cool front of composure.

"I think I'd better get dressed," she said, backing away from him.

"I've offended you." Royce's voice revealed both concern and regret. "I'm sorry."

"Offended?" Megan shook her head, and came to an abrupt halt when her bare right heel banged into the bottom step leading down into the living room. "I don't understand. Why would I feel offended?"

"The teasing. I mean, after what you've been through, for one thing." He shrugged. "Then, for another, my calling you honey." He gave a quirky smile. "I know a lot of women object to that these days."

"Uh, no...I, uh, no, I'm not offended," she said, slightly amazed that she was not. In truth, Megan had sometimes taken exception to the occasional male usage of off-hand endearments like *honey* and *sweetie* and—shudder—*babe*. And yet, when the endearment came from Royce, she felt...flattered.

Strange. But, stranger still, in light of her recent terrifying experience, was the somewhat shocking realization that she wasn't put off by his teasing, but was in fact actually enjoying it!

"I'm glad," Royce said, his expression revealing his evident relief. "Because I meant no offense."

"I know." The really funny part was, Megan did know. It was all much too strange, and so made her feel awkward, uncertain, and as giddy as a teenager in the first flush of her first real crush.

Definitely time to get dressed, she scolded herself, again absently tugging on the hem of her nightshirt.

"Ah, if you'll give me a few moments," she babbled, sliding her heel up the riser to the bottom step, "I'll dash into my room and throw on some clothes, then make you breakfast."

"That's not necessary," Royce said, unconvincingly, turning away to lift the comforter from the chair and begin folding it. "I can grab something to eat on my way home."

"You certainly will not," Megan said indignantly. "Making you breakfast is the least I can do to repay you for your trouble." An impish grin played over her lips. "Most especially the discomfort you endured in that chair.'' Not giving him a chance to respond, she whirled around, took the top two steps in one long stride, and went running to her room.

His soft laughter ran after her.

Seven

Breakfast was an unqualified success. The French toast was a perfect golden brown, the small sausage links were tangy, not too spicy, the coffee was rich and delicious.

Cradling his refilled mug in his hands, Royce sat back in his chair, stretched his legs out and smiled his utter satisfaction at his hostess.

"That was great," he told her. "You're really a very good cook. I feel almost human now."

"Thank you." A becoming flush of pleasure tinged Megan's cheeks. "Almost human?"

"Hmm…" Royce nodded and took a tentative sip of the still-steaming brew. Washed by last night's misty rainfall, the morning had dawned sparkling. The sunlight streaming through the windows shot gleaming red highlights through the long, loose strands of Megan's hair and enhanced the color pinkening her cheeks. Quashing an impulse to reach across the table and stroke the spiral curls, and her soft skin, Royce explained, "I'll feel a lot more human after I've caught a few hours' sleep."

"Oh, Royce, I'm sorry." Megan looked both downcast and embarrassed. "I'm such a wuss."

"Bag that, honey," he ordered, gently. "Your reaction to that phone call was perfectly normal," he assured her. "Whatever the hell normal is."

The shadows lifted from her eyes. A tiny smile kissed her full, luscious lips. Royce envied the smile.

"You don't know what normal is?" she asked, raising one naturally arched auburn eyebrow chidingly.

"No," he admitted easily. "I used to think I knew, but—" he shrugged "—the longer I live, the more I realize how little I do know." His expression grew wry. "Hell, I used to think I knew most of the answers. Now the only thing I really know is that I don't even know half the questions."

Megan laughed—which, of course, was the response he had worked for. She was so damned appealing when she laughed. Come to that, she was damned appealing when she didn't laugh. Like earlier this morning, he reflected, sensation stirring at the memory of Megan, her enticing form barely covered by that oversize nightshirt.

Not that she wasn't alluring in the soft jeans and baggy sweatshirt she had "thrown on" after beating her hasty retreat into the bedroom, Royce allowed, surreptitiously caressing the outline of the breasts concealed beneath the shirt. But, oh, her long, long legs... Megan's legs were the stuff of his wildest erotic fantasies.

Smothering a yearning sigh, and a leap of life in the lower section of his body, Royce took another sip of coffee...in reality, a big gulp.

"It is rather ironic, isn't it?" she said, her tone as wry as his expression. She was apparently innocently oblivious of his lascivious mental meanderings. "The older we grow, the less we know. Kinda like that old Pennsylvania Dutch saying— The faster I go, the behinder I get."

"Yeah." Royce chuckled, finished off his coffee in two long swallows, then, drawing back his legs, jackknifed to his feet. "I'm headed for home and bed." He leveled a questioning look at her. "You'll be all right now, on your own?"

"Yes, thank you." Megan gave him a bright and brave smile. "At the risk of sounding trite, I suppose things always do look brighter in the light of day, don't they?" She returned his questioning look.

"Trite, maybe, but true," Royce agreed, bending over the table to collect his plate, cup and utensils.

"No!" Megan ordered, reaching across the table to place a staying hand over his. "I'll do that."

"You cooked," he reminded her unnecessarily, feeling his skin begin to prickle and grow warm beneath her palm. "I don't mind clearing up."

"I appreciate the thought," Megan said, flexing her hand over his in a reassuring squeeze. "But you've done enough. Go home, Royce. Get some sleep. You have to work tonight."

"Yeah." Royce nodded, and stifled a yawn, along with a responsive groan at her touch. "Okay, I'm outa here." He straightened, dislodging her hand from atop his. His flesh immediately felt cooler, robbed of warmth. "Is my jacket in the foyer closet?"

"Uh, yes!" Unfastening her gaze from her now-empty hand, Megan jerked around and made a beeline for the hallway. "I'll get it for you."

Sauntering after her, Royce pondered the significance of the fleeting, almost bereft, expression that had flickered over Megan's face as she stared at her empty hand. A curl of hopeful excitement unwound inside him. Could it be possible? he wondered, catching his breath as the excitement ribboned along his nervous system. Could Megan possibly be feeling as strong an attraction to him as he felt for her?

Heady stuff, thoughts like that, Royce told himself, feeling suddenly revived, alert, not at all sleepy. His eyes sought hers as he came to a halt. Megan met his questioning stare for an instant, then lowered her eyes and thrust her hand forward, nearly tossing his jacket at him.

Without taking his contemplative gaze off her, Royce caught the garment and shucked into it. Why couldn't she look at him? he mused, absently fastening the jacket. The curl of excitement inside him flared into full-blown desire when the only reasonable answer sprang to mind.

Megan *was* attracted to him, maybe even strongly attracted to him. A thrill skittered down Royce's spine; hope sprouted in his mind like a spring blossom.

Him and Megan. Together.

An image rose in his imagination, complete in every sensuous, body-tormenting detail, of him and Megan, naked, entwined, together. Maybe. Someday.

Royce's chest muscles contracted, cutting off his breath. His arms ached with the longing to hold her. His palms burned with the need to touch, caress, every inch of her. His mouth tingled with the yearning to kiss her. The rest of his hurting body didn't bear thinking about.

Royce moved to go to her. Then he caught himself up short, pivoted and strode to the door.

Dammit, Wolfe, Royce railed at himself. *Stop reacting like a libido-driven idiot. The absolute last thing Megan needs right now is more emotional trauma.*

Get out. Go home. And grow up.

"Thanks again for breakfast," he said, hating the dry, strangled sound of his own voice.

"Thanks again for staying," Megan replied, sounding almost as strained and affected as he felt.

His fingers fumbled with the dead bolt and the safety lock. Damn. He hadn't fumbled with anything, or anyone, since his fourteenth summer. "Glad to be of service," he muttered, sighing in relief when, at last, the door swung open.

"Will you..." Megan's voice faded on an uncertain note, forcing him to glance around at her.

The shadows of confusion and doubt in her blue eyes tore a hole in his gut. Royce wanted nothing so much at that moment as to pull Megan into his arms, cradle her protectively against his hard body.

Make love to her.

Run for it, Wolfe, before you run to her.

"What?" he asked, sidling through the doorway.

"It's mild!"

"Huh?" Royce blinked.

"The day. The weather." Megan gave him a helpless look. "It's mild outside."

"Oh." Now who was confused? Royce thought, knowing the answer. Collecting himself, he stepped outside to test the air temperature. Damned if it *wasn't* mild, springlike. "Yeah," he said. "Feels good."

"Too good to stay indoors."

Royce frowned. "You're planning on going somewhere?"

"I need to do some grocery shopping," Megan said, reminding him of her empty refrigerator. "Why?"

"You have no wheels," Royce answered, in turn reminding her of her wrecked car. "You're welcome to use my car," he offered. "You could drop me—"

Megan silenced him with a quick shake of her head. The sunlight caught and tangled in her hair again, seemingly turning it into a fiery mass framing her face.

Royce curled his fingers into his palm to keep from reaching out to entangle them in the flamelike strands.

"...in the garage," she was saying.

"I beg your pardon," he admitted apologetically, "but I missed the first part of what you said." Idiot!

"I said—" Megan spoke distinctly "—thank you, but that's not necessary. My father's car is in the garage. He asked me to drive it every so often, anyway."

"Yeah, it's not good to let it sit." Royce frowned. "What had you started to say before?"

She mirrored his frown. "Before when?"

"You said 'will you...' and then stopped." He lifted one eyebrow. "Will I what?"

Megan looked uncomfortable, embarrassed. She flicked a glance at him, then immediately glanced away again. She wet her lips, cleared her throat, then shook her head. "It was nothing. I, uh, never mind...."

"C'mon, Meg," Royce said on a long sigh. "It must have been something. And you should know by now that you can ask me anything. What is it?"

Still she hesitated, her soft mouth twisting in a self-mocking grimace. "I, uh, can I?"

"Can you what?" he asked, thoroughly confused.

"Ask you anything."

"Didn't I just say you could?" Royce was experiencing a distinct sensation of going around in circles. "Ask."

Megan drew a breath, and began slowly, "I was just wondering...well..." She paused, the went on in a rush. "I was wondering if you were thinking of stopping by tonight, you know, when you're done working?"

Royce felt hard-pressed to keep from laughing. "You had to work up your courage to ask that?" he said, losing the battle to hold back a teasing smile.

"Well..." She shrugged. "I have no right to ask you to look out for me in your free time."

"But you didn't ask," he pointed out. "Not initially. It was my idea to stop by last night, remember?''

"Yes, but—"

"So," he said, blithely interrupting her, "I'll stop by. I was planning to, anyway." His teasing smile grew up, into a grin. "Were you thinking about offering me a reward for dedication to duty above and beyond the call?"

"Reward?" Megan frowned. "What sort of reward?"

On the spot, Royce decided that Megan was the only woman he knew who looked appealing when she frowned. But then, he decided, she looked appealing most of the time. Too appealing for his peace of mind. A response to her appeal stirred, in his emotions, in his body.

That was when he decided he had better stick to the discussion at hand. "Well, since I usually have a snack when I get home from work," he said, "a cup of decaf coffee or hot chocolate and a couple of sandwiches would be nice."

"A couple of sandwiches!" Megan exclaimed on a choking bout of the giggles. "At that time of night?"

"Hey, honey, give me a break, will ya?" Royce groused, in patently false aggrievement, deciding her giggle was appealing, as well, and that he had really better get going...and soon. "Look at me." He swept his arm down to indicate his tall form.

"I'm a big man. How far do you think one small sandwich will go in filling me up?"

"I see your point," Megan conceded solemnly, her gleaming blue eyes belying her somber tone. "I will be happy to prepare a snack for you."

"You've got yourself a deal," Royce said. "I'll—" He broke off, just then noticing the shivering tremor in her body. He cursed himself for not noticing sooner. "You're cold. It's not quite spring yet. Go inside. I'm going home to bed." He started for his car, but called back to her over his shoulder, "By the way, I like most kinds of luncheon meats, but most especially baked ham with cheese."

"You'll have it, Sergeant," Megan promised. "Whatever turns you on."

Laughing, Royce gave her a quick wave, slid behind the wheel, fired the engine and backed out of the driveway. His laughter ceased abruptly as soon as he was out of her sight.

You'll have it, Sergeant. Megan's promise replayed in his mind. *Whatever turns you on.*

Not hardly, Royce thought, reflexively tightening his grip on the wheel. He liked ham-and-cheese sandwiches, but they did not turn him on.

Megan turned him on.

His libido was at full throttle and humming along at way above the legal speed limit.

Royce wanted Megan so bad, so very much, it shocked him. The very intensity of his desire for her was startling, for he had never before in his life felt anything quite like it, not even during his supposedly most potent, late-teen years.

Royce made it home safely to his bachelor apartment, driving by rote, with automatic expertise. He had had no doubts about making it home safely.

But being able to get to sleep while his imagination created explicit fantasies around Megan—that he *did* have serious doubts about.

His doubts proved well-founded.

Royce tossed and turned, grunted and groaned, and didn't sleep worth a damn.

But he did enjoy the fantasies.

Megan had a wonderful time grocery shopping. In no hurry, she wandered up and down the aisles, perusing the items on the shelves, making both careful and impulsive selections.

Which just went to highlight how long it had been since she had shopped for food for anybody other than herself, she mused, frowning indecisively at the price on a packaged thick-cut Delmonico steak.

Deciding Royce deserved the expense, she tossed the package into her already piled-high basket and pushed it farther along the meat section.

Four tiny lamb chops followed the steak into the cart; they were for her. Remembering that Royce liked ham, she added a breakfast ham steak to the growing mound.

Megan didn't so much as blink at the cost of feeding Royce, but merely smiled benignly at the pleasant clerk as she handed over the stack of bills.

Considering all he had done, and planned to continue doing, in addition to his caring, gentle concern for her, Megan figured the least she could do was provide not just adequate but delicious sustenance for him.

Besides, she had discovered that morning that she enjoyed cooking for a man. Well, not simply a man, or any man, Megan qualified, grunting as she bullied the stuffed shopping bags out of the cart and into the trunk of her father's car.

She enjoyed cooking for Royce.

What did that tell her?

The question caught Megan unawares as she settled into the driver's seat and pulled the door shut after her. Her expression pensive, she examined the question. The exercise did not overtax her capabilities, even though the answer that presented itself did surprise her somewhat, in light of the fact that she had known him only a few days.

Megan admitted that she enjoyed cooking for Royce because she liked him.

Liked?

Okay, she conceded to the inner prod. She more than liked him; she felt a strong attraction to him…an emotional, as well as physical, attraction.

But how could that be? After what she had been through a few nights ago, how could she even contemplate the attractions of any man, regardless of how nice he might be?

Biting her lower lip in consternation, Megan switched on the engine and drove off the parking lot. The jarring sound of a blast from the horn of an oncoming car shattered her mental distraction.

Geez! Megan thought, shuddering in reaction. She had missed plowing into that other car by mere inches! The very idea of wrecking her father's car, so soon after totaling her own—not to mention the possible damage she could have inflicted on her own, more vulnerable person—was enough to jerk her into giving her full, undivided attention to her driving.

But a genuine concern about damaging her father's car, a rather expensive top-of-the-line that her father took great pride in, simmered at the edges of Megan's mind as she carefully tooled toward home.

And it was that concern that impelled Megan to impulsively pull onto the lot of a new-and-used-car dealership located along the highway just outside of Conifer.

The car behind her, a beat-up piece of junk with a bad muffler, sped past as she made the turn onto the lot. Megan automatically glanced at the driver, and for an instant, an eerie, uneasy sensation flickered in her mind. There was something about the look of the dark-haired man hunched over the steering wheel.

But the sensation was fleeting, overshadowed by the image of a racy red sports car in the forefront of her mind. Shrugging off the feeling, Megan brought the car to a stop near the entrance to the showroom.

Although the day was mild, Megan knew it certainly wasn't warm enough to affect the meats and frozen foods she had stashed in the trunk—at least not for the short amount of time needed for her to inquire if the dealer had in stock a car the exact style and color of the one she had totaled.

The dealer didn't, to his expressed dismay. But, while he offered to order one from the factory for her, he also was quick to point out the attractions of the wide range of sports styles and colors available and on display, there in the showroom and outside on the lot.

Feeling vaguely as if by merely driving onto the lot she had committed herself to at least looking, Megan allowed the man to escort her around. And, to her surprise, she did find herself admiring another model, in a sleek silver-gray.

Still, undecided, she gave the salesman a bright smile, and a tentative promise.

"I'll, ah, think about it," she said, heading back to her father's car. "I'll come back later in the week," she went on, deciding to ask Royce to accompany her and give her his opinion of the vehicle.

Luckily, the salesman refrained from pressuring

her, and simply offered her his card, along with a request that she see him when she returned.

Fair enough, Megan figured as she drove off the lot and into the sparse midday traffic. Telling herself that she had better finish her current project, since she would definitely need the money to put toward whatever car she eventually bought, she sedately drove home.

Megan really didn't breathe easy until after she had unloaded the groceries and shut the garage door, closing her father's car safely inside. Then, after stowing away the foodstuffs, she went to her worktable.

Lost in the advertising layout, Megan was unaware of the passage of time. It was only when long rays of sunlight slanted through the wide windows that she became aware of the waning day, and the emptiness of her stomach.

Standing, she stretched the cramps from her shoulder and back muscles, experiencing a feeling of deep satisfaction as she studied the work in progress.

It was almost finished. And it was good. Megan allowed herself a self-satisfied smile. It was more than good, she thought, congratulating herself.

So there.

Laughing to and at herself, she left the room and went to the kitchen to rustle up supper for one. The prospect held little appeal, but she had to eat.

Meeting Royce, sharing a couple of meals with

him, had changed her perspective on dining alone. For some reason, food seemed to look and taste better when Royce was seated opposite her at the table.

Thinking about Royce brought him near; it was almost as if Megan could sense him close by. A thrill tingled along her spine, igniting sparks of warmth throughout her body.

She liked him.

No, Megan told herself, absently eating the ravioli she didn't even remember heating and dishing out for herself. What she was feeling toward Royce had progressed way beyond liking. It was scary, but it was even more exciting.

She glanced at the clock and felt her pulse rate increase; only five or so hours, and Royce would be there. In a futile attempt to bring a measure of order to her errant pulse, and bring herself down to earth, Megan collected her thoughts and made a mental note to ask him about going with her sometime to look at that silver-gray sports car.

With her hunger appeased, and feeling a pleasant afterglow instilled by the satisfaction of a good day's work accomplished, Megan hummed while she washed her few dishes and straightened the kitchen.

The phone rang just as she was centering a bowl of fruit on the table.

Going stiff with reawakened fear, Megan stared at the instrument mounted on the kitchen wall.

Barely breathing, she listened as it rang, twice, three times, four times. Then, impatience flaring at her own trepidation, she stormed across the room and snatched up the receiver.

"Hello?" she snapped in a sharp-edged, somewhat threatening tone of voice.

"Megan?"

Relief washed through her at the puzzled sound of Jefferson Clarke's voice. "Oh, Jeff, it's you!" Megan replied, giving a light burst of relieved laughter.

"Yes," he said, still sounding puzzled. "Were you expecting a call from someone else?"

"No!" she said, too quickly.

"Megan, you sound strange. Is something wrong?"

For one brief moment, Megan was tempted to pour out her tale of woe to Jeff, but then the moment passed, and she shook her head, denying herself the self-indulgence. What purpose would be served by her dumping her troubles on Jeff, when he was in New York and she was in Pennsylvania?

Besides, Royce's shoulders were broader than Jeff's.

Rolling her eyes at the unfairness of the comparison, even though it was valid, Megan hastened to reassure him.

"Not a thing," she prevaricated. "I was, uh, preoccupied, and the ringing phone startled me."

"I see," he murmured. "I think."

"Are you calling to harass me about being late with the layout?" she asked, changing the subject.

"You are over deadline," Jeff reminded her gently. "But that isn't the only reason I called. I was concerned when you didn't return my call. That isn't like you."

"Uh, well, I'm sorry, but..." A low buzz sounded, indicating that there was another call waiting. "I've been busy," Megan went on, ignoring the buzz. "But I have good news. I'm almost finished with the—" The buzz sounded again.

"Perhaps you had better answer that," Jeff suggested, obviously annoyed by the interruption.

"Okay, hang on," Megan said, sighing, as she depressed the disconnect button.

"Hello?"

Nothing.

"Hello?" Megan repeated, thinking only that Jeff was waiting, very likely with mounting impatience.

Again there was silence.

Sighing once more, Megan punched the disconnect button. "Jeff, are you still there?"

"Yes, I'm here," he answered, testily. "Was it someone important?"

"No. As a matter of fact, whoever it was got impatient and hung up," she told him, silently praying that it hadn't been Royce trying to reach her. "Now, where were we?"

"You were telling me you were almost finished with the layout."

"Yes!" she said happily. "I expect to finish tomorrow and put it in the mail to you the day after."

"I have a better idea," he said softly.

"Really?" Megan frowned. "What's that?"

"Why don't you bring it over?" he asked. "We could see a show, have a late dinner, talk over drinks."

And go round and round again about deepening their relationship, having an affair, Megan thought, filling in the blanks he'd left unspoken.

"Oh, I don't know, Jeff," she began, even though she did. But there was no way she'd consider anything other than platonic friendship with him now, after meeting Royce.

"Will you at least think about it?"

There was a note of abject pleading in his tone that was so totally out of character for the usually ultraurbane Jeff that Megan didn't have the heart to respond with a flat no.

"Yes, I'll think about it." Though she'd reluctantly agreed, Megan felt it was only fair to add a qualifying warning. "But please don't build up any expectations, Jeff."

"We'll see," he murmured. "It's enough for me to know that you'll think about it."

"I will."

And Megan did think about it, for all of ten seconds after they said their goodbyes.

After that, she only had thoughts for Royce, thoughts of concern that the call waiting had been from him trying to reach her to tell her that he wouldn't be stopping by after all.

For Megan, the following hours seemed like days, which indicated a great deal more than she was ready to face about her growing feelings for Royce Wolfe.

But she did derive one benefit from the long wait. In a bid to fill the dragging hours, Megan went back to work.

The project was finished!

Eight

Royce slowed the car to make the turn into Megan's driveway, and cast a quick glance in the rearview mirror at the vehicle that had been following behind him ever since he turned off the interstate some miles back.

At any other time, the presence of the car probably wouldn't even have caught his attention, but at 12:05 in the morning it was unusual.

Though Royce occasionally passed a car, or, more often, a truck, on the interstate on his way home from work, as a rule he seldom did once he had entered the limits of the town, which for all intents and purposes rolled up its sidewalks along about 10:00 p.m. or so.

The car following Royce—a beat-up junker, from what he could see of it—also slowed down, then, with a rumble from the muffler, speeded up again.

Someone lost on the side road? Royce mused, toying with the idea of backing out of the drive and trailing the vehicle. Or someone interested in a particular driveway leading to the home of a certain woman?

The question bothered Royce, for three reasons. The first was the information he had received earlier that evening from the municipal patrolman, concerning a couple of calls to the station from residents in this area, reporting complaints about an unfamiliar car with a noisy muffler, cruising the area with apparent aimlessness.

The second reason it bothered Royce was the very fact that Megan was alone in a house set in the very center of the area from which those complaints had come.

The third, but by no means the least, of those reasons was the persistent memory of the phone call Megan had received late last night. For all his downplaying of the importance of that call to her, Royce had a nagging, uneasy suspicion that the call had not been the result of some drunk's inability to punch in the correct numbers. Instinct, or intuition, or *something,* made him feel certain the call had been placed deliberately by Megan's attacker.

Or was he simply getting slightly paranoid due to his increasing personal interest in Megan?

But the car did have a noisy muffler.

That thought settled the issue for Royce. His personal interest aside, he was first and foremost a law officer. Throwing the car into reverse, he backed out of the driveway and shot down the road after the vehicle.

Fifteen frustrating minutes later, Royce pulled into the driveway again. His pursuit had proved fruitless; he hadn't been able to find sight or sound of the car.

Knowing the driver of the car could have sought cover in any number of places in that secluded, heavily wooded area exacerbated the tension and sense of unease mounting in Royce with regard to Megan's safety.

If anything happened to her...

Clamping a lid on his thoughts, Royce exited the car and strode to the house.

Nothing was going to happen to Megan, he assured himself. Because he was going to make damn sure nothing happened to her, even if he had to cuff her to his wrist to do so.

That thought, and the image that came with it, brought a wry smile to Royce's lips.

Wolfe, old son, you really have got it bad, he told himself, raising his hand to rap his knuckles against the door. Too bad you can't put the woman in your pocket.

The door opened. Megan stood there, a flowing silk caftan caressing her body, her red mane framing her lovely face, a smile of welcome on her inviting lips.

Better yet, too bad you can't pick her up and put her in your bed, Royce thought, feeling every molecule in his body respond to the sight of her.

"Hello."

Her soft voice shivered through Royce, causing a chill in his spine, and a fire in his loins. Suppressing a groan, he worked his lips into a smile.

"Hello. Everything all right?"

"Yes, everything's fine." Megan stepped back, swinging the door wide. "Come in. It feels like the night air stole the promise of spring from the day."

"Yeah," Royce agreed, following her inside. "But it sure felt good for a change."

"Yes, it felt wonderful." She lowered her gaze to his chest, frowning when all she saw was his shirt. "Where's your jacket?" she asked, then answered for him. "In the car."

"Right." Royce grinned.

Shaking her head in despair, all the while grinning along with him, Megan turned and started down the hallway. "Hungry?" she asked, continuing on, as if certain of his answer.

"Starved," Royce admitted, conceding to her certainty. "I made do with a doughnut for dinner."

"A doughnut!" Megan stopped dead to shoot an appalled look at him. "I thought you were the guy who needed a lot of food to fill up his big body.''

Royce laughed. ''I am.'' His lips curled into a blatantly wicked smile. ''The doughnut had a rich cream filling.''

''Oh, wonderful.'' Megan rolled her eyes. ''Empty calories, fats, all that good stuff.''

''I only ate it to stave off the hunger,'' he explained, losing the fight against another grin. ''I wanted to save it for the snack you promised me tonight.''

''Then consider yourself lucky that I did go grocery shopping today,'' she retorted, striding into the kitchen. ''I have everything ready,'' she said as he stepped up to her side. She motioned with her hand, indicating the food laid out on the countertop. ''As you can see, there's ham and cheese, lettuce and tomatoes, pickles and olives, chips and pretzels, mayo and mustard and bread and rolls.'' She moved her hand slightly to indicate the refrigerator. ''I also bought small containers of potato and macaroni salad, as well.''

''You *were* shopping,'' Royce said over a low, appreciative grumble from his empty stomach.

Evidently hearing the noise, Megan laughed and moved closer to the counter, and the cutting board she had placed there in readiness. ''If you'll tell me what you want on your sandwich, I'll make it for you.''

''Ham, cheese, lettuce, tomato and mayo on a

roll," Royce recited. "Pickles, olives, chips and potato salad on the side." He raised one eyebrow. "What's to drink?"

"Decaffeinated coffee, tea, soda, beer, fruit juice, milk or water," Megan said, spreading butter on a kaiser roll. "The coffee's fresh, in the pot, and the other drinks are in the fridge. Help yourself."

"Are you going to join me in this repast?" he drawled, ambling to the refrigerator.

"Yes." Megan shot a quick grin at him. "I didn't eat much for dinner, either. I, er, wanted to get back to work."

"You have been busy," he murmured, returning her grin as he pulled the salad containers and the pickle and olive jars from the appliance. "Make any headway?"

"Yes." Megan's voice held a deep vein of satisfaction. "As a matter of fact, I finished the project, so this midnight snack is something of a celebration for me."

"Hey, that's great. Congratulations," Royce said, verbally applauding her. "So, what's on the agenda?" he asked, while continuing to gather together food, plates and glasses, then carry them to the table. "Another project?"

"Nope, nothing," Megan answered, turning away from the counter to frown at the table. "Do you want to bring those plates over here? The sandwiches are ready."

"Oh...sure," Royce said agreeably, ambling back to her side with the plates. "Looks good," he told her, his mouth watering at the sight of the food. "You build a mean-looking sandwich, lady."

"Thank you kindly, sir," Megan said solemnly. Then she went on, impishly. "So, let's not stand here admiring them, let's demolish them."

And that was exactly what they did. And while they did, the conversation was reduced to a minimum.

"Actually, I do have one thing on my agenda," Megan said casually as they worked together clearing away afterward.

Alerted by the almost too casual note in her tone, Royce slanted a probing look at her. "Yeah, what's that?"

"I stopped by the dealership on Commerce Avenue on my way home from the supermarket," she said, slowly.

"And?" He arched his brows.

Megan fidgeted with the dishcloth. "I, er, saw one model that I kinda liked."

"But?" he nudged.

Her fingers twisted the cloth. "But, um, I'd really appreciate another opinion. A man's opinion."

Royce grinned. "Mine?"

"If you wouldn't mind?" she asked, hopefully.

"Honey, I wouldn't mind at all," he assured her, feeling inordinately please by her request.

"When would you like to go, tomorrow morning?"

"It already is tomorrow morning," she pointed out, appearing both relieved and as pleased as he felt.

"So it is," Royce conceded, glancing at the clock. "And time for me to get out of here and let you get to bed." Tamping down an impulse to take her into his arms and suggest they get to bed together, he moved to the kitchen doorway.

"I am sleepy," Megan admitted, trailing along the hallway behind him. "I didn't get much sleep last night."

Tell me about it, Royce thought, recalling his own discomfort the night before, both in the recliner and in his mind and body. Come to that, he reflected, turning to her when he reached the front door, the way she looked in that silky caftan was making him pretty damned uncomfortable right now.

"Ah, let's see," he said, shooting a look at his watch. "It's going on two. Suppose I pick you up around eleven-thirty? We can take a look at the car, then have lunch."

"Is your mind always on food?" she asked teasingly, her eyes bright with inner amusement.

Not hardly, Royce answered in silent longing, while aloud he replied, "No, not always." Unable to resist a sudden urge, he raised his hand to slowly brush his fingertips across her cheek to the corner of her mouth, his touch a light caress against the faint bruises marring the perfection of her creamy skin. Anger, hot and biting, for the man who had inflicted those bruises twisted inside Royce.

He kept the rage from coloring his voice by exerting all the control he possessed. "My mind is often on other things, Megan," he murmured.

"Wh-what kinds of things?"

The anger merged with desire. Royce felt a pang in his chest, a constriction in his throat. Megan's eyes were wide, luminous…vulnerable. He wanted, so very badly, to take her in his arms, cradle her, protect her, make love to her.

But he couldn't allow himself the pleasure that holding her, loving her, would give him. Because the pure light of trust also shone out of her eyes.

Megan trusted him; Royce would rather die than betray that trust.

"Maybe I'll tell you, someday," he replied, smothering a sigh as he drew his index finger over the sweet curve of her lower lip. "But not today."

"I…I don't understand," she said in a soft, plaintive little murmur.

"I know." Royce smiled, and let his hand fall away from her tempting mouth. "Hell, I'm not certain that I do." Shrugging, he turned to open the door. "I'll see you at eleven-thirty," he said, stepping into the cold night air. "Good night, Megan. Lock up tight. Sleep well."

* * *

Sleep well.

Fat chance.

Megan shifted position, again. Over an hour had passed since Royce had left her with those parting words, an hour in which she had continued to thrill to his tantalizing touch, while puzzling over his enigmatic remark.

My mind is often on other things...

What had he meant? What other things? Personal? Professional? Megan wondered. More important, did those unmentioned other things involve her in any way?

Excitement, uncertainty, confusion, were a mixed bag inside Megan's stomach.

She hoped, and feared to hope. She yearned, and was afraid of the yearning. She needed, and...

And what?

Megan shifted position yet again, made uncomfortable and restless by her own thoughts.

But there were thoughts, emotions, desires and, yes, fears that had to be confronted and examined. Otherwise, Megan knew, there was a danger of closing herself off from any normal contact and association with members of the opposite sex.

Sex.

The word loomed in Megan's mind.

Intuition told her that the other things on Royce's mind were all directly related to that one

word—intuition, and physical and emotional reactions.

Her lips burned with the imprint of Royce's caress.

Royce had touched her, in a sensuous, intimate
manner, and she had not cringed, had not felt revulsion, had not been filled with stifling panic, as
she had feared she would be upon ever again being
touched by any man.

Quite the contrary. To Megan's utter surprise,
she had responded to his caress, going all soft and
quivery inside, breathless from the wonder of it all.

Physical attraction?

Sex?

In spades, she acknowledged. But it was more
than mere sexual attraction—much, much more.

Megan wasn't as yet quite ready to delve into
the depths of just what that much, much more entailed, but the shadow of it was there, hovering at
the edges of her consciousness, haunting her as
effectively as some persistent ghost.

The analogy brought a frown to Megan's brow.
The day of reckoning would come, the day when
she would have to face the truth of her feelings,
emotions, fears and hopes.

But this wasn't that day. It was too soon, Megan
told herself, absently raising her hand to smother
a yawn. Maybe tomorrow, or the next day, she
mused, curling onto her side as her eyelids drifted
shut.

Maybe.

* * *

The ringing phone woke Royce at 8:14.

Groaning, he stretched out his arm, groping for the instrument set on the nightstand by the bed.

"'lo," he mumbled into the receiver around a wide, noisy yawn.

"Did I wake you?" The deep voice held a definite note of amusement.

"Naw," Royce replied, his lips twitching into a rueful smile. "I always sound like I have a mouth full of cotton in the morning." Blinking the sleep from his eyes, he shimmied up the bed to prop his shoulders against the headboard. "What's up, big bro?"

"Let's not go into that," Cameron drawled, eliciting a chuckle from his younger brother. "I was wondering if you had talked to Mother."

"Not in nearly a week," Royce said, a spark of alarm stealing the chuckle, and much of the moisture, from his throat. "Why? Is something wrong?"

"No, no. Don't go into a tailspin, Royce," Cameron hastened to assure him. "Mother's fine."

Royce let his breath out on a sigh of relief, before launching an attack. "Well, dammit, Cam, if everything's fine, why did you wake me up to ask me if I had talked to her? You had me close to a cold sweat."

"You always were the overconcerned one,"

Cameron said dryly. "Must get your mother-hen personality from the mother hen."

"You're a laugh a minute, you know that?" Royce retorted. "Now, if nothing's wrong at home, would you mind telling me the purpose for this inane call?"

"I am never inane, little brother." Cameron's voice contained both steel and utter conviction.

The damn thing was, his brother's statement was as solid as the Rock of Gibraltar, Royce silently conceded. The bottom line was that if Cameron said something was so, then it was so.

"I know, I know," Royce admitted. "But cut me a break, will ya? I'm not quite with it."

"Tell me about it," Cam taunted.

Royce sighed. "Look, Ca-me-ron," he said, in tones of rigidly imposed patience. "I worked the late shift. I didn't get to bed until 2:30. I want to get back to sleep. Did you call me for a real reason, or just to see if I was still here?"

Cameron laughed.

Royce decided it would be very easy to actively dislike his older brother...if he didn't practically worship the very ground Cam set his size twelves upon.

"Okay, here's the scoop." Cameron's voice was now brisk, if still overlaid with amusement. "Jake's in love."

"I'll alert the media," Royce retorted, yawning loudly into the mouthpiece. "But I already knew.

For crying out loud, Cam, Mother told me about Jake way back last fall, and has been giving me periodic updates ever since.''

"I'm talking *seriously* in love, Royce."

"Well, hell, I figured that," Royce said. "Didn't I just say Mom's been keeping me posted?"

"I mean, *marriage* serious," Cameron said. "Did you know that?"

"Marriage?" Royce sat bolt upright.

"Appears so."

"When?" Royce stared in bemusement at the opposite wall, seeing an image of his youngest brother with his inner eye. Jake, the baby, was getting married?

"Late spring." Cameron's soft laughter conveyed amusement and indulgence. "Seems we're going to have a June wedding."

"I'll be damned," Royce murmured.

"Likely, but that's beside the point," Cameron drawled. "Mother will probably be calling with the news any minute now. Act surprised, will you? She's waited a long time for a wedding in the family, and I don't want to ruin her fun. I do hate to steal her thunder."

"Yeah, sure," Royce agreed vaguely, distracted by the image of young Jake traipsing down the proverbial aisle. "I'll give her an award-winning performance."

"Thanks." Cameron was quiet a moment, and then he asked, "So, what do you think about it?"

Royce frowned. What did he think about it? "I don't know. I haven't decided yet." He shrugged, then laughed. "Do you think Jake gives a damn what I think...or what you and Eric think, come to that?"

"No, and rightly so," Cameron said, laughing with him.

"Right," Royce concurred. "I've been curious about Sarah ever since Mom told me about her. Now I can't wait to meet her."

"Well, you won't have to wait too long. You'll be meeting her at the gathering of the Wolfe pack in June." Cameron's voice turned brisk. "I've got to go, I've got another call. You can go back to sleep now, Royce. Talk to you later."

"Yeah, later, bro."

Marriage.

The word stood, bold as brass, in the forefront of Royce's mind, barring a return to slumber. There was a lot of tossing, a lot of heaving his long frame from one position to another position, but no escape into sleep.

"Damn."

Cursing beneath his breath, Royce finally gave up the battle and crawled out from under the tangled covers on his king-size bed.

Marriage. And Jake. The youngest of the four Wolfe progeny; the first to take the plunge into matrimony.

Who would have thunk it?

Shaking his head in bemusement, Royce left the bedroom, heading for what he hoped would be a reviving shower.

Marriage.

The word seemed to get stuck in a mental groove, revolving and repeating inside Royce's head while he wallowed in a long, leisurely, stinging-hot shower.

The one-word refrain persisted as he made faces at himself in the bathroom mirror, contorting to find and scythe every tiny trace of morning stubble.

He was picking up Megan for car-looking and lunch.

After selecting, then discarding, several combinations of pants, shirt and sport jacket, and eventually settling on the fifth ensemble he put together, Royce wandered into the minuscule kitchen in his apartment to make a pot of coffee.

But would lunchtime ever come?

The clock on the stove read 10:17.

Royce exhaled a deep sigh; almost an hour to kill before he could leave to pick up Megan.

In the interim, Royce polished off two pots of coffee and a hearty number of slightly stale English muffins. Toasting eliminated the staleness. After eating, he filled in the remaining minutes cleaning up the kitchen, making his bed and rehanging his clothes in the bedroom, and tidying up the living room—which didn't take long, since it was only marginally larger than the minuscule kitchen, and a great deal smaller than the spacious bedroom.

Which just went to prove that, in the case of space allocation, Royce had his priorities straight.

When, at last, Royce strode from his apartment, he felt he now knew precisely the feelings of a felon being sprung from the slammer.

Marriage.

Though less bold, thus less demanding of his immediate attention, the word was there, comfortably ensconced at the back of his mind.

All in relation to Jake...of course.

The day was fine, the breeze cool but scented with the promise of spring, hovering just around the corner.

Megan was waiting for Royce on the front stoop, her face raised to the strengthening warmth of the sunlight. Smiling, she drew in a deep breath, trying to capture the elusive scent teasing her senses. Her smile curved into a frown at the discordant sound of a bad car muffler disturbing the late morning peace and tranquillity.

The crunching noise had a familiar ring.

Now, where...

Megan's emerging thoughts took flight as a dark green car made a smooth, purring turn into her driveway.

Royce.

Thinking his name brought a flutter to her pulse,

a soaring sense of joy skittering throughout her being. Her lips curved into a bright smile of pleasure at the sight of him.

The effect on Royce was gratifying, to say the least.

He looked stunned, bemused, bewitched. He also appeared incapable of movement. Bringing the car to a stop alongside her, he simply sat, staring into her smiling face.

Laughter bubbled up Megan's throat and over her lips. The sound of her amusement dancing on the mild spring air, she opened the passenger-side door and slid onto the seat next to him, her laughter taking on a teasing note.

"Cat got your tongue?" Megan asked when he just sat there, staring at her.

"No," Royce said in somber seriousness. "Your smile stole my breath."

His bold admission rendered Megan as speechless as he had been. For an eternity of seconds, they merely sat there, staring into each other's eyes.

The flutter in Megan's pulses accelerated into a thundering gallop that thrummed in every nerve ending. Her breath was shallow, her heartbeat deep.

She suddenly ached...everywhere.

The exquisite pain shattered her trancelike state.

"Ah..." Megan paused, swallowed, cleared her throat. "I guess we'd better get going."

Royce released his visual lock on her with flattering reluctance. "Yeah." His voice was strained, ragged; his fingers betrayed a fine tremor when he reached for the key in the ignition.

The engine fired, and he slanted a glance at her. Then, drawing a deep breath, he set the car into motion.

Megan sat, still and contemplative, throughout the drive to the car dealership. Not knowing quite what to think of the strange interlude they had shared, she tried not to think about it at all.

But that didn't work, because she could still see his eyes, the bright blue darkened by emotion.

It was all very thrilling...and rather scary. Scary enough to keep her quiet, thinking, while trying not to think.

Apparently Royce was experiencing similar difficulties, for he remained as quiet as Megan.

Shopping for a new car was decidedly anticlimactic. Royce approved the silver-gray sports car, and Megan made arrangements to buy it. It was all cut-and-dried.

After becoming lost inside blue eyes intent on peering into her soul, Megan could hardly feel thrilled by the prospect of becoming the owner of what, in fact, was nothing more than a piece of metal with wheels.

The sports car was beautiful, but inanimate.

Royce Wolfe was real.

Now *that* was something to think about.

And Megan did think about it, long after Royce had driven her back to the house after lunch, through the even longer afternoon, and into the silence of the night.

She thought about nothing else except Royce until the silence of the night was broken by the innocent-sounding ring of the telephone.

Certain it was Royce, Megan snatched up the receiver and blurted out a breathless "Hello?"

"I'm coming for you, bitch."

Megan's breath ceased at the familiar sound of the harsh voice—the haunting sound of her attacker. Panic clutched at her throat; fear froze her in place.

"And when I get there, I'm going to…"

Megan's stomach roiled, threatening to reject her light supper, at the obscene description the man spewed out of what he was planning to do to her.

The sour taste of bile filled her mouth, and with a whimpered protest Megan slammed down the receiver. Terrified, sobbing, she grabbed it up again and punched in the number Royce had given to her so that she could reach him at work.

"Sergeant Wolfe," he answered on the second ring.

"Royce!" Megan cried, her voice high with rising hysteria. "He's coming for me. That man, that hulking man, he's coming for me. He said…he said…"

"I'm on my way."

The line went dead.

Caught in the gripping claws of fear, Megan stood, the telephone receiver pressed to her breast, afraid to move, her body shaking, waiting for deliverance.

Royce.

Nine

"**M**egan!"

The razor-edged sound of Royce's voice, overlapping a sharply delivered rapping against the front door, pierced the fear-induced trance holding Megan's mind captive.

A shudder of awareness quaked through her. The phone falling away from her nerveless fingers, she whirled and ran from the bedroom to the foyer. His call rang out again as she dashed across the chill flagstone inlay to the door.

"*Me-gan.*"

There was now a new note in his voice, a note she had not previously heard before, a note rife with abject, unadulterated fright.

"I'm here," she called in immediate response. "I'm all right," she hastened to assure him.

Fumbling with the lock, Megan shoved to the back of her mind the intriguing speculation on the possible meaning for the sound of sheer panic coloring his tone.

"Open the damn door," he ordered.

"I'm...I'm trying!" Megan heaved a sigh of relief as the lock gave way. Cranking the knob, she stepped back and pulled the door open.

This time, she did not fling herself against him. She could not, for with the first opening crack in the doorway Royce strode inside and swept her into his arms, crushing her to his tension-taut body.

Safe. Safe.

The words repeated inside Megan's mind as she clung to the solid strength of the man she now trusted without question or doubt.

But even Royce's solid strength revealed the ravages of emotional fear. Locked within that uncompromising embrace, Megan could not help but notice the fine tremor shivering through his long frame. In truth, she could barely tell which of them was trembling more, she herself or Royce.

"I want you to tell me exactly what happened." Even his voice betrayed his inner unsteadiness.

"At first...when I answered the phone, there was nothing, just silence," Megan said shakily, tilting her head back to look up, into his sternly set face. "But then...then," she went on, her voice gathering speed and panic as she continued, "he called me 'bitch' and said he was going to..." She broke off, eyes widening, then cried, "Royce, he knows who I am! He knows where I am! He's coming here to...to... He intends to finish what he started last Friday night!"

"Like hell he will." Royce released her with confusing abruptness. "You're getting out of here."

"But...oh!" Megan exclaimed, starting when he grasped her hand and literally yanked her along with him as he strode into her bedroom.

"Where's your bag?"

"Bag?" Megan blinked. "Wha—"

"Suitcase, carryon, garment bag." Keeping a tight hold on her hand, he moved to the double closet set into the bathroom wall. "Anything to throw a few things into."

"But...but..."

"Dammit, Megan," Royce exploded, whipping around to pin her with blue eyes blazing with impatience and flat-out fury. "Don't stand there sputtering at me like a motorboat running out of fuel. I'm getting you out of here. Now. You can think of it as protective custody. Where do you keep your bags?"

"On the shelf in that closet," she said, flicking her free hand at the double doors. "But where are you taking me?" she demanded. "To the lockup?"

"The lockup?" Royce gave her a sour look,

then turned toward the closet doors. "Get real, Megan," he said, releasing her hand to pull the doors open. "Get some things together and get dressed." He pulled her nylon carryon from the shelf and thrust it into her hands. "I'm taking you to my place."

His place.

Megan stood in the center of the small living room, feeling nervous, uncertain, and rather ridiculous.

She wasn't even properly dressed, for pity's sake, she thought, clutching her full-length wool coat to her shivering body as she glanced around her.

Beneath the coat, all Megan had on was the nightshirt she'd been wearing when that terrible person called, a pair of sweatpants she had pulled on under the shirt, and low-heeled, soft leather slip-ons she had barely had time to slip on before Royce hustled her out of the house and into his car.

Megan was cold, a condition attributable more to her emotional state than to the outside air temperature of forty degrees or so. This chill was inside, not outside.

Still, she huddled beneath the coat, seeking comfort from the warming wool.

"You can relax now," Royce murmured, shucking out of his jacket. "You're safe." Tossing the jacket aside, he slowly walked to her, coming to a stop mere inches from her.

"Yes." Megan managed a smile, faint but real, for him. "Thank you, Royce."

"You're welcome." His answering smile was tender, compassionate, understanding. "You can take your coat off now."

"I..." Megan shivered and wet her lips. "I'm cold."

"I know, but the coat won't contain the chill." He held out his hand. "And you know it."

Megan drew a quick breath, hesitated, then raised her trembling fingers to the coat buttons. It seemed to take forever to unfasten the four plain black buttons. Royce didn't try to help her or hurry her. He stood there, quiet and patient, until the coat's panels gaped apart. After she removed the garment and handed it to him, he turned away to carefully drape it over the back of an oversize— Royce-size—club chair.

The minute the coat was off, Megan wished she had it back. Her shiver intensified into a teeth-rattling tremble.

"R-R-Royce," she began, her muscles clenching against the reactionary shakes. "I—need..."

Suddenly Royce was there, drawing her into his arms, taking the place of the coat, enfolding her within the warmer cocoon of his presence.

"I know, I know," he whispered, his breath ruffling wisps of hair at her temple. "But it's all right now.'' He stroked one hand down the length of her spine. ''You're all right now.'' His lips brushed from the corner of her eyebrow to her quivering cheek. ''I won't let him, or anyone else, hurt you, Megan. Depend on it.''

Clutching him every bit as tightly as she had clutched her coat, Megan burrowed against him, into him, seeking the strength of his body, as well as his conviction.

The chill permeating her body slowly lessened. And still she trembled, but now the tremors were activated by a shiver of unvarnished sensual awareness of him.

His soft voice dissolved her fears; his stroking hands unlocked her clenched muscles; his caressing lips ignited a fire that consumed her.

Slowly, but inevitably, like a tightly closed early-spring bud, Megan responded to Royce's caring ministrations, unfolding like the flower in the warmth of the sun.

''You will stay here, with me, safe from harm, for as long as it takes,'' he murmured, the light movement of his mouth on her cheek causing ripples of sensation from her face to the outer edges of her tingling toes.

Megan didn't need to ask what he meant; though he hadn't said so, she knew he meant she was to stay with him until her attacker was apprehended and confined.

"I...I can't. I don't expect you to..." She broke off on a softly gasped "Oh!"

His lips had drifted to the corner of her mouth. "I know," he said, tantalizing her lips with the feather-light touch of his mouth. "I want to do this, keep you safe, protected, for myself, my sanity, as well as for your peace of mind."

Peace of mind! Megan quivered. At that moment, her mind was anything but at peace—not to mention her senses! Her mind was a chaotic whirl, her senses running riot.

His nearness, his unmistakable arousal, the allure of his mouth, were playing havoc with every feminine impulse Megan possessed.

Royce continued to murmur words of comfort and reassurance that she no longer heard. All her powers of concentration were centered on his lips, teasing the edges of her own.

Suddenly, the world of harsh reality retreated, banished by the forward charge of the realm of sensuality. Her overriding priority was the compulsion to taste his mouth.

A whimper shuddering from the depths of her throat, Megan turned her head, bringing her lips into contact with the mouth she craved.

"Megan?" Royce's voice could only have been described as raw. "You're understandably upset." He drew another soft whimper from her as he raised his head to stare into her eyes. "Are you certain this is what you want?"

A firm affirmation sprang to her lips, just as a startling thought sprang into her mind. The thought spilled from her mind to her tongue.

"Are you afraid I just want to use you to forget?" she asked, biting her lower lip in consternation.

The glow that deepened the blue of his eyes, and the smile that drifted across his lips presaged his answer.

"Honey, feel free to use me for anything. A hand to hang on to, a buffer against fear, an opinion on the choice of a car—" his voice went low, intimate, sexy "—a body to warm you, soothe you, fulfill you."

"Royce." Megan's voice was barely there, so she let her eyes speak of her needs.

"Use me, honey," he murmured, slowly lowering his head, his mouth, to hers. "Please, please, use me."

His lips touched hers, tentatively, testingly, sweetly. Megan shuddered from the thistledown impact.

Gentle. His kiss was the most gentle blending of two mouths imaginable. And seductive. Royce's very gentleness seduced not Megan's body, but her mind.

Feeling utterly safe, secure within the warm haven of his embrace, she divorced herself from concern, and surrendered her being into his care.

Royce moved; Megan moved with him.

Lost inside the blue heaven of his eyes, she didn't notice the details of his bedroom, or even the kingly size of his bed. She didn't notice the coolness of the air against her bare skin when he carefully removed her nightshirt, her sweatpants and her panties.

The mattress was firm, a solid support for a big man. Megan didn't notice that, either. She was too fascinated with watching Royce undress to take note.

He was a beautiful sight in the natural state. She could not discern an ounce of excess weight on his long, muscular body. His shoulders and lightly haired chest were broad, his waist and hips were narrow, his belly was flat, and his long legs were straight and well shaped.

His fully aroused manhood was of a size scaled to the rest of his body.

The overall effect of him was formidable.

Megan suffered a twinge of disquiet.

"Easy, Megan, easy," he murmured, stretching his length out next to her on the bed. "I'm not a boy, or an animal. I will not clutch, or grab." Shifting to his side facing her, he stroked her shoulder, her arm, the back of her hand, her fingers.

Megan felt his feather-light touch in the depths of her being—felt it and responded to it.

"I'm…I'm not afraid," she said, secretly willing away the tiny flare of trepidation.

"Of course you are, and understandably so."

His eyes and smile were soft with compassion, and a hint of sadness. "I want to make love with you, Megan, probably more than I have ever wanted anything else before in my entire adult life." He drew a deep, shuddering breath. "But I have nothing to prove here, no issues to resolve." Acceptance now tinged his tone. "Say the word, anytime, and I'll back off. I can live with frustration. I could not bear living with the thought of having frightened or hurt you in any way."

"Oh, Royce." Thoroughly reassured, and disarmed, Megan blinked away the sting of tears in her eyes, and raised her hands to cup his face to draw his mouth to hers. "Come to me," she whispered against his lips. "Make love with me."

Royce was incredibly gentle. Even so, memory sparked and Megan tensed when he eased into position between her thighs.

He went still. His hands braced at either side of her head, he stared into her eyes a moment, then began slowly to withdraw from her.

"No." Megan shook her head, and clasped his hips, holding him in place. "I'm all right. It's all right."

He frowned. "Are you sure?"

"Yes. I trust you, Royce. I'd trust you with my life." She managed a smile. "I know I can trust you with my body."

"Yes. You can," he said. "I swear it."

And he proceeded to prove his assertion.

Slowly, and with infinite care, Royce brought himself to her, joining his body with hers in gentle possession. His mouth claimed hers, and then, in unison, his body and tongue stroked in ever-increasing thrusts, fanning the flames of desire into a blaze raging out of control.

Megan experienced a different form of tension, a spiraling, crackling tension born of sensual excitement. Suddenly, she felt as though she *were* the flame, burning brightly for him, only for Royce.

There was no past. There was no future. There was only the here, and the now, the instant, striving for the next instant, and then the next, toward the ultimate goal of perfect harmony, complete freedom. Oneness.

The ultimate attained, Megan cried out in sheer wonder at the beauty of the moment. Royce's hoarse-voiced exclamation echoed her own.

He might have made a very costly mistake.

Royce stood in the bedroom doorway, his expression pensive, his feelings in conflict, as he stared at the woman asleep in his bed.

In the cold, clear light of midmorning, the smoky haze of last night's passion took on a different and unsettling hue. He had slept better, deeper, than he had in nearly a year. But what, he mused, was that sleep going to cost him?

A sigh expanded his chest as he stared bleakly into the sleeping woman's face.

Megan looked so vulnerable, so defenseless, so gut-wrenchingly appealing, in slumber. It took all his considerable control to keep from going to her, joining her on the bed, losing himself in the joy of loving her.

Loving Megan.

There it was, the root cause for the messed-up condition of his thought processes.

When had the wanting turned into love?

Royce released the pent-up sigh.

What did when, or even why matter?

He was in love with her.

The acknowledgment scared the hell out of him.

Megan sighed in her sleep. A soft smile curved her lips. Then a whisper hit him with the force of a scream.

"Royce."

He winced at the beguiling sound of his name on her lips. He knew he had satisfied her, in a physical sense. But had he touched her emotionally, engaged her affections?

Did Megan care for him in any meaningful way?

The question kept him standing in the doorway, wanting to go to her, yet hesitant, afraid the answer might turn out to be the one he didn't want to hear.

Big tough cop. Royce derided himself. If your brothers could see you now, he mused, they'd laugh themselves sick.

That didn't matter, either. Hell, it was easy to be tough professionally. On the job, his emotions weren't involved. Well, as a rule his emotions weren't involved.

Megan just happened to be a special case, with the potential to turn *him* into a basket case.

Royce had been close to being in love before, and had been rejected. It had hurt like hell. Now, after nearly a year, he knew the blow had been mainly to his pride, his ego. He also knew that his feelings for Megan were different, deeper, permanent.

If he declared himself to Megan, and she rejected him, he would be devastated. Royce knew that, as well.

She murmured his name again in her sleep.

Royce backed away from the doorway, calling himself a coward with each retreating step.

Later, he justified his action—or lack of same. Megan had endured a traumatizing ordeal. She needed time to heal, not more emotional baggage to weigh her down—and most especially not *his* emotional baggage.

But, damn, not knowing how she felt, whether or not she cared, was tearing him apart.

Megan woke feeling vaguely disoriented, dissatisfied and definitely disgruntled.

A quick glance around her clarified her disorientation. She was ensconced in Royce's bed. Determining her sense of place clarified her dissatisfaction. What she and Royce had shared had been wonderful—and she wanted more of it. The acknowledgment of need clarified the disgruntlement. She was building up a head of angry steam.

Damn that hulking man, Megan fumed, tossing back the rumpled covers. Damn that attacker of women, for casting her in the role of victim, a supplicant for protection from the one man she could give herself to completely and unconditionally.

Railing against the unfairness of it all, she scooped her nightshirt from the floor and stormed into the bathroom.

Megan's mind spun its wheels the entire time required to shower and shampoo.

Making love with Royce had been more than wonderful; it had been everything she had ever dared fantasize being intimate with a man could be. In point of fact, it had been even more than that, for, with absolute honesty, Megan knew that she had been more than making love with Royce; she was deeply in love with him. And the more she thought about it, the angrier she became.

Her ire at full arousal, Megan stormed back into the bedroom, collecting her carry-on bag from the living room as she whirled through.

Her blood heating to a roiling boil as she hastily dressed in slacks and a loose-knit midthigh-length sweater, Megan continued to mentally lash out at the fate that had placed her in her present predicament.

After years—and men—that had been totally

discouraging, she had finally found the man who embodied every one of her secret dreams of the ideal partner—kind, caring, compassionate, intelligent, humorous, and sexy as the very devil.

And Megan loved Royce. Of course she loved him. She was destined to love him.

Dammit, she protested, against her situation and against the tug of the brush she yanked through her tangled hair.

She loved, but... Megan gritted her teeth. But because of that...that thing who dared to impersonate a man, she was very much afraid that the driving force behind Royce's response to her owed more to the kind of man he was, the embodiment of all his fine qualities, than to his loving her in return.

But Megan couldn't know Royce's thoughts or feelings. She did know that he had not once so much as hinted at, never mind mentioned, love.

And therein lay the cause of the anger eating away at her, anger directed not at Royce, but at that despicable hulking man whose presence overshadowed every facet of her life.

Well, enough was enough, Megan decided, stamping into ankle boots. She was done with cowering and hiding.

She wanted her life back.

She wanted Royce.

First things first.

Where was Royce, anyway?

The phone rang as Megan left the bedroom.

Following the muted sound of his voice, Megan crossed through the living room and came to a halt in the kitchen doorway. Royce stood with his back to her, his shoulder resting against the wall, talking on the phone.

Lord, he looked gorgeous.

"You're kidding."

Megan noted the surprise in his voice, but really didn't pay too much attention to what he was saying. She was too distracted by the effect of the sight of him, his powerful effect on her senses.

Merely looking at him made her feel all hot and melty inside, and all shivery outside.

Love? Megan was hard-pressed to keep from laughing out loud, and not in genuine amusement. She was suffering every one of the classic symptoms.

Love?

In spades.

"A June wedding, huh?"

That snagged her attention. Megan's ears perked up. A June wedding sounded perfect.

"Are you serious? Of course I'll be able to make it. I'll put in a request for vacation for the first week in June, when I go back to work tomorrow."

Tomorrow? Megan frowned.

"Yeah, Mom, I'll take care." Royce shifted away from the wall. "You too. And pass along my congratulations to Jake. Tell him I can't wait to meet Sarah." He chuckled. "She's got to be some kind of woman, if she's willing to take on the job of housebreaking that maverick."

Megan's frown melted into a smile at the underlying note of true affection in Royce's tone. The evidence of his love for his family was unvarnished, and unashamedly voiced.

She liked that in a man.

Royce turned as he hung up the receiver, and caught sight of Megan's misty smile.

"Hi." His voice was now low, intimate.

Megan felt a responsive thrill; it affected her own voice, making it throaty. "Hi."

"Sleep well?" While his voice remained low and even, his eyes bored into hers with intent.

"Yes." Megan's frown crept back to steal her smile. "Did you?"

"Oh, yeah, terrific." His reply came too quickly, and was much too glib. But he turned away before she could question him on it. "There's fresh coffee," he said, going to the tiny counter next to the sink. "Are you hungry?"

"No." Megan shook her head, even though he couldn't see her. "I'll just have coffee, thank you." She hesitated, bit down on her lip, then blurted out, "Royce, what's wrong? Are you sorry about last night?"

Ten

"**S**orry?" Royce whipped around to stare at her. "No, I'm not sorry, but..." He shrugged.

But. Megan felt a sick sensation in her stomach. It was the *buts* in life that did you in.

"I see." Somehow, she managed to keep the pain from spilling over into her voice.

"No, I don't think you do." Royce gave a sharp shake of his head. "Megan, honey, it's this damnable situation. You're so fragile right now, so vulnerable, and..." He paused, as if groping for just the right words.

She didn't give him time to find them. Mentally backing away from the abyss of unthinkable pain, she put on her brightest morning face.

"I know, I know." She flicked her hand, dismissing the subject. "I couldn't help overhearing part of your telephone conversation," she went on, rapid-fire. "Your brother is getting married?"

"Huh?" He frowned, then, shifting mental gears, caught up with her. "Oh. Yes. That was my mother on the phone. Jake and his lady have set the date to take the fatal step on the first Saturday in June."

The fatal step. Megan's spirits took a nosedive. His phrasing said just about all there was to say concerning his opinion of the marital state. Or was he simply trying to tell her something, something direct and personal? Well, so much for hopes and dreams and fantasies.

Keeping her bright morning face in place was growing more difficult by the second. "That's nice. I, er, hope they'll be very happy." She smothered a sigh and worked up a faint smile of thanks for the cup of steaming coffee he poured for her. "Did I also hear you say something about not having to work today?" She raised the cup to her lips, and her eyebrows in what she hoped was an expression of casual interest.

Royce nodded. "Today and tomorrow are my scheduled days off." He paused an instant, then went on. "But I have to go out for a while. I have some things to do."

Recognizing opportunity when it stared her in the face, Megan grabbed for it.

"Do you? Well, I'm going to call the car dealer to ask if my car's ready for me," she said off-handedly. "If it is, would you please drop me off there, so I can pick it up? And if it isn't," she rushed on, "would you drop me at home?"

"No." Flat. Unequivocal. Final.

"No?" Megan had never taken well to flat, unequivocal and final. "I beg your pardon?"

"I don't want you going back to the house." Royce's features were locked into an expression of stern determination.

"But I must go home," she argued. "I brought only one change of clothes with me. Besides, I have to package my illustrations for mailing and get them to the post office."

"No, Megan." He slowly shook his head. "It's not safe for you to go back there. If you'll tell me what clothing you'll need, and how you want the illustrations packaged, I'll take care of everything for you."

Indeed? Though Megan kept the biting response inside her head, it burned like fiery anger on her tongue. But the bitter anger was directed more at herself than at him—even if he was getting a tad too heavy-handed.

Royce had been wonderful from the beginning—taking care of everything since that dreadful night. From standing by in the hospital to driving her home, then stopping by every night to check up on her, he had been there for her. He had gone way beyond the call of duty.

And Megan had greedily availed herself of his offer to use his body to lose herself. She had used him shamelessly, she admitted to herself in all honesty. She had used him eagerly, joyously, wantonly. She had used him for all he was worth—and in the process, she had returned his generous offer by giving freely of herself, for all she was worth, body, mind and soul.

Megan loved Royce, was now deeply in love with him, but acknowledged that Royce could in no way be faulted if he did not love her in return. *If.*

Megan clung to the word. To her way of thinking, so long as there was an if, there was a hope, a hope to build a friendship, a relationship, and possibly even a mutual and deeply committed love, upon.

But—the dreaded but—first she had to reclaim her independence, her life, the way it had been before that beast posing as a man robbed her of it.

And to begin with, Megan was done with running—literally, as well as figuratively. Lifting her chin to a defiant angle, she stared Royce directly in the eyes.

"I *am* going," she said distinctly.

Royce was noticeably unimpressed by her show of bravado. His blue eyes placid, he stared right back at her.

"For*get* it," he told her, mimicking her tone. "I will not allow you to place yourself in harm's way."

"Really?" Megan arched one auburn eyebrow. "How are you planning to stop me?"

That gave him pause, but only for a few moments of visible frustration. Then he smiled. It sent an apprehensive shiver up her spine.

"I could take you into protective custody, citing fear for your life. Or I could take a different but equally effective route, and simply handcuff you to something solid, out of reach of a phone." His smile tilted, much too engagingly. "But I'd much prefer to have your word to me that you won't leave the apartment."

Mulling over whether or not he actually could legally confine her, Megan made a performance of considering the options he'd presented to her. Then she heaved a loud, defeated-sounding sigh of surrender.

"Okay, Wolfe, you win."

"You'll stay put?"

Loath to commit herself verbally with an outright lie, she nodded her head once in agreement.

"Say it, Megan." His voice was pure steel.

She glared at him in sheer disgruntlement at his persistence. He stared back. Seconds ticked by, and then she again gave way, while crossing the first two fingers of her free hand in childish self-exoneration.

"Okay, okay, I'll stay put."

Royce maintained his steely regard for a few seconds longer. Then he smiled, stirring a sickening sensation of guilt inside Megan. "Okay," he said, extending his hand, palm up. "If you'll give me your door key, I'll get to it."

Chagrin washed over her; she hadn't thought about the necessity of relinquishing her key. Fortunately, she then recollected the spare key her father kept hidden in the garage for just such contingencies. Her sense of chagrin evaporated in the warmth of her smile.

"I'll get it," she said, placing her cup on the table before turning to the doorway. "It's in my handbag."

"Can I get you something to eat before I leave?" Royce called after her.

"No, thank you," she called back. "I'm still not hungry. I'll have something later."

"Okay. Feel free to rummage through the fridge and cabinets." There was a pause, and then he called out again. "Megan, make a list of the clothes you want me to gather for you."

Even though she felt certain she wouldn't need them, at least not here, Megan dutifully pulled a notebook from her purse and jotted down an assortment of casual garments. Then, after unfastening the door key from the case, which also held the garage key, she left the bedroom.

Royce was waiting for her at the front door.

"The sooner I get moving, the sooner I'll get back," he said, once again extending his hand, palm up.

Crossing to him, Megan placed the key and the scrap of paper in his palm, then launched into instructions on exactly how she wanted her illustrations packaged.

"Will do." He hesitated, as if unsure. Then, bending quickly to her, he brushed his lips over hers, murmuring, "Be good."

Megan felt bereft when he raised his head, and lonely the second the door closed behind him. Her lips tingling, hungry for more of his kisses, she stood staring bleakly at the solid panel, agonizing over the possibility that what she was about to do could cause an irreparable rift between them.

But she had to do it, Megan assured herself, bolstering her courage. She had to assert herself, make her own decisions, take back control of her existence.

Swinging away from the door, she went directly to the phone and punched in the number of the car dealership. If her car was ready, she would have to walk there to take possession, but needs must be met. Besides, it was a small town, after all, and the dealership was located only a little more than a mile from Royce's apartment.

The car was ready. Megan hung up the receiver. A satisfied smile curving her lips, she headed for the bathroom to apply some color to her face. It was to be the old shoe-leather express, but that was okay, she told herself. She could do with the exercise.

The day was mild, the air faintly scented with the elusive fragrance of early spring. Megan strode forward, looking for all the world as if she didn't have a care. In reality, she raked her eyes over each and every male she passed on the street, searching for, and yet fearful of spotting a large, hulking form looming up before her.

There were no hulking forms...or dark-browed males.

Megan's step faltered as she strode onto the car lot. Dark-browed males? Now why had she thought...?

A vision flashed into her mind, and she could see her attacker, clearly defined as he arced over her in the car, his lips curled into a snarl, his eyes narrowed and mean beneath lowered dark brows.

And she felt positive she would recognize him if she saw him again!

Megan shivered, and felt grateful for the sight of the salesman, a broad smile creasing his rather homely face, raising his arm in greeting as he hurried to meet her.

Mere minutes were required to dispense with the paperwork, during which Megan's attention was diverted from thoughts of mean eyes and dark brows to the more pleasurable and exciting prospects of a sparkling new sports car.

The formalities over with, Megan slipped into the contoured seat behind the steering wheel, gave a final wave to the grinning salesman and fired the engine.

It purred like a well-fed tiger.

Megan's spirits purred along with it. Taking it slow and cautious, she eased the silver beauty to the lot's driveway, inching forward as she checked the roadway for oncoming traffic. There was a string of vehicles coming toward her.

Waiting patiently, she began to hum, but the sound dried on her lips as a niggling memory sprang to life at another, discordant sound—a rattling muffler on a car midway in the line of oncoming cars.

Frowning in concentration, Megan peered through the windshield at the badly dented car. The sight of the driver of the car, viewed in profile, caused a burst of memory that sent fingers of panic curling around her throat.

It was him! Megan knew it as surely as she knew her own name. Suddenly she recalled taking note of the noisy car the first time she had visited the dealer, feeling a vague uneasiness about the look of the driver.

Without thought or hesitation, Megan pulled the sports car into the end of the line, determined to follow the rattling junker to its destination.

One by one, the other cars in the string turned off, until only one car remained between Megan and her target, which was headed on a direct course for her parents' home.

Her nerves feeling as if they were literally jumping wildly beneath her skin, Megan clutched the steering wheel with sweaty hands and maintained a discreet distance from the battered and noisy vehicle.

She felt sick to her stomach, and wanted nothing so much as to whip the sports car into a U-turn and beat a hasty retreat to the safety of Royce's apartment.

Royce. Thinking of him brought his mission to mind. He had said he had some things to do, but he had also promised to stop by the house to pack her illustrations and collect clothing for her. Maybe Royce was at the house now.

Distracted by her thoughts, Megan wasn't aware of the truck cutting her off at an intersection until it was almost on top of her. Reacting automatically, she sheered away from the large vehicle, avoiding a collision by a hairbreadth.

Shaken and trembling, she pulled to the side of the road and sat, still gripping the wheel, gulping in deep, composure-restoring breaths, while the driver of the truck went merrily on his way, unaware that he had come within mere seconds of wiping her off the face of the earth.

It wasn't until a measure of her calm was restored that Megan was struck by the realization that she had lost sight of the rattling car she had been tailing.

How long, she wondered, had she been sitting there, collecting her composure? Five minutes? Ten? Longer? As long as twenty minutes? She had to get moving. If Royce was at the house, and that man was headed there…

"Damn." Muttering the curse aloud, she set the car in motion again, and drove at a careful yet steady pace the rest of the distance to her parents' home.

Megan spotted the battered car again when she was less than a city block's distance from her destination. She couldn't miss it, for it was moving at speed, along the driveway, heading away from the house.

She took in the scene and comprehended its portent at once. The driver, the man she was now certain was her attacker, was on the run, fleeing from another man, who was at that moment diving into a distinctive dark green car parked to one side of the double garage.

"Royce!" Megan cried, knowing he couldn't hear her, knowing, as well, that, though officially off duty, he was in pursuit of a suspect—and the suspect had a head start.

The battered car was nearing the end of the driveway that Megan was approaching. And so she did the only thing she could think of to do. Without a qualm, she stamped down on the gas pedal. The silver sports car responded like an Indy race car. The purr accelerating into a growl, it shot forward, a silver streak aimed at intersecting the rattling junker.

With a cool she hadn't previously realized she possessed, Megan deliberately drove her brand-new car directly into the junker, crumpling the already battered front end.

The air bag deployed.

Though once again shaken, and slightly stunned, Megan was miraculously uninjured. She was performing the deep, composure-restoring routine when the door beside her was yanked open with a force nearly strong enough to tear it from its hinges and Royce thrust his head into the car.

"Dammit to hell, Megan, are you trying to kill yourself?" he shouted, directly into her face.

Recoiling from the assault on her ear drums, she tilted her body to the side, away from him. Then, realizing what she was doing, she shifted the other way, bringing her face so close to his that she could see the fine pores in his skin.

"No, I'm not trying to kill myself!" she shouted back at him. "I was trying to help you!"

There came the loud wail of a police car siren. Royce yelled above it.

"Help me? How? By hurting yourself?"

"I'm not hurt!" she yelled back.

"You gave me your word, Megan." Harsh accusation accented his raised voice.

"I crossed my fingers." The excuse sounded lame even to her own ears.

Royce made a disgusted face; it was not pretty. "You crossed your fingers," he repeated in a mutter. "Lord, I don't believe you." Shaking his head in despair, he straightened away from the car. "Are you sure you're all right?"

It was only then, as he stood back, that Megan noticed the reactive tremors cascading the length of his body. Feeling small, and not particularly bright, Megan nodded in answer. "What about him?" She turned to look at the man slumped over the wheel of the other car. "Maybe you'd better check on him."

Royce gave a sharp, backward jerk of his head as the patrolman came to a tire-screeching stop behind him. "Let the local law handle it. I'm off duty."

The local law officer did handle it, and very well at that. After assuring himself that Megan had not suffered any visible injuries, he proceeded to take charge of the situation.

Approaching the other vehicle apprehensively, Megan made a positive identification of the driver as the same man who had attacked her the previous Friday night.

Through it all, Royce stood by her side, close but withdrawn, asking no questions, offering no comments, making her nervous and fearful with his stoic silence.

The only time he spoke was when the patrolman told Megan she would have to go to the police station to file a criminal-assault complaint against the man.

"I'll drive her in," he said, immediately turning to walk to his car. "Let's get it over with, Megan."

There was something ominous, final-sounding, about his voice, his manner, that caused a queasy feeling in Megan's stomach, and a certainty in her mind that what he wanted to get over with involved more than the filing of a complaint.

Thanking the patrolman, Megan trailed after Royce, scared witless that with her rash action she had ruined the tenuous relationship they had begun.

"What about my car?" she asked, settling into the passenger seat beside him.

"The patrolman will have it towed."

His indifferent tone was less than encouraging. Nevertheless, Megan persevered. "You're really mad at me, aren't you?"

He shot a weary-looking glance at her. "Later, Megan." His voice was dull, flat with finality. "I don't want to talk about it here, en route to the police station."

"But...but I did help you catch that man!" Megan cried in her own defense.

"Yeah."

The disillusionment contained in that one small word effectively silenced her.

The formalities at the police station seemed endless, but finally Megan was told she could leave. Feeling wrung out, listless, and fighting a need to simply sit down and cry, she followed her still-silent escort to his car.

"I'll take you home now." Cynicism laced his tone. "Then we can talk about it."

Megan felt the bottom fall out of her tenuous hold on hope; his attitude did not bode well for the hours ahead, or the future, come to think of it.

The sports car was gone by the time they returned to the house, as was the rattler and its driver. Megan sighed as they made the swing into the driveway, the spot where she had run her new car into the junker.

"Your insurance premiums are going to go up like a Fourth of July rocket," Royce said, hearing her sigh.

"I know." Megan smothered another sigh. "But it was worth it to apprehend that terrible monster."

"Was it?" he demanded, bringing the car to a stop directly in front of the house.

"Yes, of course," she insisted, scrambling after him when he got out without a backward glance at her. "Royce, you must agree that it was worth it."

"Must I?" He turned from the door, which he had unlocked with her key, to give her a cool look. "Why must I?" He pushed the door open, stood aside, and motioned her to precede him.

Impatience and anxiety driving her, Megan hurried inside, then spun to face him as he followed and shut the door.

"Royce, please be reasonable about this," she said, prepared to plead with him if necessary. "I only wanted to help."

"You lied to me, Megan."

"But…" she began.

"Do all women lie to get their way?"

His voice held such anguish, it cut through her like a knife. Megan stared at him, and suddenly knew that he had been hurt, deeply hurt, by another woman who had lied to him.

"Royce, I…" she began again, but once more his voice sliced through hers.

"Dammit, Megan, I trusted you, believed in you." Striding to her, he grasped her by the shoulders. "You gave me your word, and then broke it the minute my back was turned."

"She hurt you very badly, didn't she?" Megan murmured, raising her hand to stroke his quivering face.

"Yes," he said bluntly. "But it was a shot to my ego and pride, not an emotionally lethal blow." His voice went low, soft and tender. "But it was nothing in comparison to the agony and trauma you've endured."

It was the opening she needed, and she grabbed for it. "But that's just it, Royce. It was because of the uncertainty and fear that I broke my word to you.''

He frowned.

Megan rushed on. ''After the way I fell apart last night, when that man called, I felt I had to do something to normalize my life, reclaim my sense of self. I just couldn't go on, being afraid of shadows, hiding behind you.'' She drew in a ragged breath. ''Please, try to understand.''

Royce's frown gave way to a rueful expression. ''I do, now. And I'm sorry I yelled at you.''

''I'm sorry, too.'' Megan hesitated, then asked the question she had to have answered. ''Are you still missing her?''

''She doesn't matter anymore.'' His response came with satisfying swiftness. ''She hasn't mattered for a long time. But you did.''

Megan felt a searing twist of pain at his use of the past tense. Had her rash action destroyed her attraction for him? A rush of tears stung her eyes. ''Did I?''

''Didn't last night prove that to you?''

''I thought,'' she said in a tear-choked whisper. ''I hoped.''

''I hoped, too.'' His fingers flexed, sinking sensuously into her soft flesh. ''It's been nearly a year since I've been intimate with a woman.'' A wry smile slanted his lips. ''Her defection left me feeling empty, sexually disinterested.'' His smile gentled. ''Then I met you, and from that morning I came to interview you in the hospital, you filled me, brought back the wanting.''

"Oh, Royce..."

"I know I have no right to dump my feelings on you, after what you've been through, but—" He drew a quick breath, then blurted out, "I'm afraid I'm falling in love with you, Megan." He gave a sharp shake of his head. "No, I know I'm in love with you."

The sensations that exploded inside Megan at his declaration were too glorious to be described. So she didn't even try. Instead, responding to them, she threw her arms around his neck and laughed in sheer joy and relief.

Royce reacted to the sound of her jubilation by releasing his hold on her arms to draw her close to him, very close. "Does this mean you don't mind?"

"Mind?" Megan's laughter peeled out again. "Oh, Sergeant, you big, beautiful man," she sang out when her laughter had subsided. "I'm very much afraid I'm in love with you, too. And the only thing I'd mind was if you didn't..."

His mouth claimed hers, drowning her voice, stirring her senses, sealing her fate. When, satisfying moments later, he raised his head, her eyes were shining with love for him as she finished what she'd begun to say.

"Want me, Wolfe."

* * * * *

WOLFE WEDDING

One

Why hadn't they ever gone to bed together?

Cameron Wolfe peered over the top of his gold-framed reading glasses at the woman elegantly poised in his office doorway.

Sandra Bradley was well worth peering at.

At age thirty-one—or was it thirty-two now?—Sandra was in her glorious prime. Tall, slender, gorgeous, and smart as they came, she was one fantastic piece of work, a delight to the eyes and senses, and a worthy opponent into the bargain.

What more could any red-blooded American male ask for in a woman?

Compliance?

Cameron repressed a smile at the immediate response his brain threw out to his silent query. He could readily imagine Sandra in any role she chose to perform—any role, that is, except one of acquiescence.

An unabashed feminist and a damn sharp lawyer, Sandra was light-years beyond the outmoded traditional concept of femininity—which answered his original question about why they had never gone to bed together. He and Sandra had a professional relationship, and Cameron never mixed business with pleasure. The combination could be explosive, thus devastating. Besides, his view of women was as unabashedly traditional as Sandra's was nontraditional.

Pity.

"Well, hello," he drawled. "To what do I owe the singular honor of your visit?"

"Hello yourself." Sandra's voice always thrilled. Low and throaty, she could drawl along with the best. "It's a courtesy call." She strolled with languid grace into the room.

Attired in a severely tailored jonquil yellow suit, combined with a silk shirt, scarf, shoes and handbag in leaf green, she appeared to bring the mild freshness of Denver's early-spring weather into the room with her.

Up close, she was even easier on the eyes.

Her features were clearly classic—sculptured bone structure, beneath satiny skin with a magnolia-creamy complexion. Her well-defined, full-lipped mouth alone could have, and probably had, turned hordes of men's minds to mush, and another part of their anatomy to steel.

Her long-legged, curvaceous figure wasn't bad, either. In truth, it was muscle-clenching.

Feeling the predictable thrill, and the tightening effect, in every atom of his being, Cameron covered his reaction with the equally languid-appearing motions of first rising, then removing his glasses.

"How intriguing." He allowed a hint of a smile to shadow his lips. Laying the specs on top of the papers he had been reading, he flicked a hand to indicate the two functional chairs placed in front of his desk. "Have a seat," he said, arching one gold-kissed, tawny eyebrow. "And explain."

"The courtesy?" Matching his expression with a raised brown brow that was as dark as his were light, Sandra sank onto a chair and crossed her legs, causing her long, narrow side-split linen skirt to hitch up to reveal an enticing length of thigh.

"Er...yeah." Cameron's voice was dry, because his throat was dry, parched by the heat of his reaction to her display of one sheer-nylon-encased leg.

Lord, what his imagination could conjure around her legs, should he give it free rein. And most of the conjuring would involve those long, shapely limbs, that tapered to slender ankles, curling around him.

The fleeting thought occurred to him of how amused—surprised? shocked? amazed?—his family, friends and acquaintances would very likely be, should they be able to tap into the desire of his imagination to indulge in erotic flights of fantasy about her.

With the possible exception of his mother, who knew him best, and tended to peer beneath the surface, nearly everyone who knew Cameron believed him to be a confirmed woman-hater, as well as a confirmed bachelor.

He wasn't, of course. But having been burned once, a long time ago, he was not only wary of involvement, he was extremely selective in his choice of female companions—who had been few and far between for some years. And even then, he had never had a dalliance with anyone remotely concerned with his professional life.

Sandra, however, was something else again. There had been instances, too many for comfort, when temptation lured, desire swirled, and his imagination fought against his self-imposed control in a burning bid to soar free. To date, his control had proved stronger. Today was no different.

Imposing that hard-fought-for iron control, Cameron didn't free his imagination. With a silent sigh of regret, he reined it in instead.

"What courtesy, and why?"

Her luscious mouth curved into a knowing smile of genuine amusement, and appreciation for his discernment. Sandra had never made the mistake of taking him for anybody's fool.

"The courtesy of letting you know that you'll be getting a break from tangling with me for a while...possibly a long while."

He frowned; instead of clarifying, her explanation compounded his confusion. His expression mirroring his feelings, Cameron dropped into his desk chair, leaned forward and fixed a piercing stare on her.

"You want to expand on that cryptic statement?"

Sandra's smile took on a teasing quirk; her soft dark brown eyes danced with laughter lights. "You mean, what in hell am I talking about?"

Cameron gave a judicious nod of his head, and absently raised a hand to brush back the thick lock of tawny hair that tumbled onto his forehead. "Yeah, that would clear up the issue for me."

"I'm taking a leave of absence from my work and the firm," she answered with a simple candor. "A sabbatical, if you will."

Her response brought him to a full stop for an instant. The low sound of her throaty laughter jarred him out of his bemusement.

"Leave of absence?" His voice had lost the slow and easy drawl, and now held unabashed and blatant disbelief. "A sabbatical?"

Sandra made an elaborate show of glancing around the office. "Do I detect an echo in here?"

"Clever. Real clever." Cameron gave her a dry, droll look. "If you're through playing straight ma—person," he said chidingly, "are you ready to tell me what in hell you *are* talking about?"

She chided him right back. "Exactly what I said. I'm taking a leave of absence."

"Why?" His brow furrowed in a frown. "You're the best lawyer in the firm."

"Thank you for that." Sandra inclined her head in acknowledgment of the compliment. She knew they were few and far between from Cameron Wolfe.

"You're welcome. Now tell me why."

"I'm tired." Her answer came without hesitation, and with determined adamancy. "I need a break."

His eyes shadowed with brooding intent, Cameron absently toyed with one of the earpieces of his glasses as he mulled over her response.

Sandra certainly didn't look tired, he mused, studying her face in minute detail. In point of fact, she looked as bright and sparkling as the spring sunshine that was pouring through the wide office window and splashing butter yellow color on the utilitarian gray carpet.

For all the depth of his shrewd observation, Cameron could not detect the slightest sign of stress or strain in her smooth features, or in the calm, clear eyes returning his inspection.

"You don't look tired," he voiced his assessment. "Matter of fact, you look pretty good."

Sandra laughed; it was another sound that never failed to thrill. Low, throatily exciting, her laughter had always had the power to light the darkest and most secret depths of his being.

"Two compliments from you in one day." Her eyes sparkled with amusement. "Must be a record."

"A stranger overhearing you might be forgiven for thinking me some kind of ogre," Cameron said in gentle reproof. "Am I really that cold?"

"No." She shook her head, setting her sleek, stylishly bobbed sable hair swirling. "A tad remote, perhaps, but not cold." Her soft mouth curved into a teasing smile. "But for as long as I've known you, you have never been fast and loose with the compliments."

"I never saw the point in sweet-talking anyone," he said with blunt honesty.

"Yes, I know. You call them as you see them."

"Right." He gave a sharp, emphatic nod of his head, once again flipping the shock of hair onto his forehead. "So, now that we've established my forthrightness," he drawled, absently brushing back the unruly hair, "I'd like to hear the bottom-line reason for your taking a leave of absence."

Sandra shook her head despairingly, and sent another ripple of throaty laughter dancing around the room and down his spine.

"You're a hoot, Wolfe," she said, a smile remaining after her laughter subsided. "You're like a journalist in hot pursuit of a fast-breaking juicy scandal—you just don't quit, do you?"

"Quitting doesn't get you anywhere."

"Touché," she said, acknowledging his pointed barb. "But you see, the bottom line is, I am tired." A frown drew her perfectly arched brows together. "I'm more than tired. I'm burned out. I need a break."

Cameron stared at her pensively while he assimilated the depth of the shading in her voice. Sandra was saying a lot more than she was saying, he concluded, loosening his visual grip on her steadily returned stare.

"This last case get to you?" he asked, setting his reading glasses aside once more to rake long fingers through his already finger-ruffled hair.

"Yes." Her flat response was immediate, unequivocal. "It got to me."

Cameron knew the feeling; boy, did he know the feeling. The strange, almost eerie thing was, the case he had just wrapped up had gotten to him, too.

Odd, the two of them feeling the strain at the same time. Odd, and a bit weird.

He made a quick movement of his head, as if trying to shake off the uncanny sensation. Coincidence, he assured himself. Nothing but coincidence.

But was it?

Cameron's built-in computer went to work, tossing out facts and figures, irrefutable and unarguable.

He had been transferred to Denver by the Bureau the year that Sandra joined the law firm of Carlson and Carlson, a mother-and-daughter partnership handling primarily what Cameron thought of as "women's cases."

Throughout the intervening years, he had observed Sandra's dedication and work with what he hoped was a dispassionate objectivity. They had clashed and tangled on several occasions—whenever one of his cases evolved into one of her cases.

Sandra had always maintained the highest level of professionalism and the strictest moral and ethical code of behavior—as, in fact, he did himself.

In Cameron's opinion, Sandra was not just one of the best attorneys he knew but also one of the best human beings. He admired her, and genuinely liked her, more than a little—which was why he kept a professional barrier between them.

But, at the same time, he also kept close tabs on her, following her career and cases.

And her last case had been a real beaut.

Sandra had represented the mother in a child-custody battle. The divorced combatants had been equally determined to attain sole custody of the innocent party, a lovely little girl of five.

The father, one Raymond Whitfield—a man

Cameron personally and secretly considered an arrogant and overbearing bastard—had been confident of winning the battle, due to his wealth and his position in the city.

The mother—made timid and fearful by years of marriage to a psychologically abusive man—had somehow worked up the courage to seek help from Carlson and Carlson, after reading an article in a national magazine about the successful record of the firm, and the skill in the courtroom of Sandra Bradley.

Sandra had not only accepted the woman as a client, she had marshaled all her formidable intelligence and talents to bring them to the case.

Sandra, the mother and, most importantly, the five-year-old child had won. The bastard had lost—with much huffing and puffing, and not a whiff of dignity.

But the battle had obviously taken a great toll on Sandra—although there was little evidence of it in her appearance or demeanor.

"He didn't lose graciously, did he?" he said, referring to the man's public harrumphing.

"No, he didn't." Sandra lifted her shoulders in a helpless shrug. "Probably because he genuinely believed he couldn't possibly lose."

"Seeing as how he comes from a very old and well-established family, with friends in high places, I suppose that's understandable."

"More like predictable," she murmured, grimacing. "He is really not a very nice man."

"Did he make any threats, open or veiled?" Cameron demanded, alerted by a hint of something in her tone, her expression.

Sandra flipped her hand in a dismissive gesture. "He was just blowing off steam."

"What did he say?"

"It wasn't important, all big—"

He cut her off, repeating his hard voiced question. "What did he say?"

"Cameron—"

He again cut her off. "Sandra. Tell me."

She heaved a sigh, but answered, "He muttered something about getting me, winning out in the end." She made a face, looking both wry and bored. "I'm sure he meant that he'd see me in court again, maybe even the Supreme Court."

"Maybe," he agreed, making a mental note to keep tabs on the man, just to be on the safe side.

"At any rate, it's over, at least for now," she said, giving him a faint smile. "And I'm tired. I've earned a break, and I'm going to take it."

"Well, at the risk of repeating myself, it doesn't show. You don't look tired."

She responded with a spine-tingling laugh.

While absorbing the effect of her laughter on his senses, Cameron couldn't help but wonder if his own weariness and uneasy sense of pointlessness were manifesting themselves in his expressions or his actions.

After more than ten years as a special agent for the Federal Bureau of Investigation, he was experiencing more than disillusionment; he was feeling jaded and cynical.

He didn't like the feeling.

Cameron sprang from a family with a history of involvement in law enforcement. Pennsylvania was his birth state. His father had been a beat cop in Philadelphia, and had been killed in the line of duty by a strung-out dealer during a narcotics bust several years ago. Cameron still ached inside at the memory.

The eldest of four sons, he was proud of his younger brothers, all three of whom were in law enforcement. The one nearest to him in age, Royce, was a sergeant with the Pennsylvania State Police. The next brother, Eric, was on the Philadelphia police force, working undercover in the narcotics division, which he had transferred to after the death of their father. His youngest brother, Jake, after years of worrying Cameron with his rebellious attitude and footloose-and-fancy-free life-style, had finally come to terms with himself.

To the relief and delight of the entire Wolfe family, Jake had recently joined the police force in their hometown of Sprucewood, some fifteen miles from Philadelphia. In addition to settling into law enforcement, Jake had further surprised the family a short time ago by being the first one of the brothers to fall in love—really in love, seriously in love.

Baby brother Jake was getting married.

While Cameron was delighted that his brother had apparently found his niche in life and, according to their mother, whose judgment none of them ever doubted, the perfect woman to share his niche, there was a growing niggling sense of dissatisfaction inside that was beginning to concern Cameron.

Over the years, he had had some strange, even some weird, cases to contend with in his work for the Bureau. The last one in particular, which also had been wrapped up two days ago, had been both strange and weird. Disquieting, as well, since it had seemed to indicate, at least to him, the fragile mental state of the world in general, and some individuals in particular.

For weeks, while Sandra fought her case in court, Cameron had been on the trail of a real wacko, a wild and daring young man who believed himself the reincarnation of some legendary Western outlaw.

Instead of a horse, the man—who called himself Swift-Draw Slim—had jockeyed a four-wheel-drive Bronco. Slim got his kicks from holding up small-town banks throughout the Midwest and the Southwest. Which was bad enough, and reason enough to involve the FBI.

Cameron had been drawn into the case when

Slim abducted a fourteen-year-old girl and took her
across state lines, from New Mexico into Colorado.

Although Slim had led all the local, state and
federal authorities on a merry chase, by the time
he finally caught him, literally with his pants down,
Cameron hadn't been laughing. In fact, he'd been
mad as hell, disgusted, and about ready to throw
in the towel—or throw up.

Gazing into the somber brown eyes of Sandra
Bradley, Cameron suddenly decided that he needed
a break, too. A sabbatical. *If you will.*

And he had accumulated vacation time due
him—six weeks' time, to be exact.

He had been planning to use some of the time,
two weeks or so, to fly East for his brother Jake's
wedding. Jake had done him the singular honor of
asking him to be his best man. The wedding was
scheduled for the beginning of June, just four and
a half weeks away.

But if he requested and was granted his time
beginning the end of this week, which was the last
full week in April, that would give him four weeks
to play around with before Jake took the marriage
plunge, and two weeks after the celebration to re-
cover from the festivities.

Hmm...

His brooding gaze fixed on the delectable
woman seated opposite him, Cameron mentally
frowned and contemplated the advisability and
possibility of playing around with Sandra Bradley.

The prospect had definite appeal, and an immediate drawback. Cameron was at once hard, hot and ready. Appearing cool, calm and in command required all the considerable control he possessed.

"I can't help wondering what you are thinking about." Amused suspicion colored Sandra's voice. "You have a decidedly devilish look about you."

Go for it.

"I was just thinking," he said, acting on the prompt that flashed through his head. "What are your plans? Anything definite in mind?"

"Yes." Sandra smiled; he swallowed a groan. "I'm going to run away, hide out for a while."

"Any particular destination?"

She nodded, setting her hair—and his insides—to rippling. "I've been given the use of a small cabin in the mountains for as long as it takes."

Cameron frowned. "For as long as it takes to do what, exactly?"

Sandra laughed. "In the words of my boss, For as long as it takes to get my head back on straight. She's convinced I simply need some breathing space."

"And it's more than that?" Cameron asked, with sudden and shrewd insight.

She hesitated, then released a deep sigh. "I honestly don't know, Cameron. I was prepared to chuck it all. I had even typed up my letter of resignation." Her lips quirked into a wry smile. "Barbara refused to accept it. In fact, she tore it in two the instant she finished reading it. That's when she handed me the keys and directions to her retreat in the mountains.''

Hmm… A mountain retreat. Springtime in the Rockies. Wildflowers blooming. Birds singing. Butterflies fluttering. The alluring Sandra, and perhaps, Cameron mused, a male companion—namely him. Nature taking its course. Interesting. Exciting.

But would she?

Find out.

''Ah, when are you leaving?'' he asked, in as casual a tone as he could muster.

She gave him an arch look. ''The firm or the city?''

''Well…'' Cameron shrugged. ''Both.''

''I've already left the firm.'' Her lips twitched in amusement. ''On granted leave. I wanted to clean out my desk, just in case I decided to stick to my original plan not to return. Janice nearly went into a decline.'' She chuckled. ''And Barbara wouldn't even talk about it.''

''Uh-huh,'' he murmured, prudently keeping his opinion of the mother-daughter team to himself. After all, he cautioned himself, being brutally honest at this particular moment could hardly advance his cause.

From all indications, Sandra liked and respected both the mother and daughter of the team.

And, though he would willingly concede that

they were excellent lawyers, Cameron privately considered both women, Barbara, the senior member, and her daughter, Janice, to be feminists in the extreme. Although he agreed with the concept of equality of the sexes, he did find the extremist element of the movement a bit tiring.

"Okay," he went on, "when are you planning to leave for the mountains?"

"Day after tomorrow," Sandra answered, readily enough, while fixing him with a probing stare. "Why?"

Here goes.

Cameron grabbed a quick breath.

"Want some company?"

His soft query was met by stillness. The room was still. The air was still. Sandra was the most still of all...for about ten seconds. Then she blinked, and frowned, and blurted out a choked laugh.

"You?" She stared at him in patent disbelief. "The legendary Lone Wolfe?"

"Me," he admitted. "And can the Lone Wolfe bull."

"Are you serious?" Her velvety voice had grown a little ragged around the edges.

"Quite serious," he assured her, tamping down the urge to elaborate.

"But..." She shook her head, as if trying to clear her mind, and gave another abortive laugh. "Why?"

Cameron arched a brow in chiding. "A little R and R. Fun and games. Unadulterated pleasure."

"In other words," she murmured, the ragged edges in her velvety voice smoothed out, "Sex, sex, and more sex?"

"A sensual sabbatical." Even he could hear the enticement in his soft voice. "If you will."

Two

She would!

Sandra stood beside her bed, a bemused smile curving her lips, a filmy flame red nightgown dangling from her nerveless fingertips.

Had she actually agreed to Cameron's outrageous proposal to have him stay with her in Barbara's cabin? she asked herself for perhaps the hundredth time since leaving his office a few hours ago.

In a shot!

Some folks might have accused Sandra of being aloof, but no astute person had ever accused her of being stupid—and she wasn't about to start now.

Her smile evolved into a soft, excited laugh.

It was spring. And how did the old saying go? In the spring, a young man's fancy, and all that. Well, didn't the same apply to young women, as well?

An anticipatory thrill moved through her. The filmy gown undulated through her fingers, bringing awareness of the sexy garment. Laughter again tickled the back of her throat. Contemplating the possible—hopeful?—ramifications of wearing the revealing scrap of nothing for him, she folded the nightie and tucked it into the suitcase lying open on her bed.

Imagine, she mused, the legendary Lone Wolfe expressing a desire to spend time in seclusion for an unspecified time...with her!

Wild.

How long had she been secretly lusting for the oh-so-cool-and-self-contained Cameron Wolfe?

Sandra laughed once more, low and sultry. She knew full well how long it had been. She had wanted Cameron from the very first day she met him, six long years ago. And wanting him had ruined her chances of forming a deep romantic relationship with any other man.

From the very beginning, it had had to be Cameron, or no one. And the passage of time had not diminished her desire for him. On the contrary, getting to know him, learning about some of the facets of his character—his honesty, his high personal moral code, his dedication to duty—had only deepened the attraction she felt for him.

She wanted him, and it was as simple as that. Foolish, maybe, but that was the way it was.

And now...and now...

Anticipation expanded into an effervescent sensation inside her, rushing through her bloodstream, intoxicating her mind and senses. Reacting to the stimulant, she turned and two-stepped across the room to her dresser, pulling open the drawer containing her mostly ultrafeminine lingerie.

Humming an old and very suggestive love ballad, she moved around the room, from the dresser to the closet to the bed, with side trips into the bathroom, filling the suitcase and a large nylon carryon with the things she wanted to take to the cabin.

Originally thinking to do nothing more strenuous than take short, brisk hikes in the foothills surrounding the cabin, Sandra had planned on packing only what she thought of as loafing-around clothes—jeans, sweatshirts, sweaters, parka, boots and such. But at one point, while she was removing an old cotton shirt, soft from many washings, from the closet, her glance had touched, then settled on, a new, more alluring outfit.

Sandra had never worn the two-piece ensemble. It bore a Paris label—a thirty-second-birthday gift she had received over a month ago from her parents, who were spending a year in France, both working and having a grand time, while her father set up international offices there for his business firm.

The reason Sandra had never worn the outfit was that there had never been an occasion suitable for her to do so. The set was too darn alluring for just any old gathering of friends.

Fashioned of sand-washed silk in shimmering swirls of fuchsia, orange and mint green, the outfit consisted of a voluminous-sleeved poet-style shirt and a belted, full-flowing skirt.

Viewed on a padded clothes hanger, the ensemble appeared innocent enough. But, upon trying it on for fit, Sandra had been mildly shocked by the appearance she presented in it.

The first button on the shirt was placed at mid-chest, a plunging vee revealing the cleavage of her high, fully rounded breasts. And, although there was an abundance of material to the skirt, when she moved, it swirled around her long legs, the clinging silk caressing every curve from her waist to her ankles.

At the time, Sandra had stared at her mirrored image in wide-eyed amazement, deciding on the spot that the outfit was too blatantly sexy for just any casual get-together. It was definitely for something special.

An impish glow sparkled in her dark eyes now as a thought flashed through her mind.

The Lone Wolfe was someone special. And being with him would most definitely be special.

Sandra carefully folded the two pieces and tucked them into the case.

How much farther could it possibly be?

Sandra frowned as she maneuvered her one-year-old front-wheel-drive compact around yet another sharp bend in the narrow, rutted, mud-and-slush-covered dirt road. Although spring had arrived at the lower elevations, shallow mounds of snow still lay in patches on the ground and beneath the trees in the foothills of the mountain range northwest of Denver.

A quick glance at the dashboard clock told her that thirty-odd minutes had elapsed since she had made the turn off the major highway indicated in the directions Barbara had written down for her.

By Sandra's reckoning, she should soon be seeing the signpost indicating the private road leading to the cabin. Even though she knew what to expect, she laughed aloud upon sighting the sign with the words *Escape Hatch* printed in bold letters on it.

The private driveway leading to the cabin was in worse condition than the dirt road, the slush concealing potholes that caught her unawares and caused the vehicle to lurch from side to side.

Sandra heaved a deep sigh of relief when the cabin came into view around a gentle curve in the road.

Seemingly built into the side of the hill, the log cabin looked as if it belonged there, nestled in amid the tall pines. A broad porch fronted the cabin. A wide window overlooked the porch and the valley beyond.

Anxious to see the inside of the place, Sandra stepped from the vehicle and tramped through the diminishing snow cover to the three broad steps leading up to the porch. The sunshine was warm on her shoulders, and turned the snow to mush beneath her hiking boots.

Around the base of the cabin, yellow and white jonquils raised their bright faces to the spring sunlight, while at the base of the stalks, shoots of delicate green grasses poked through the melting snow.

Smiling at the harbingers of spring, Sandra mounted the stairs to the porch and strode to the front door, key at the ready. Unlocking the door, she turned the knob, pushed open the door, stepped inside, and came to an abrupt halt, a soft "Oh…" whispering through her parted lips.

The cabin was everything she had dared to hope for, and more. Barbara had warned that the place was rustic, and it was. And yet the decorative touches—a flower-bedecked, deep-cushioned sofa and two matching chairs, sun yellow curtains, and a large rug braided in colors harmonizing with those in the furniture and the curtains—gave the place a snug, homey warmth, even though the still air inside felt at least ten degrees colder than the spring-washed air outside.

Sandra longed to investigate, but, deciding to deal with first things first, went directly to the thermostat to activate the heater, which, Barbara had assured her, had a full supply of fuel. Hearing the heater kick on, she turned and retraced her steps outside to collect her gear and the groceries she had purchased before leaving the city.

In all, four trips were required from the cabin to the vehicle, and Sandra was panting for breath by the time she set the last two bags of groceries on the butcher-block table in the small kitchen.

Whew! Was she getting old—or was she just terribly out of shape?

Pausing to catch her breath, she ran a slow, comprehensive look over the room. Her perusal banished consideration of encroaching age and deteriorating physical condition. A smile of satisfaction tilted her lips at what she observed.

Though small, the kitchen was compact, every inch of space wisely utilized, with fitted cabinets above and below the sink, and a small electric range and refrigerator. A full-size microwave oven was tucked into a corner of the countertop, and next to it sat the latest in automatic coffeemakers. A small, uncurtained window above the sink looked out over a smaller replica of the front porch, and the stately pines dotting the gentle incline of the foothills. A bottled-gas-fired grill stood on the wood-railed porch. Its domed lid wore a thin layer of snow.

Hmm... Sandra's mouth watered as she envisioned the steaks she'd bought, sizzling to a perfect medium-rare on the grill. Thinking of the steaks brought awareness of place and time—and it was time to put the food away, unpack her cases and familiarize herself with the place that would be her home for several weeks.

But first, she could do with a cup of coffee.

Humming softly, she washed the glass pot, then dug out of a stuffed-full grocery bag one of the cans of French-roast coffee she had bought. While the aromatic stream of dark liquid trickled into the pot, she loaded perishable foods—meat, cheese, eggs, milk, and fresh vegetables and fruits—into the fridge. Onto the bottom shelf she slid the two bottles of wine, one white, one red, that she had thought to pick up. The dried and canned articles went into the overhead cabinets.

When the foodstuffs were stashed away, Sandra poured coffee into a rainbow-decorated ceramic mug and carried it into the cabin's single bedroom, where she had earlier dumped her suitcase and carryon, and the shopping bag into which she had jammed sheets and towels.

Measuring approximately twelve feet by fourteen, the room was far from spacious. And yet the sparse furnishings, a double bed, a small nightstand

and one standard-size chest of drawers, lent the illusion of roominess.

Another brightly colored braided rug covered most of the pine board floor. As in the living room, the colors in the rug were picked up in the bedspread and curtains at the room's two windows, one of which faced the north side of the cabin, the other the mountains to the rear.

All in all, not bad, Sandra decided, hefting the large suitcase onto the bed, then plopping onto the mattress and bouncing to test the resiliency of the springs.

It would do quite adequately, she thought, shivering in response to the thrill of anticipation that scurried up her back as an image of Cameron Wolfe filled her mind, along with the realization of what the bed would be used for, besides sleeping.

The temptation was overwhelming to forget every other concern and to settle back, wallowing in the comfort of the mattress…and exciting speculation.

But, being disciplined and responsible, Sandra resisted the temptation. With an unconscious sigh of longing, she heaved herself from the bed.

It was now midafternoon on Thursday, and there was work to be done before Cameron's scheduled arrival. He had told her to expect him sometime around noon, give or take an hour or so, on Saturday.

Sandra flicked the clasps on the large suitcase and flipped it open. She had to get her tush in gear. She had to unpack, put away her clothes, make up the bed with her own sheets. And then start scrubbing.

Barbara had given Sandra fair warning that, as she hadn't been to the cabin since the beginning of December, the place would need a thorough cleaning.

Barbara had not been overstating the case. Even with her quick initial perusal of the place, Sandra had noted the layer of dust that coated every flat surface, lamp, appliance and knickknack...not to mention the tile and fixtures in the bathroom.

It was immediately obvious that neither Barbara nor her daughter was very neat or very much inclined toward cleaning up after themselves. Fortunately, that was not reflected in their professional work or their workplace.

But at the time of her employer's offer, delighted with the idea of having the use of the isolated retreat, Sandra had shrugged and readily agreed to doing the necessary work involved.

Still, being willing to do the housekeeping chores and actually doing the work were two entirely different things, especially when one was not, either by nature or by training, particularly domesticated.

Sandra heaved another sigh as she began removing her clothes from the case. She did not *do* housework. With the jam-packed client schedule she carried—or had been carrying up until now—she didn't have time to do housework, even if she was so inclined. She paid a hefty amount to a professional service to *do* for her.

But the cleaning service was in Denver, and she was here, in this isolated cabin. So, Ms. Professional, she told herself, systematically stowing her things in dresser drawers and closets, you'd be well advised to get your act together and get it done.

Sandra was nearly undone herself when she pulled open the narrow drawer in the bedside nightstand. As small as it was, the gun inside the drawer looked lethal—which, of course, it was.

Naturally, she had known it was there. Barbara had told her it was there. Still…

Sandra hated guns. She knew how to handle them, how to use them properly, simply because the use of them had been included in a self-defense class she took while in college. Even so, she hated them.

Shuddering, she slipped the paperback novels she'd brought with her into the drawer, shoving the weapon, and the accompanying box of cartridges, to the back, out of sight. Then, firmly erasing the ugly thing from her thoughts, she turned to begin working on the bed.

Did she want Cameron to think she was a slob?

"Your man flew out of Denver in a private plane at 6:35 this morning."

"Heading where?" Cameron asked tersely into the phone. He slanted a glance at his watch. It read 6:51; his operative was right on top of his assignment, as he had fully expected him to be.

"Chicago."

Cameron breathed a sigh of relief; if Whitfield was off to Chicago, on business or whatever, he couldn't very well be harassing Sandra.

"Thanks, Steve," he said. "Who will take over surveillance there?"

"Jibs."

"Okay. I'll be out of town for a couple of weeks, but I'll be in touch."

"I'll be here." Steve hesitated, then asked, "You going on assignment or vacation?"

"Vacation."

Steve let out an exaggerated groan. "I should be so lucky. Enjoy."

A slow smile played over Cameron's lips as an image of Sandra filled his mind.

"Oh, I intend to," he said, anticipation simmering within him. "Every minute."

After cradling the receiver, he shot another look at his watch. It read 6:59. He had another call to make, back East, but it was still too early.

Turning away from the kitchen wall phone, Cameron poured himself a fresh cup of coffee, then headed for the bedroom. He also still had some packing to finish, the last-minute things he had left

for this morning. Sipping the hot brew, he sauntered into his bedroom.

Pack first, call later.

The job of finishing up the packing required all
of thirteen and a half minutes—Cameron was nothing if not both neat and efficient.

In addition to being a supremely competent and
confident law-enforcement agent, recognized as
one of the best operatives in the field, he was a
proficient cook *and* did his own laundry.

Cameron was firmly convinced that his talents
when it came to law enforcement were in his
genes—although he was the first to credit his father
for his early training along those lines.

But his domestic talents were definitely attributable to the concentrated efforts of his indomitable mother. From day one, son one, Maddy Wolfe
had stoutly maintained that any idiot could learn
to pick up after himself, and that included each one
of her sons.

Having lived a bachelor existence from the day
he left home for college, at age eighteen, Cameron
had numerous times given fervent, if silent, thanks
to his mother for her persistence.

He had spent more than a few day-off mornings
on his knees, scrubbing the kitchen or bathroom
floor of whatever apartment he happened to be living in at the time.

Though this was one of his days off, both his
kitchen and bathroom floors were spotlessly clean,

as was everything in his current apartment, thanks to the professional housekeeper he now paid to do the chore.

He shot yet another quick look at his watch; all of five minutes had elapsed since his last look. What to do? He had made his bed over an hour ago and, except for washing up the few dishes he had used for breakfast, there was really nothing left to do.

So, wash the dishes.

Draining the swallow of coffee remaining in the cup, Cameron left the bedroom and headed for the kitchen. Fifteen minutes later, with the dishes done and put away, and finding himself wiping the countertop for the third time, he literally threw in the sponge, or in this case the abused dishcloth.

Impatience crawled through him. He fairly itched to go, from the apartment, out of the city, into the foothills, in a beeline to Sandra.

Although he had committed them to memory, he dug from his pocket the piece of paper on which he had jotted Sandra's directions to the cabin. A piece of cake, he decided, tossing the scrap of paper on the sparkling clean table.

Now what? Cameron heaved a sigh and sliced a glaring glance from the clock to the phone.

The hell with it. Early or not, he was placing the call.

Maddy answered on the second ring. "Hello?"

"Good morning, beautiful," Cameron said

smoothly, heaving another silent sigh of relief at the wide-awake sound of his mother's voice. "How are you on this bright spring morning?"

"It's storming here, but I'm fine, just the same," she returned dryly. "How are you?"

"As usual," he answered—as usual. "I didn't wake you, did I?"

"Wake me?" Maddy laughed; it was a rich, deep sound that he had always loved. "I've been up for hours. But you did catch me in the middle of mixing pie crust."

"Pie crust." Cameron mentally licked his lips; Maddy did make tasty pies. "For shoofly?" Shoofly pie was his all-time favorite.

She laughed again—a mother's laugh. "No. Not today. I'm making lemon meringue." She chuckled again, and this time the sound was different, loaded with amusement and self-satisfaction.

Cameron frowned. What was she up to? He knew full well that lemon meringue was his brother Eric's all-time favorite. But why should that amuse his mother?

"Eric coming for dinner?"

"Not today. Tomorrow," she said, and now her voice was rife with an alerting...something.

"Okay, Mom, I give up," he said, his curiosity thoroughly aroused, as he knew she had deliberately set out to do. "What's the story with Eric?"

"He's coming for dinner tomorrow."

Maddy did so enjoy teasing her overgrown sons—teasing and testing.

Despite his impatience to get under way, Cameron had to laugh, enjoying his mother's enjoyment.

"And?" he prompted when she failed to continue.

"He's bringing Tina with him."

Tina. He should have known. Cameron administered a mental self-reprimand for missing the clue Maddy had given him.

Lemon meringue. Not only was the dessert Eric's favorite, but also, from what Maddy had told Cameron, the object of a friendly rivalry between his mother and the young woman his brother had met last fall.

At Maddy's invitation, Eric had brought the woman home to meet her at Thanksgiving. Tina had brought along a lemon meringue pie as her contribution to the feast.

After the holiday, when Maddy relayed the information to Cameron, she had graciously conceded that Tina's pie was first-rate...almost as good as her own.

Cameron hadn't been fooled for a moment. He knew at once that Maddy didn't give a rip about the pies, one way or the other. But what she did care about was the possibility of a serious relationship growing between Eric and Tina, who, she claimed, was a lovely young woman.

Cameron was also fully aware that his mother

lived in hope of first seeing her sons settled into marriages as strong as her own had been, and second spoiling the hell out of her grandchildren—of whom she had expressed a desire for at least eight.

And now Eric was bringing the woman home to mother for a second visit.

Hmm, he mused, recalling that, to his knowledge, Eric had never brought a woman home twice.

First Jake. Now Eric?

"Does this portend something?" he asked after a lengthy silence, realizing that his mother had calmly been waiting for him to assimilate the facts.

"I sincerely hope so," she answered. "Keep in touch, and I'll keep you informed."

"Yeah, well, as to that," he said, interested in being brought up to speed on his brother's love life, but a lot more interested in pursuing his own, "I'm not sure when I'll be able to get back to you. I'm going out of town for a spell."

"I see." Not a hint of concern tainted her voice; after thirty years of living with a police officer, she had long since learned to conceal her fears. "Well, then, I'll talk to you when I talk to you." She paused, then added softly, "Take care, son."

"I will." A gentle smile tugged at his lips as he hung up the phone. In his admittedly biased opinion, Maddy epitomized the best of the female sex.

Female.

Sex.

Sandra.

Swinging away from the phone, Cameron strode from the kitchen. He collected his bags, glanced at, then deliberately shifted his gaze away from his beeper, which was lying atop the bedside table. He wouldn't need that where he was going. Gear in hand, he gave a final sweeping look around the room, then left the apartment.

"Dammit." Cameron wasn't even aware of swearing aloud; he was too busy making the turn to head back. He had driven only a few miles from his apartment when he knew he just couldn't do it. He just could not leave town for two weeks without his "connection" to the office, and the weapon that had grown to feel almost a part of him.

Muttering to himself that the two items had taken on the semblance of adult pacifiers, he strode into the apartment and directly to the bedside table.

After snatching up the beeper and the shoulder-holstered agency-issue revolver, he shoved the beeper into his pocket and, gripping the weapon, pivoted and retraced his steps to the door.

Something, an uneasy sensation, halted him midway to the door. What was it? he asked himself, raking the living room with a narrowed look. What was wrong? Nothing had been disturbed in the bedroom. Pacing to the kitchen, he ran a slow, encompassing look around. The entire place was exactly as he'd left it a half hour ago.

Still...

Sandra.

Telling himself he really did need a vacation, Cameron shrugged off the odd sensation, patted his pocket and once again exited the apartment. After stashing the gun in the rear of the vehicle, he drove away.

Now he was on vacation.

Maybe he'd stop somewhere along the way to the cabin and pick up a bottle or two of good wine, and a couple of six-packs of beer, he mused, anticipation crawling along his nerve endings, arousing all kinds of wicked thoughts and exciting reactions.

It wasn't until he was well out of the city, the wine and beer stashed in the back of his almost new Jeep Cherokee, that Cameron gave some thought to his brothers—and one in particular.

While talking to his mother, he had mused about his brothers. First Jake, the baby of the Wolfe pack, and now Eric, the third of the brood. But, on reflection, he recollected a phone conversation that he had had several weeks ago with Royce.

At the time, something—more what Royce hadn't said than what he had, a trace of distraction in his manner—had bothered Cameron.

Now, on reflection, he wondered whether Royce could possibly be involved with a woman, and whether his emotions were seriously engaged. Of course, he could have been reading his brother's voice incorrectly. But Cameron seriously doubted it; he knew his brothers.

And now, here he was, impatiently maintaining the legal speed limit, as anxious and excited as a teenager in the first throes of passion about spending a couple weeks alone in the mountains with Sandra.

Hmm…

Did this portend something?

Cameron's question to his mother came back to haunt and taunt him.

It's physical, my attraction to Sandra is purely physical, he assured himself, while trying to ignore the tingle that did a tango from his nape to the base of his spine.

Wasn't it?

Three

"**W**hoosh…" Sandra exhaled a deep breath and swiped the back of her hand across her damp forehead.

Damn, housecleaning was hard work, she thought, but at last she was finished. The interior of the cabin virtually sparkled as a result of her concentrated efforts of yesterday afternoon and all of today.

Going into the now-gleaming kitchen, she crossed to the fridge for a diet cola. She was sweaty. She was thirsty. She was hungry. And, boy, was she tired.

Was Cameron Wolfe worth her feverish flurry of activity? Sandra asked herself, dropping limply onto a lemon-scented, polished chair.

Damned right he was!

Laughing to and at herself, she downed the last of the cola and heaved her wilting body from the chair.

Tomorrow.

Cameron should—would—be arriving in less than twenty-four hours.

An anticipatory chill invaded her body.

It was rather shocking. Sandra scowled at herself, at her involuntary physical and emotional response to the mere thought of Cameron's forthcoming arrival.

Honestly, she chided herself. If her thoughts, feelings, could have been monitored, a stranger, or friend, could have been forgiven for looking askance at her. She was a full-grown woman, mature, intelligent—well, usually. And here she stood, shivering, in the center of the kitchen, figuratively and literally itching to get her hands, among other body parts, on Cameron Wolfe.

Pitiful.

Sandra grinned.

So it was pitiful. So what?

She wanted the Lone Wolfe in the worst way… and the best way…every way there was.

Hell, for all she knew, maybe she was actually in love with the man.

Now there was a sobering speculation. Sobering and scary. Who knew what love was? Or even if love, romantic love, really existed outside the fantasies individuals dreamed up for themselves?

Sandra had never run across that impossible-to-describe, elusive emotion.

The affliction called love certainly couldn't be clinically diagnosed. Nor could it be smeared on a slide and studied under a microscope. Come to that, as far as Sandra knew, the feverish fancy had never been nailed down by an absolute definition.

That being the case, how was one woman supposed to know if and when the emotion struck, replacing common sense with uncommon appetites?

Appetites.

Her stomach rumbled.

There were appetites, and then there were appetites.

Sandra laughed aloud. Here she stood, quite like a twittery teenager, mooning over a man, when what she should be doing was rustling up some food.

Of course, Sandra was well aware that feeding herself, getting a shower, shampooing her sweat-stiffened hair, then having a good night's sleep, were all ploys to distract herself from contemplation.

She didn't want to think about love, in any way, shape or form.

Sex, yes.

But love?

That really was too scary.

Sandra did sleep well, surprisingly well, considering her mental upheaval during the hours prior to her crawling between the sheets.

The questions of the evening, most especially the questions about motivation, were banished by the exciting, erotic dreams that visited her in slumber.

She awoke refreshed, eager to embrace the bright spring morning, and the man who hopefully would be joining her in the retreat by lunchtime.

After a leisurely breakfast of juice, toast and coffee, Sandra switched on the radio, and proceeded to while away the hours by alternately pacing from room to room and staring out the wide front window and along the road leading to the cabin.

He was late.

It was past noon.

Had he changed his mind?

Sandra bit her lip and peered down the driveway.

It was exactly 12:46 when she spied his Jeep; Sandra knew, because she shot a quick look at her wristwatch as she made a dash for the door to greet him.

She stepped onto the deck as Cameron stepped from the Jeep. The sun felt warm on her face. The sight of him made her feel warmer all over.

The Lone Wolfe.

Lord! He looked delicious.

Good enough to eat.

Sandra promised herself a taste.

He was dressed for the outdoors—tight jeans, denim jacket and desert boots. He waved and strode toward her, looking long and lean and dangerous.

Sandra shivered in the sunshine.

"Hi."

Cameron's voice, low, intimate, was more dangerous than the look of him. Her pulse leaped. Her heartbeat went thumpety-thump. Her breath fluttered from between her parted lips on a whisper.

"Hi."

He took the steps in two long bounds.

Nervous as a crab dodging a rake, she skittered sideways to the door. "Come in."

He was right behind her.

The strains of an old love ballad blared from the radio. She started toward it to turn down the volume. One step, and then: "Oh!" She yelped as a strong arm curled around her waist, turning her around, bringing her hard against his harder body.

"Dance with me, I want my arms about you...." He sang along with the instrumental rendition of the song in a low, seductive voice.

Sandra gave herself up to the moment, and the dance, and the thrill of moving in time with him.

They danced together very well, as if they had been doing it for years. Bemused, beguiled, Sandra

found herself thrilling to the prospect of their being
so attuned to one another in the more intimate
dance of love.

"I'm hungry," the Lone Wolfe growled into her
ear.

She shivered. "I...I'll make you lunch."

"I don't think so." His soft laughter was pure
incitement. "I'll have you for lunch."

"M-m-m-me?" Sandra drew her head back to
stare at him; the raw passion blazing from his eyes
ignited a liquid fire in the core of her, and burned
her inhibitions to smoldering flinders.

"You. Me." He trailed a hand down to the hol-
low at the base of her spine, aligning her body to
the fullness of his. "Let's feast on each other."
His warm breath caressed her lips as he slowly
lowered his head.

Barely breathing, Sandra parted her lips an instant before his mouth touched hers. His lips were
firm, still cool from the outdoors and sweet with
the taste of spring.

She moaned and raised her arms to capture his
head in her hands.

His tongue dipped, then dipped lower still to her
throat.

Her fingers dug into the thick strands of his hair,
tugging him closer, closer.

His free hand teased the outer curve and the un-
derside of her breast.

She arched her back, inviting exploration.

His lips hardened, plundering her soft mouth as his hand curled around the soft mound.

She shuddered at the sensations caused by his teasing fingers, and scraped her nails against his scalp, from crown to nape.

"Yes."

She felt his response, whispered into her mouth, leaping against her body.

"Yes," she replied in kind, murmuring into his mouth, arching into his arousal.

In a haze of desire, time lost relevance. Their clothing was swept away, unnoticed, unmissed.

"The bed?" Cameron's lips moved around the tightness of one nipple.

"This way." Grasping his hand, she stepped back, and turned toward the hallway.

Scooping up his jeans from the floor, Cameron followed her to the bedroom.

Neither noticed nor cared that the front door was left standing wide open.

She released his hand by the side of the bed, then stepped back to look at him.

Unembarrassed in his nakedness, the Lone Wolfe stood tall and proud, magnificent in his masculine glory.

He was beautiful. Sandra's throat and lips suddenly felt hot and dry. She skimmed her tongue over her lips to moisten them.

"You're beautiful." His voice was rough-edged, exciting in its intensity.

"So are you." Her voice was barely audible. He smiled.

She raised a hand to stroke his chest; her fingers tingled to touch the tight whorls of dark burnished-gold hair. Emboldened by the tremor her touch sent through him, she slowly skimmed her fingers down the narrowing trail of hair, to flatten her palm against the tightening muscles of his concave belly.

Cameron sucked in his breath. "Don't stop there," he said in a raw whisper. "Please, don't stop there. Find me. Hold me."

Watching the fire of desire leap higher in his eyes, Sandra glided her hand lower, through the silky curls surrounding his manhood. He moaned and shuddered when her fingers encased him.

"Good. That feels so unbelievably good." Cautioning, "Don't let go," he moved closer to her and, cradling her breasts in his hands, bent his head to suckle each rigid nipple in turn.

Responding to the sensations rioting inside her, the heat building in the core of her femininity, Sandra arched into his hungry mouth and caressed his silky-smooth, throbbing flesh.

Her mind, her body, every atom and molecule of her, was ready for him when he coiled an arm around her waist and lowered her to the edge of the bed. Before she realized what he was doing, he'd dropped to his knees between her parted, quivering thighs.

"Cameron?" She protested when he grasped her

shoulders and gently moved her back, onto the mattress. "What are you doing?" she said raggedly when he pressed his lips to her belly, stabbed his tongue into her navel.

"I want to taste you," he murmured against her skin, moistening it as he slid his tongue lower. "Every sweet, intoxicating inch of you."

"Cameron." Though her voice betrayed the uncertainty she was feeling, her hands speared into his hair, anchoring his head to her body.

"You'll love it," he promised, swirling his tongue around the tight curls covering her mound. "I'm going to send you soaring."

Sandra could hear her own harsh breaths, and knew they were caused by anticipation, not trepidation. She had never allowed this intimacy, never granted the right to any other man.

But this was Cameron. The Lone Wolfe. A man of the law, and a law unto himself.

His tongue tasted the moist heat of her.

Sandra surrendered herself to the law.

Moments later, Cameron delivered on his promise. Ripples of unimagined and unimaginable pleasure cascading through her, Sandra went soaring into the no-time, no-space realm of ecstasy.

The flight was spectacular, but it soon became apparent to Sandra that the journey into sensuality was far from over.

Cameron had an agenda of his own to pursue.

Vaguely, at the fringes of her consciousness,

Sandra heard the faint rustle of clothing, the quick, distinctive sound of foil being ripped. Then he was looming over her, moving her limp, depleted body lengthwise onto the bed, settling his taut-muscled form between her thighs.

"That was beautiful to watch," he murmured, stroking the tremor from her legs. "You're beautiful to watch." He slid his hands beneath her and raised her hips, aligning her body with the probing tip of his manhood. "Now, I want to watch you do it again, with me."

Sandra knew it was possible; at least she had heard it was possible, although she had never experienced the sensation of a repeat release. In truth, she had only ever experienced a single release, on a rare occasion. But, grateful for the exquisite pleasure he had given to her, she was willing to try, to be the vessel of his ultimate release and pleasure.

He entered her slowly, delicately, allowing her still-pulsating body to adjust to the fullness of his, making her feel treasured, not at all a mere vessel, a convenient depository for his passion.

To Sandra's surprise, her own desire flared anew when he began to move, carefully pacing his rhythm to her response, tightly reining his own needs, while fanning the flames of the smoldering spark of passion.

The look of him enhanced the tension spiraling inside her. In the throes of rigidly controlled passion, Cameron was a sight to behold.

His hair was ruffled from his earlier attention to her pleasure, one gold-streaked swath sweeping his forehead. His eyes were narrowed, intent on the emotional reactions revealed in her expression. His face was strained, and his bared teeth were clenched in determination. The strain was reflected in the tendons and veins throbbing in his arched throat, the muscles bunched in his chest.

He was working, hard, denying himself the soaring experience in an effort to stir her to the point of flying with him.

Beads of sweat stood out on his forehead and darkened his hair. His sun-bronzed skin shimmered, slick and moist from perspiration. His flat belly slid, wet and silky, against hers.

Everything about him, the look of him, the intensity he revealed, heightened the tension, the excitement revitalizing her, driving her to match his ardor.

She could barely breathe, and yet she felt exhilarated. The muscles in her body, which had felt slack and weak moments ago, now felt strong, energized.

Tightening her legs around his thighs, Sandra grasped his hips and arched high, into the measured rhythm of his thrusting body.

Without missing a beat of his driving motion, Cameron suddenly lowered his head to her breast, to capture one turgid nipple between his teeth.

The sensations his nipping teeth created inside

her tore a gasping moan from her throat. Her heart-beat thrummed against her eardrums. Her pulses stampeded. Her body clenched around him.

A low, growl-like sound rumbled deep in his throat. "If you do that again, I can't be held accountable," he warned, in a harsh, tension-strained whisper.

A sense of sheer feminine power filled Sandra. Testing him, his control, she sank her nails into the spare flesh stretched over his hipbones, and this time deliberately clenched around him.

"Sandra, have mercy," he pleaded, teeth snapping together, veins now prominent in his forehead.

Once again she clenched, inwardly drawing on him. In response, Cameron thrust to the hilt, while simultaneously thrusting a hand between their bodies to stroke the aroused center of her femininity.

"Wolfe!" Crying his name in a strangled exclamation, Sandra went off like a rocket, blasting into space, convulsing wildly around him.

Within a heartbeat, she heard her own name cried in a harsh exaltation of joy, and felt the throbbing heat of his powerful release.

Sandra was exhausted. Every muscle and nerve in her body quivered. She could hardly breathe. She felt drained, hot and wet. Cameron's weight crushed her, pressing her into the damp sheet beneath her.

It was wonderful.

"Now...that's...what I call...a greeting," he said, between harsh gasps for breath. His tongue swept over her nipple, sending a shiver cascading through her. "And one spectacular way to begin a vacation."

Startled by the instant response of her body to the caress of his lips, Sandra gasped and wriggled her hips; his response was just as instantaneous. She felt the leap of life deep within her.

"Again?" Awe colored her tone, and surprise widened her eyes as she met the glittering gaze he fixed on her.

"Amazing, ain't it?" Laughter, and more than a hint of masculine pride, threaded his voice. "Are you game for another gallop?"

"That depends on the inducements offered to me to ride," she rejoined, laughing along with him.

"Suppose I say please?" he asked, but without giving her time to answer, he heaved himself up and over, hauling her with him.

Sandra found herself in the saddle—so to speak. "Please would be nice," she said, drawing a moan from him by settling onto his hair-roughened thighs, and settling him firmly inside her.

"Please, Sandra," he said, retaliating by arching high off the bed, thrusting deeply into her. "Ride with me into the fires of ecstasy."

Before many more moments elapsed, it was Sandra who was crying "Please" and "More" and "Hurry" and then "Oh, Cameron, Cameron!"

Four

Sandra surfaced from a light doze to the tingling sensation of long fingers combing through her hair.

She curled closer to the man beside her, to press her lips to his chest.

The combing fingers stilled. The chest beneath her parted lips expanded.

"I'm sorry if I woke you." Cameron's warm breath ruffled her hair, and her pulse.

"S'okay," she mumbled, in a voice still slurred by sleep. She yawned, and felt a tremor ripple through him from the movement of her mouth against his skin. "It's chilly in here." Sandra shivered, then frowned. "Where is that cool air coming from?"

"I'm afraid we left the front door wide open," he said, moving away from her to first pull the comforter over her trembling body, then roll off the bed. "I guess I'd better go shut it before we find ourselves sharing the place with little forest critters."

The possibility held very little appeal for Sandra. "Critters?" she yelped, tossing back the comforter and springing to her feet. "What kind of critters?" she cried, scurrying about to find her robe.

"Oh, squirrels, and raccoons, and skunks, and… maybe a snake or two."

Turned away from him, she didn't see the devilish gleam in his eyes, but she couldn't miss the laughter threaded through his voice. Even so, she responded to his teasing bait.

"Snakes!" She whipped around to stare at him in abject horror. "Do you really think—?"

"No, of course not," Cameron quickly interrupted to reassure her. "I was only teasing."

"Teasing? You, you—" She burst out laughing, while trying to sound angry. Unsuccessful at her attempt to appear incensed, she threw her robe at him.

Laughing with her, and nimbly stepping out of the line of fire, Cameron made a hasty retreat from the room.

He should have looked ludicrous, trotting through the doorway as naked as a newborn, Sandra mused, staring after him. But he didn't. Quite the contrary, she realized. To her eyes, he appeared utterly natural, in his element, breathtaking and magnificent.

The Lone Wolfe.

Sandra shivered; her reaction owed nothing to the chill in the spring air.

"Is it safe for me to come in?" Cameron called from the hallway. "Or are you clothing-armed and to be assumed dangerous?"

"I'm unarmed, Officer," she called back, suppressing an urge to giggle like a teenager. She felt good—wonderful. No, glorious, more vibrantly alive than she had ever felt before. "And I'm escaping into the shower," she went on in sudden inspiration. "You won't catch me, Copper."

Cameron burst into the room like a member of a SWAT team on a raid, immediately assuming the position, legs apart, knees slightly bent, arms extended straight out in front of him, hands clasped, as if around the butt of a revolver.

Sandra's expression of wide-eyed surprise was unfeigned; Cameron's appearance, buck naked, in that familiar stance, was more than surprising, it was flat-out hilarious. She clapped a hand over her lips to contain her laughter.

"Don't move, lady," he ordered, in a low, menacing voice. "I've got you covered."

"Not yet," she responded, laughing through her spread fingers. "But I do have hopes in that regard."

Cameron's blue eyes glittered with sheer devilment. "I'm afraid I'm going to have to take you into protective custody." He indicated the bathroom with a quick movement of his head. "In there, lady."

"Whatever you say, Officer." Tossing aside the nightshirt she'd pulled from a drawer along with her robe, which she'd been holding in front of her nude body, Sandra started toward the bathroom in a sashaying stroll. Glancing back over her shoulder, she gave him a smoldering look and a throaty invitation. "Walk this way."

"Well, if you insist," he said doubtfully. "But I'm going to look pretty silly." Lowering his arms, he straightened and crossed the room to her, mimicking her hip-swaying stroll.

Sandra lost it.

So did Cameron.

Roaring in laughter, he swept her up into his arms and carried her into the bathroom, there to indulge in what she would later decide was probably the longest shower on record, possibly in history.

She reveled in every minute of it.

"That was wonderful." Sandra patted her lips with a paper napkin, then dropped it onto her empty plate.

Several hours had elapsed since their shower-lovemaking marathon. Long spears of late-afternoon sunlight lent a mellow glow to the room.

After an energy-restoring nap, they had dressed, picked up their clothing from the living room floor, unloaded and unpacked his gear, then headed for the kitchen for much-needed sustenance.

Cameron had insisted on preparing the repast.

"Thank you, ma'am. I aim to please." He grinned at her over the rim of his coffee cup.

"No, I'm serious," she said. "That western omelet was perfect, golden brown outside, creamy inside. You really are a very good cook."

"Thanks again," he said quietly, setting the cup on the table. "But I owe it all to my teacher."

Sandra's eyes widened in surprise. "You went to a cooking school?"

"No." Cameron shook his head, dislodging a lock of hair as golden brown as the omelet had been. "My teacher was a mother who firmly believed that being born a male did not excuse a child from lessons in the basics of domesticity." His quick, soft chuckle was threaded with loving remembrance. "She insisted that her sons be house-broken."

"Sons?" Sandra asked, suddenly realizing how very little she knew about him, this Lone Wolfe who was now her lover. "How many are there?"

"Four." He pushed back his chair and got up to walk to the countertop. Sliding the glass carafe from the heating plate of the coffeemaker, he returned to refill their cups. "I'm the eldest."

"Four sons," she murmured in awe, absently lifting her cup to take a careful sip of the hot liquid. "The mere thought of raising four boys is daunting."

Cameron laughed, and began collecting dishes and cutlery. "Believe me, it would have taken a lot more than us kids to daunt my mother."

Sounds formidable, Sandra mused—a veritable shining example of the traditional wife and mother, old-fashioned and outdated now, but fondly recalled, if Cameron's expression was anything to judge by. The total opposite of her own mother, she ruminated, rising to help him clear the table. Her mother had been a career woman to the oval tips of her fingernails. She'd been forced into an early retirement a few years ago, due to a heart condition—which, thankfully, was not life-threatening—and probably would have gone into a decline if faced with the very thought of taking on the role of housewife and mother to four children.

"At present, she's eagerly looking forward to whipping her grandchildren into shape."

Cameron's laconic remark ended Sandra's introspective reverie.

"How many grandchildren are there?" she asked, looking away from the flow of water churning the detergent into a mound of bubbles in the sink.

"None." He moved his shoulders in a light shrug, then grabbed a dish towel from a wall-mounted hook in readiness. "That's why she's so eager. But she believes that now, at long last, she has reason to hope." He took the dripping plate she handed him and applied the towel as if he were an old hand at the chore.

Sandra finished rinsing the second plate and frowned as she handed it to him. "Why?" She shook her head, confused. "I mean, why does your mother now believe there's reason to hope for grandchildren?"

"Because my youngest brother, Jake, is getting married in June." He laughed. "It's kinda funny. The lastborn of Maddy's sons will be the first one to marry."

"All four of you are still single?" The dishes done, she moved to wipe the table.

"Yes, at least for a little while yet." He tossed the damp towel adroitly onto the hook. "I may be reading it all wrong, but something tells me things are heating up between my other two brothers, Eric and Royce, and their respective ladies." He grinned at her; she felt the effects to the tingling soles of her bare feet. "I believe my mother's thinking along the same lines," he explained. "She sounded suspiciously smug when I talked to her early this morning."

"Do you talk to your mother often?" she asked,

thinking about her twice-monthly, insubstantial telephone chats with her own mother.

"At least once a week." He paused, then shrugged. "When I can."

Sandra didn't require further explanation; she understood the demands of his profession.

"That's nice," she murmured, meaning it. But then she flashed a teasing smile at him. "You're a good and considerate son."

His own smile flashed; it had a wolfish look. "I'm good at a lot of things." Appearing deceptively lazy, he strolled to her. "Exciting things."

"Really?" Concealing a sizzling inner response behind an expression of wide-eyed innocence, Sandra watched with mounting anticipation as he closed in on her.

"Hmmm..." Cameron came to a halt with his chest just brushing her already tingling breasts. His eyes were dark, hooded, sultry. "You need more proof?"

"Much more proof and I'll probably die from intense ecstasy," she said breathlessly.

"Yeah, but, as the old saying claims," he whispered, slowly rubbing his chest against the hardening tips of her breasts, "what a way to go."

Sandra could barely breathe; she couldn't think of anything at all—except for the riot of erotic images seducing her mind and thoughts.

"Wanna go with me?" His voice was so low, she could hardly hear him, but still she understood,

understood and responded, almost violently, to the sexy intonation in his voice.

"To...to the bed?" Silly question.

"The bed. The couch. The floor." He made a quick hand gesture. "The kitchen table."

She blinked. "I've never made love on a kitchen table. I've heard of it, of cour— Oh!" she softly exclaimed as he deposited her on top of the table.

"I'll be happy to expand your experience," he said, unfastening her jeans and tugging them down, over her hips. Within seconds, her jeans and panties were lying in a heap on the floor, and his jeans and briefs were bunched somewhere around his knees.

Sandra sucked in a breath as Cameron moved into position between her thighs; in comparison to his aroused body, the table didn't seem nearly as hard as it had moments before.

Bending over her, he tormented her into readiness for him with his body and his mouth.

Sandra moaned, deep in her throat, when his teeth gently raked her aching nipple and the tip of his manhood nudged against her mound.

Hot and moist, eager to again experience the thrill of feeling him inside her, filling her, Sandra raised her hips, inviting his possession.

There was an instant's pause, the rustle of clothes as he kicked free of his jeans, the sound of tearing foil, then a murmured curse from Cameron.

Reaching out, Sandra stroked his hips, his tautly muscled buttocks and thighs.

Cameron shuddered in response, then plunged, deep, straight to the core of her desire.

It was fast, and furious, and utterly satisfying. In unison, they cried out in joyous release.

The purple shadows of encroaching evening dimmed the interior of the cabin as Cameron gently cradled Sandra in his arms and carried her into the bedroom.

Pearly pink dawn revealed a tangle of bedclothes and bodies sprawled across the bed.

The softly creeping light bathed Cameron's face, waking him. In turn, he woke Sandra with a creeping series of soft kisses, to her face and neck and breasts.

She stirred, stretched, and languidly wound her arms around his neck.

"You missed my mouth," she scolded, pouting.

"You're right," he agreed, kissing his way to her lips. "I missed it all night."

His morning kiss was cool, gentle, heart-wrenchingly tender. A warm moisture stung her eyes.

"That was lovely," she murmured on a sigh when he raised his head to gaze into her misty eyes.

"And so are you," he said, swooping to brush his lips over her sparkling wet lashes. "I could continue kissing you all day…'' He lifted his head again, and gave her a teasing smile. ''But you'd soon get tired of the growling demand for food from my stomach.''

Sandra smiled back at him. ''Is this your way of telling me that you're hungry?''

''Famished.'' Startling her with the sudden swiftness of his movement, Cameron swept back the covers and literally leaped from the bed. ''I'll cook,'' he offered, striding for the bathroom. ''Why don't you go back to sleep until breakfast is ready?''

''Wait!'' Her cry brought him to a stop, hand extended for the doorknob. ''I'm slept out.'' Scrambling from the bed, she slanted a twinkling glance at him. ''Besides, I'd much rather shower with you.''

His eyes narrowed suspiciously. ''I'm not sure I can trust you. Do you promise to be good?''

Her smile mirrored the one he had given her in the kitchen last evening.

''I promise to be terrific.''

Laughing and kissing, Sandra and Cameron lathered, and bathed, and satisfied each other's bodies.

Cameron cooked steaks on the outside grill for breakfast. Firmly refusing to even consider fat and calorie content, Sandra prepared fried potatoes and scrambled eggs on the side.

The meal was every bit as satisfying as their romp in the shower, if in a different manner.

After the meal was finished and the dishes were cleared away, they donned jackets and hiking boots and left the cabin to explore the terrain surrounding the building nestled in the foothills.

Their laughter ringing on the crisp spring air, they trudged hand in hand, stepping with care on the squishy ground and the patches of lingering snow along a steep mountain trail.

The outing was both exhilarating and exhausting. Sandra was panting from the exertion when they returned to the cabin.

"Time for lunch," Cameron said, after making a trip into the bedroom to hang up their jackets.

"Past time." She glanced pointedly at the clock; it read 1:45.

"And then a nap?" He leered at her.

"You're insatiable!" Laughing, she went to the cabinet to take out a can of soup.

"Hungry, too," he drawled, turning to the fridge. "You want a sandwich with your soup?"

And that was how the following days played out, slowly unwinding in an atmosphere of domestic tranquillity and sensuous bliss.

On Saturday evening, happy and content with each other, Sandra and Cameron decided to make a celebration of their first week together.

Sandra donned the two-piece confection her parents had sent her from Paris for her birthday; Cameron dressed casually but elegantly in brushed-denim pants and a crisp white silk shirt. The effect of their sartorial efforts on one another was immediate appreciation.

Seated opposite one another at the dinner table, they devoured each other with their eyes, while devouring grilled salmon, crisp salad, and the pale gold wine Cameron had brought with him.

Later that night, all her appetites sated, Sandra lay curled against Cameron's warmth, awake while he slept, musing on the sweet satisfaction of two individuals in seemingly perfect harmony.

Maybe, she thought muzzily, floating in the nether area between sleep and wakefulness, just maybe, there really could be such a thing as an equal, balanced, happy and mutually satisfying marriage between two independent, career-minded people.

She floated off to sleep in a contemplative bubble of contentment.

As all bubbles eventually do, Sandra's burst. The deflating pinprick came early Sunday morning, in the form of a summons from Cameron's beeper. The muted beep penetrated her unconsciousness; the noise Cameron made fumbling with the bedside phone drew her to the surface; the sound of his voice brought her to awareness.

"It's Wolfe. What's up?"

Well I am, for one, Sandra grumbled to herself, shifting into an upright position in the bed.

"When?"

When what? she asked herself, covering a yawn with the palm of her hand. And what was so all-fired important that it warranted a call at this time of the morning?

"Damn it all to hell!"

She blinked. Whatever the call was about, from the tone of Cameron's voice, it sounded serious.

"Okay, thanks, Steve." He heaved a sigh. "Yeah, I'll be careful."

Careful? About what? Or whom? Her curiosity aroused, Sandra watched as he replaced the receiver and sat still for a moment, staring into space. His very stillness sent an apprehensive shiver down her spine.

"Cameron, is something wrong?"

He heaved another sigh before turning to her; the look of him intensified the shiver.

"What is it?" she asked, impulsively reaching a hand out to him.

"*It* is a man," he said, curling his hand around hers. "And it means the end of our time here together."

Sandra's spirits did a swan dive. Her hand tightened on his. "You must leave?"

"Yes." His voice was flat, which said a lot about his spirits.

"Work-related?" Sandra knew better than to ask for anything other than the bare essentials.

"Yeah."

She nodded in acceptance, expecting no further explanation, but he surprised her with his willingness to be more forthcoming.

"While you were waging your custody battle in court I was chasing a two-bit bank robber turned kidnapper and rapist." The shadow of a wry smile flickered briefly on his lips. "I caught him, too." He jerked his head to indicate the phone. "That call was from another agent, informing me that the felon escaped from the lockup where he was awaiting trial."

"And the Bureau wants you to suspend your vacation to track him down?"

"No." Cameron shook his head. "That call wasn't official. But the agent thought I should know about the situation, since the felon had sworn to track me down if he ever gained his freedom."

"But...I don't understand." Sandra frowned. "I mean, we're secluded here. This man, this felon, can't possibly know you're here. Why would you leave and put yourself in harm's way?"

"I have a duty, a responsibility to—"

"Your responsibility in this instance is to yourself," she said, interrupting him. "What are you thinking of doing—making yourself a sitting duck, using yourself as live bait to lure the criminal?"

A smile flittered over his lips again. "Something like that," he admitted.

"That's nuts!"

"Perhaps, but—"

"Cameron! Will you listen to yourself? Surely you don't believe you're the only agent capable of capturing this...this outlaw?"

"No, of course not," he immediately replied. "And I wasn't thinking of playing the macho hero and going after him alone. But I should be part of the team."

"Why?" she demanded, fearful for his safety, and incensed by his adamancy. "I could accept your attitude if the call had come from your superior, ordering or even requesting your help, but your deciding to use yourself as bait doesn't make sense."

This time he didn't smile; he grinned.

"What's so funny?" she asked suspiciously.

"You." He gave her hand a quick squeeze. "You sound just like a prosecuting attorney grilling an unfriendly witness."

She gave him a dry look. "I was trained to apply logic, and reason, and good old-fashioned common sense, you know."

"And you apply it to advantage."

Sandra's spirits surfaced from the depths into the sunshine. "You'll stay?" She didn't try to contain the breathless, hopeful note in her voice.

"Yes." He nodded, then quickly cautioned her, "At least for a day or so, until I hear how the hunt is progressing. But if it turns out that they could use me..." He let his voice trail away.

"I understand." Giving his hand a final squeeze, she slipped away from his hold and left the bed.

"Where are you going? It's still early—why not catch a little more sleep?"

"I'm awake now," she said, heading for the bathroom. "And I'm hungry."

"Yeah, well, so am I." He grinned suggestively. "That's why I wanted to stay in bed."

"Guess you'll have to settle for pancakes."

Laughing, Cameron leaped from the bed and tracked her into the bathroom.

Five

It began raining early Sunday afternoon, a gentle spring rain—or at least that was what Sandra and Cameron believed it to be.

Sometime during the night, after they fell asleep, the temperature took a sudden plunge and the rain turned first to sleet, then to ice.

They awoke Monday morning to an unnatural stillness outside, and an eerie grayish-white light seeping into the cabin.

"Snow?" Cameron guessed, padding barefoot and naked to the window.

"Possible," Sandra mumbled, burrowing deeper under the covers; she had experienced many Colorado spring blizzards.

"Not this time," he returned sourly, peering sleepy-eyed through the frost-rimmed pane. "We've got ice—boy, have we got ice."

"Ice?" Sandra repeated, tossing back the covers. Shivering, she came up behind him to stare over his shoulder. "Why, it's beautiful!" she exclaimed, entranced by the glistening coat weighing down tree branches, shimmering on the surface of their surroundings. "It's a winter wonderland out there."

"Yeah." Cameron sounded unconvinced. "The problem is, everything's frozen, and we're in the mountains."

"Oh, it is spring, you know," she said, dismissing his obvious concern. "It won't last long."

By midday, Sandra's assurances appeared prophetic. Although the sky was heavy with dark clouds, the distinct sound of melting ice rattled through the drainpipe from the roof, and small puddles of mud-swirled water dotted the driveway.

Braving the wet and slippery terrain underfoot, they ventured forth for a short walk, laughing as they took turns singing bits and pieces of "Slip Slidin' Away."

After dinner, content to be alone and quiet together, they didn't bother, or even think, to tune in to the radio or TV for a weather forecast, deciding it would be more interesting, and a lot more fun, to get comfortable on the floor in front of the crackling fire and play a few hands of strip poker.

Except for his shoes and socks, Cameron was still fully clothed while Sandra had lost to the tune of everything but her panties and bra, when his beeper once again shrilled an intrusion.

Sandra frowned to make clear her dissatisfaction with the annoying device.

"Duty calls, and all that," Cameron said, making an obvious effort to sound casual as he rose and sauntered into the kitchen to use the wall-mounted phone.

Suddenly cold, Sandra tugged the patchwork afghan from the couch and wrapped it around her chilled body.

Cameron stood facing her, and though she couldn't hear what he was saying, she could see his expression, and it was not an encouraging sight.

She read his lips when he bit out a socially unacceptable expletive. Then he turned his back to her, intensifying the chill permeating her being.

Hugging the soft wool throw to her shivering body, Sandra waited in dread for him to finish the call and return to her, certain the news was not good.

She was right. Still, he startled her with his first statement.

"You're going to have to leave here first thing tomorrow morning."

"Leave?" Sandra blinked. "Tomorrow? Why?"

"Because as long as you're with me, you are

not safe.'' Cameron stood over her, scowling, and raked his fingers through his burnished hair. ''That call was from the agent I talked to earlier. He told me that my apartment was broken into and ransacked this afternoon.''

''And they believe it was that escaped criminal you told me about?''

''Yes. And they also believe he is tracking me.''

Clutching the afghan, Sandra struggled to her feet to stand before him. ''But then, why leave here? As I think I pointed out before, we're secluded here, and—'' She paused when his hand sliced through the air, effectively cutting off her reasoned argument.

''And I'm afraid he knows exactly where we are,'' Cameron inserted, his voice heavy with disgust.

''That's ridiculous,'' she argued. ''He's been in jail. How could he possibly know about Barbara's hideaway, or even me, for that matter?''

''So far as this place belonging to Barbara and you personally are concerned, he couldn't know,'' he readily agreed. ''But he does know that I'm here. He knows, because I inadvertently told him.''

''You told him!'' Sandra cried, suddenly understanding that his obvious disgust was self-directed. ''But how? You certainly couldn't have talked to him...could you?''

Cameron was shaking his head in denial before she had finished speaking. ''No, I haven't talked to him. But what I did do was just as stupid." He heaved a sigh. "I left the written directions to the cabin lying in plain sight on my kitchen table."

"And your apartment was broken into and ransacked," she said flatly.

"Exactly."

"It's not going to require a lot of tracking ability on his part to find you, then, is it?"

He gave a quick, sharp nod. "Which is why I have got to get you out of here."

"But—"

He again cut her off. "At once." Pivoting, he started for the bedroom. "So I think you had better get busy packing."

"No." Sandra's soft but firm refusal brought him to an abrupt halt.

"No?" Cameron slowly turned to stare at her, his expression one of sheer disbelief.

"No." Sandra met his narrowed stare with cool composure, determined that she would not be panicked by the possibility of a criminal arriving on the scene. Nor would she tolerate being ordered about, not even by Special Agent Cameron Wolfe.

"What do you mean, *no?*" he asked, in a tone of controlled calm.

"I mean, no, I'm not leaving," she answered, in an equally calm tone. "I'm not afraid." That wasn't quite true. Still, while she felt a mite apprehensive about the situation, she felt an even deeper sense of anger and resentment at being summarily ordered to get packing.

Her calm demolished his calm.

"Dammit, woman, will you think?" He paced back to within a foot of her. "You're too bright to pull a childish rebellion act."

"Thank you...I think," Sandra said, maintaining her cool, while containing an impulse to slap him silly for the insult implied within the compliment. "Nevertheless, I won't change my mind." She arched her eyebrows. "Didn't you relay the same directions to this place to the agent you spoke to?"

"Certainly, but—"

"There you are, then," she said, coolly interrupting him. "Wouldn't you say that, even as we speak, there are any number of law enforcement officers, federal, state and local, converging on this place?"

"Probably, but—"

She interrupted him again. "I'd say definitely. So...not to worry. You may leave if you like, of course, to join your fellow officers in the chase, but I...am...not...budging," she said, her firm tone emphasizing each word. "And don't call me 'woman.'"

Apparently rendered speechless, Cameron glared at her from glittering blue eyes, giving her the impression that at any moment smoke might well steam from his ears and nostrils.

Girding herself to withstand an onslaught of ranting and raving, Sandra clenched her muscles and drew her composure, along with the afghan, around her chilled and quaking body.

But Cameron didn't rant or rave. He heaved a deep sigh and gave her a knowing, cynical smile.

"I see. You're not pulling a childish act of rebellion at all, are you?" he observed, coolly and rather tiredly. "You're doing your in-your-face-and-be-damned ultrafeminist shtick. Right?"

Sheer rage swept through Sandra, a rage born of his blatant stupidity. How could he? she railed, literally shaking from the emotions roaring in protest inside her. After the days and nights they had shared, how could he dare to accuse her of now making an equal-rights stand? Didn't he know her primary concern was for him? His safety? And, if he didn't know, why didn't he know? Or why hadn't he at least asked?

So much for symbiosis and domestic harmony.

Sandra felt wounded, the pain running astonishingly deep. Freezing inside, she drew the mantle of hot fury around her.

"You're a fool, Wolfe," she said, concealing her pain with disdain. "And I can't be bothered sparring with fools."

Her budding hopes for their future killed by the frost of his cynicism, she gave him a dismissive once-over, then circled around him.

"Sandra?" There was a new, altogether unfamiliar and surprising note of uncertainty in his voice. "Where are you going?"

"To bed," she snapped, heading for the bedroom. "So if you're leaving, you'd better get your stuff together and out of the bedroom."

"I'm not going without you," he called after her, the note of uncertainty giving way to one of anger.

"Your choice." Sandra marched into the bedroom, tossed aside the afghan, pulled on her robe, then went to the linen closet to collect a quilt. Then, snatching his pillow from the bed, she marched back to the living room and threw the bedding at him.

"You're kidding." Cameron's eyes flashed blue fire at her; she deflected it with a cold smile.

"Laugh yourself to sleep." Swinging around, she strode from the room.

"Sandra!" He was right behind her—but a step and a half too late.

She turned the door lock an instant before he grasped the knob.

"Now you *are* being childish," he said, raising his voice to penetrate the barrier.

She didn't deign to answer.

"I won't beg," he threatened.

"I never thought you would."

"Are you going to open the door?"

"No." Sandra bit down on her lower lip, but she held her ground.

"Good night, Sandra."

Good night? Or goodbye? Tears rushed to her eyes, and she didn't trust her voice enough to respond. The tears spilled over onto her cheeks when she heard him sigh and move away.

Standing stock-still, Sandra glanced at the bed, then quickly glanced away. The standard-size double bed looked so big, so empty, so lonely. After the thrilling nights spent in that bed with Cameron, could she bear to even think of crawling into that bed alone?

All she had to do was unlock that door and call to him, for him, an inner voice whispered.

No. She shook her head. After the closeness, the intimacy, they had shared, he had misread her motives completely, accusing her of militancy, self-interest, when in fact her concern was all for him.

Suddenly impatient, with Cameron, with herself, she brushed the tears from her cheeks with a swipe of her hand. If he was too dense to discern that she felt she couldn't leave him to face the danger alone, that was his problem, not hers.

Shrugging out of her robe, her panties and bra, Sandra pulled on her nightgown and slipped into bed. She had slept alone before…for a good many years. Like it or not, she could sleep alone again.

She didn't like it. She didn't do much sleeping, anyway. Awake and miserable, she lay, stiff and tense, listening to the pinging sound of sleet striking against the windowpanes.

But, although she couldn't know it, Sandra wasn't the only one awake and miserable.

Cameron hadn't even bothered to lie down. He felt too restless, too agitated, too damn mad to lie still and quiet; the emotions roiling inside him wouldn't be contained, had to be released by some form of action.

The first of those actions was reflexive, second nature to him after his years with the Bureau. Shoving his bare feet into his running shoes, he left the house and made his way cautiously to his vehicle. Quickly retrieving his holstered gun, he spared a moment to rake the area with a narrow-eyed sweep before returning to the house, wet and shivering from the cold, sleet-spattered rain.

Spring.

Right.

Scattering cold droplets with an impatient shake of his head, he kicked off his shoes, then padded to the couch to slip the weapon beneath the end cushion. Still shivering, he moved to the fireplace and placed another piece of wood on the dwindling flames.

The fire blazed to renewed life, radiating heat and warmth. But the warmth didn't penetrate the surface of his skin, didn't touch the cold and empty spot deep inside him; only crawling into bed beside Sandra could have warmed him to the core of his being.

The realization of how very important she had

become to him, to his physical and mental comfort, startled him, made him uneasy and even more restless.

Dammit, he cursed in silent frustration, venting his restlessness by prowling the room. What was with the woman? Oh, yeah, she had ordered him not to call her "woman," he savagely reminded himself, making a sharp turn into the kitchen.

But, hell, she was a woman—wasn't she? Oh, yeah, he answered himself. He knew firsthand, up close and personal, that Sandra was all woman.

All feminist woman, he recalled, making a sour face and a rude noise.

The very last thing he needed was to get hung up on a woman who wouldn't hesitate to whip out a little copy of her own personal Declaration of Independence every time she decided he was pulling a male-superiority act.

What kind of a masochistic idiot was he, anyway? he railed at himself, deliberately stoking his anger, to smother the disappointment and hurt he was feeling. How many times did he have to get emotionally raped by a woman before he got smart enough to keep his emotions inviolate?

And what in hell did he want in here, anyway? Cameron skimmed the nearly dark room with narrowed eyes, seeking diversion from his own thoughts.

Coffee. That was it—he needed some coffee.

He moved to the countertop—only to stand

there, blankly staring at the automatic coffeemaker. What did he think he was doing? he chided himself. Coffee would only wire him, and he was strung too damn tight now.

Spinning around, he headed for the fridge; what he really needed was a beer, maybe several beers.

Cameron never finished the first can he opened; he was too busy pacing off a path in the rug to take the time to swig from the can.

Was Sandra asleep?

He groaned aloud. Damn. Why had he thought about her sleeping? Thinking about her, in bed, sleeping or awake, caused a yawning hollowness inside him, a yearning, sharp and deep, to be there, burrowed beneath the covers, beside her, inside her.

"Sandra."

Cameron froze, startled by the whispery longing in his own voice. Hell, he had it bad...whatever *it* was.

Love?

Remaining perfectly still, he examined the word that immediately sprang into his head.

Love?

He rolled the word around in his mind. He had been in love before, years ago. Yet it hadn't felt anything near like what he had experienced these past days with Sandra. Never before had he experienced the roller coaster of sensations and emotions he had felt simply from being with her. Over the past week, his feelings had run the gamut, from the highs of euphoria, possessiveness, protectiveness and happiness, to the lows of anger, anxiety, frustration and hopelessness miring him now.

But did those varied and confusing sensations and emotions equate to love...or were they the natural response to an appreciation of really great sex?

God. Cameron was developing a headache. All this probing of his psyche was getting to him.

And none of his internal dialogue had so much as touched on the cause of his present dilemma, that of his need to get Sandra out of the cabin and harm's way.

He sighed and raked a hand through his hair. She had stated adamantly that she would not budge. Furthermore, she had sounded as if she meant it. He was fresh out of ideas as to how to go about convincing her to leave, short of tossing her over his shoulder and physically removing her from the place.

Yeah. Right.

A grim smile played over his lips as he imagined himself playing Tarzan to her Jane.

Although it held sensuous appeal, he knew he could scratch that particular fancy.

Shaking his head in despair at his dearth of ideas, Cameron retraced his steps into the kitchen to set the half-full can of beer in the sink.

It was only then, standing so close to the window above the sink, that he became aware of the wind picking up speed, and what was now mostly sleet sweeping across the deck and against the pane.

Oh, hell. What was he racking his brain for? he thought irritably. From the sound of the wind and sleet, they were going to be iced in and unable to go anywhere, anyway. Might as well try to get some sleep.

Cameron did try. He just didn't succeed too well. The couch wasn't long enough for his tall frame, and the cushions suddenly felt lumpy. Besides, Sandra wasn't curled up next to him. And, in addition to the physical discomforts, the concept of love, romantic love, the forever-after concept of love, persisted in dancing around the fringes of his mind, tormenting him with the hopelessness of a man like him, already made wary of females, falling for a blazing feminist like Sandra.

How was a man to sleep under those conditions?

Had she reacted immaturely?

The question loomed ever larger throughout the dark hours in Sandra's alert consciousness.

When it first slithered into her head, she had made a snorting sound of rejection, then flipped from one side to the other in the seemingly too-roomy bed.

But the inner probe proved impervious to rejection, continuing its stabbing forays into her attention.

By somewhere around two-thirty or three, Sandra gave up evasive tactics. Flopping onto her back, she stared into middle distance, as if expecting an answer to magically materialize, written in bold letters against the darkness by a fiery finger of illumination.

And, to a certain extent, her expectations were realized. Dawn came to Sandra's consciousness hours before it grayed the eastern horizon.

Heaving a tired sigh, she bravely faced the truth: Of course she had reacted immaturely, simply because she had reacted emotionally instead of intellectually.

Women in love were known to do that occasionally—or so Sandra had always heard.

It was a bit of a shock. Sandra had never considered herself one of the typically portrayed helplessly emotion-driven females.

Love did really strange things to people—Sandra had heard that maxim more than once, as well.

And here she was, flat on her back in bed, staring into the darkness of the predawn house, vigorously engaged in an argument with herself.

Strange indeed.

The really hard-to-take part was, she was losing the damn argument!

Having always judged herself a thoughtful and rational being, capable of stepping around emotions to examine the cold, hard facts, both in her private and professional life, Sandra now felt challenged to live up to her own intellectual capabilities.

So then, had she reacted immaturely to Cameron's marching orders?

Of course she had.

Once she'd admitted the obvious, the emotional trigger was easily identified. In point of fact, Sandra acknowledged, she loved Cameron more than she valued her own physical safety and well-being.

But, naturally, she couldn't tell him that, Sandra realized with a sinking sensation. She very much feared that, should Cameron sense even a hint of her true feelings for him, he'd back away in an instant. He hadn't been tagged the Lone Wolfe by his contemporaries without reason. In a nutshell, despite the occasional indulgence of the senses, he preferred being alone.

By the time a weak and sickly light had somewhat brightened the room, Sandra had resolved her inner conflict. In essence, she would continue as she had begun, even if that meant maintaining to Cameron what he perceived as her position of immaturity and feminist militancy.

Resigned to the role, she pushed back the covers and dragged her tired body from the bed. She had little choice but to maintain her position, she reasoned. Because there was no way in hell she'd allow him to remove her to a safe place, then return to face the danger alone—even though he was trained and paid to do precisely that. Besides, there would very likely be the nearest thing to a platoon of law officers swarming around the cabin.

A woman's got to do what a woman's got to do. A wry smile flickered over her lips as Sandra repeated the catchphrase to herself.

Her smile fading, she pulled on her robe and pulled tight the belt around her waist, literally girding herself to approach the Lone Wolfe in the living room.

He wasn't there. Sandra found Cameron in the kitchen, sitting at the table, hunched over the cup of steaming coffee cradled in his hands.

"Good morning," she said, wincing at the tone she had deliberately hardened to conceal her trepidation.

"Oh, you're speaking to me again," he muttered, glancing up at her without raising his head. "You can afford to be gracious, I suppose, now that the weather has settled the issue of contention between us."

Weather? Sandra frowned and moved to gaze out the window above the sink.

"Oh!" she exclaimed in a surprised murmur.

The scene beyond the pane was again one of a winter wonderland, every surface locked in ice, glittering in the pale light of morning.

"Yeah," he said disgustedly. "Even if you agreed to go, I couldn't take you down that road. The Jeep's great in snow, but it don't do diddly on ice."

"But then..." Sandra swung around to look at him. "It works both ways, doesn't it?"

It was Cameron's turn to frown; he produced more of a beetle-browed scowl.

She rushed on. "I mean it stands to reason that if you can't get down the road, then that man, that criminal, can't get up the road, either." She fought to keep the note of triumph from her voice; she didn't quite succeed. "Isn't that right?"

"Sure," he readily agreed. Then he delivered the pinprick that burst her balloon. "That is, of course, unless he is already up here."

Sandra grimaced; she hadn't thought of that.

Six

The day dragged even more than the previous night, and was fraught with tension.

Cameron was moody and mostly silent, deflecting her few innocuous remarks with growled monosyllables, which in turn sparked a fire of anger and discontent inside Sandra.

At regular, almost predictable intervals, he prowled to the window to glare out at the road, as if willing the ice to melt from the heat of his angry stare.

Not only did the ice not melt, but by late afternoon the temperature had plummeted, ensuring that the frigid conditions would last through the coming night and into the morning.

And throughout the day, whenever a branch creaked from the weight of the ice, or a window rattled from the gusty wind, he went stock-still and alert, eyes narrowed, muscles taut, as if readying for action.

In those moments, he was more than unnerving; he was flat-out frightening.

While preparing dinner, Sandra surprised herself by suddenly wishing for a warming trend and thaw that would set her free from her confinement inside the cabin, even if it meant being hustled back to Denver.

Being caged with a restless, disgruntled Wolfe was not her idea of a relaxing vacation.

"What are you cooking?"

Though Sandra started, she managed to hold back a yelp of surprise at the unexpected and almost human sound of his voice so close behind her. Composing herself, she slowly turned to look at him.

"Snails and puppy-dog tails?" he went on, in a peacemaking, cajoling tone.

"I'm fresh out of those," she rejoined dryly. "You'll have to settle for meat loaf."

"I love meat loaf." He gave her a tentative smile; she didn't return it.

"Most men do." She turned back to peeling potatoes. "So do I," she said, leaving him under no illusions that she had chosen the meal to pacify him.

"You're really ticked, aren't you?"

"Me? Ticked?" She swung around again, this time brandishing the paring knife. "Why ever would you think that I'd be ticked?"

Eyeing her warily, Cameron took a satisfying step back. "Careful with that thing," he murmured in warning.

"This thing?" She held the knife aloft, relishing the moment as she examined it, before giving him a droll glance. "Afraid I'll peel you along with the potatoes?"

"Feel inclined to take a strip off my hide, do you?" Amusement laced his serious voice.

"I feel inclined to tell you to go—"

His beeper sounded, overriding her need to vent her anger and resentment. Frustrated, hating the damn beeper, and pretty close to hating him at the moment, she watched him stride into the living room to where he had left the dratted thing on an end table.

Swinging around, she rinsed the potato, quartered it, placed the pieces in the roast pan with the other chunks of potatoes, carrots, onions and celery arranged around the meat loaf, then shoved the pan into the oven.

When she turned again, Cameron was standing propped against the kitchen wall, his back to her, talking softly into the phone.

More trouble? she wondered, heaving a sigh. Not wishing to appear at all interested, she took off for the bedroom, to shower and change before dinner.

She lingered beneath the shower spray, half believing Cameron might join her there.

He didn't. Nor did he enter the room while she was dressing. Optimistically hoping his call had been good news—like the information that the escaped criminal had been apprehended, thereby allowing them to resolve their differences, if that was possible, and get on with their vacation, should they still be on speaking terms—Sandra left the bedroom with her fingers crossed.

After one look at Cameron's face as she entered the kitchen, Sandra uncrossed her fingers. So much for wishful thinking, she chided herself.

"Well?" she asked impatiently, when he was not immediately forthcoming.

"You can't go back to Denver."

Perplexed at hearing him state the obvious, Sandra stared at him a moment before replying, "I know, everything's covered with ice out there."

"Even if there were no ice, you couldn't go back."

"Why not?" she asked, in a reasonable tone that she hoped concealed the impatience gathering speed inside her.

"Whitfield's back in Denver." His taciturn response was, for Sandra, as good as no response at all.

"Back from where?" Her brow crinkled in a frown of utter confusion.

"Chicago."

That terse tidbit of information meant nothing to her; she hadn't even known Whitfield had left Denver, nor would she have cared if she had known.

"Uh-huh." Her hard-fought-for reasonable tone lost ground to advancing irritation. "I don't think we're connecting here. What, exactly, whether or not he's in Chicago, does Raymond Whitfield have to do with my returning to Denver?"

Cameron raked a hand through his hair, betraying his own fraying patience. "I think Whitfield was laying down a smoke screen by flying to Chicago."

Sandra literally threw up her hands. "Well, that explains everything." Controlling herself with effort, she took a quick breath, and tried again. "Cameron, I haven't a clue as to what you're talking about."

"Whitfield," he barked. "I put a surveillance team on him. He flew to Chicago last Saturday morning, but now he's back in Denver."

"So what?" she asked, more confused than before. "And why in heaven's name put a surveillance team on him in the first place?"

"Because of the threats he'd made to you, that's why," he said, a tone usually reserved for slow learners. A tone, moreover, that she rather resented.

"But that's ridiculous!" Sandra was barely hanging on to her temper. "I told you I thought Whitfield was only making noises."

"Oh, yeah?" His blue eyes glittered beneath raised goldenbrown brows. "Well, you thought wrong." He indicated the phone with a sharp head movement. "That call was to the operative I've got tailing Whitfield. He told me he followed Whitfield from the airport, straight to your apartment."

Though she managed not to show it, Sandra was a little shaken by the news. "Still, that doesn't mean he had anything sinister in mind," she said, unsure whether she was trying to convince him, or herself.

"It wouldn't, if he had gone about it in a normal way." Cameron shook his head. "But he didn't. He sat in his car until it was dark, then he poked around, not only at the front of the complex, but the back, as well. Then he returned to his car. He was still there, just sitting and watching the place, when the agent beeped me."

Really shaken, Sandra nevertheless put up a brave front. "That doesn't prove he means me harm," she said, hoping she was right, but fearing she wasn't.

"No, it doesn't, but—" he smiled in a feral way that raised the short hairs at her nape "—I'm not taking any chances, with either Whitfield or Slim."

"Slim?" She frowned, having momentarily forgotten the escapee his fellow agents were certain was tracking Cameron. "The criminal?"

"The same." Cameron paced to the window to peer into the darkness. Grunting, he flipped the switch that activated the trouble lights positioned at either corner of the house. "As soon as this damn ice melts, I'm getting you out of here."

Sandra had gone to the stove and pulled open the oven door to check their dinner. His flatly voiced statement made her pause as heat poured over her from the open oven. "Getting me out of here?" she repeated in sheer disbelief. "But you just a moment ago told me I can't go back to Denver."

He shook his head. "I meant that you can't go back to your apartment."

"I don't want to shock you," she said with sweet reason, "but my apartment is in Denver."

"Very funny." He grimaced. "But you know what I mean. I won't allow you to stay there alone. Is there a friend you could stay with for a while? Maybe Barbara?"

"No." Sandra gave a quick, sharp shake of her head, deciding she had had enough. Allow her, indeed! Who did he think he was, her keeper? "Listen carefully, Cameron," she said distinctly. "I am not going anywhere. I am staying right here until I'm damn good and ready to leave. Now, have you got that?"

"Dammit, woman!"

"Stuff it, Wolfe," she retorted, turning to peer into the oven. "And I told you not to call me 'woman.'"

He was quiet while she spooned broth over the meat and vegetables. Ominously quiet, she thought, surprised that she didn't detect the scent of brimstone emanating from him. But the only scent assailing her nostrils was the mouth-watering aroma of roasting meat and vegetables wafting from the oven. When she slid the pan back on the rack, then shut the door, he heaved a sigh that held the unmistakable sound of defeat—if only in this round of their ongoing argument.

"How long until dinner is ready?" he asked, changing the subject. He inhaled, drawing in the tantalizing smell. "Do I have time to clean up?"

"Yes," she replied, striving for a neutral tone, grateful for the cessation of hostilities, however brief. "I figure it'll be another fifteen, twenty minutes." She shrugged. "Besides, it'll keep in a warm oven. Go have your shower."

"Right." Cameron took two steps, then paused to slant a faint but conciliatory smile at her. "How about breaking out the last bottle of cabernet? I think we both could do with a glass with dinner."

"All right," she agreed without hesitation, tentatively returning his smile.

He didn't move for a second, just stood there, staring at her. Then he nodded and strode from the room, leaving her to ponder on what he might be thinking.

Speculation ran swift and rife through her head. All sorts of unpalatable ideas came to mind.

It was now dark, heralding the approach of nighttime—bedtime. Was Cameron perhaps calculating his chances of later sharing the bed with her? Was he, by softening his voice and attitude, not to mention his request for wine, hoping to soften her, undermine her determination to remain steadfast to her principles?

Sandra loved Cameron. Although at this point in their relationship she was not prepared to admit that to him, she accepted it within her own mind and being. But loving did not blind her to the facts. She had been blessed by the sheer circumstance of birth with active intelligence, and expertly educated to dispassionately examine the facts of any matter or situation.

And so, by her very nature, she could not ignore or dismiss what she perceived as the facts in relation to her present circumstances.

The very fact that Sandra was now questioning Cameron's motives was telling, in and of itself. And what it was telling her was that she harbored grave doubts about placing her trust in him, and her heart with him.

This was a fact that did not bode well for any sort of meaningful relationship between them.

Accepting this fact was difficult for Sandra, perhaps the most difficult thing she had ever had to do. But there was no getting around it—although on a purely emotional level she longed to circumvent it.

No. Shaking her head, as if to free it of the doubts assailing her mind, she moved to busy herself setting the table for dinner.

Her dodging maneuvers were an abject failure; the doubts and questions persisted, stabbing into her mind, and thus her heart, with unrelenting reason.

Sandra had been interested in Cameron in a personal way since the moment she met him. More than interested, if the truth was faced—and in her case, it always was.

There had been between them an instant spark, a sensual recognition, a chemical reaction—whatever. She certainly had felt it; she had believed then, and believed even more strongly now, that he felt it, too.

It had been there from the first, a male-female thing, shimmering and crackling between them. That she had previously not indulged herself by exploring the intangible something had not altered or negated it. But, though she had not explored it, she had been receptive to every word spoken or murmured about the object of her interest. And the words she had heard over time about Cameron had not been encouraging.

Early on, Sandra had garnered the information

that Cameron had been more than merely involved with a woman. That involvement, moreover, had progressed to speculation about an imminent announcement of their engagement. Then, abruptly, the speculation had ceased, replaced by an undercurrent of suggestion that the affair was over and, more to her interest, that Cameron had been left devastated by the perfidy of the woman, who had apparently dumped him for another, richer man.

Cameron had obviously been hurt in the process, and in turn, now she was feeling the pain.

Sandra sighed as she uncorked the wine to let it breathe.

Unbidden, she recalled hearing a scathing comment by a woman, somewhere, to the effect that the handsome and exciting special agent did not in fact like women, but merely tolerated them when the demands of sexual appetites had to be appeased.

At the time, Sandra had dismissed the remark out of hand as the nasty barb of a frustrated woman.

Now she wondered. And the very fact that she did so said much about her state of mind.

She had now spent over a week in Cameron's company. Day in, day out, to the exclusion of everything and everyone else, and at no time had she discerned so much as a hint indicating disdain for the opposite sex.

Quite the contrary. He had proved to be excellent and entertaining company, fun to be with, laugh with, make love with...especially to make love with.

But, of course, that was precisely what he had promised, wasn't it? Sandra reminded herself. Great sex. A sensual sabbatical.

And he had delivered, above and beyond the call, beyond her wildest imaginings.

Until the call to duty had intruded, dousing the fire of sensuality with the blanket of cold reality. And now it was over. She was in the way.

But there was still tonight to get through. And Cameron appeared prepared—no, eager—to suspend reality for one more night of sensual heat.

Sandra stared at the ruby red wine in the bottle, sniffed the intoxicating scent.

Did she want to play along, close her mind to the hopelessness of the situation, lose herself in the allure of his mouth, his touch, his possession?

Yes. Sandra wanted this night with him, more than she had ever before wanted anything.

Would she allow herself the license of mindlessness for the sake of one more night with him?

She hesitated...then closed her eyes against the pain of facing the bottom-line answer.

No.

She could not betray herself, any more than she could ever betray him.

She loved him. But a one-sided love was never, could never, be enough.

Sex was one thing. Love was another. And Sandra knew that for her, to hang on to one while denying the other would be self-destructive.

Her decision reached, she gathered her strength, steeled herself for the evening ahead.

But dreams, old and new alike, die very hard, and her mettle was tested with the first step Cameron took into the kitchen.

The look of him, showered, shaved, his damp hair appearing dark, like antique gold, stole her breath, and nearly shattered her resolve.

He was dressed in faded jeans that hugged his narrow hips and waist and delineated the musculature of his long legs. A stark white loose-knit sweater defined the width and breadth of his chest.

Swallowing a sigh of regret, while repressing a surge of desire for myriad things, physical and emotional, Sandra schooled her lips into a coolly remote smile.

"Dinner's ready," she said, in a hard-fought tone devoid of inflection.

He frowned, but said only, "Is there anything I can do to help?"

"You can pour the wine," she said, turning to open the oven door. "I'll bring the food."

Blaming the heat radiating from the oven for the sting in her eyes, Sandra mentally shored up her defenses, and grabbing pot holders, bent to the chore.

* * *

He had lost her.

Cameron had known it from the moment he walked into the kitchen endless hours ago.

It was late. He was tired. And he felt literally sick to his stomach. The feeling owed nothing to the delicious meal Sandra had prepared, or to the several glasses of wine he had consumed with the meal.

She hadn't even finished the first glass he had poured for her.

She had closed him out.

During the twenty or so minutes required for him to shower, shave and dress, Sandra had erected a barrier between them, an invisible yet impenetrable wall of resistance he had been unable to breach.

And Cameron had tried with every fiber of his being to tear down that barrier.

During dinner, and afterward, right up until she bade him a cool good-night, he had tried everything he could think of: conversation, humor, charm—what little he possessed—everything short of begging, to draw the warm woman from her cold shell of assumed indifference.

And Cameron believed Sandra's indifference was assumed; he had to believe it, because he couldn't bear to contemplate anything else.

Why?

What had he done wrong?

What terrible sin had he committed?

Why had she raised a shield against him?

Those tormenting questions were the direct cause of the roiling sensation sickening Cameron.

Twice. He had been rejected twice, and both times just as he was falling in love.

No.

Cameron shook his head. No. The first time hadn't felt anywhere near this painful. That had been nothing, *nothing,* compared to the sick sense of loss he was now suffering through.

And, try as he would, he could not convince himself that Sandra's sudden about-face had surfaced as a direct result of his accusing her of childishness and militant feminism.

No. It was more than that, deeper than that.

But...what?

Something in him.

The thought was unpalatable. Cameron didn't want to examine it, let alone accept it.

But there it was, entrenched in his consciousness, stabbing into his mind.

Something in him? Some essence, objectionable to the opposite sex, that he displayed?

Hell. Cameron raked stiff fingers through already wildly disheveled hair. He had had affairs with women other than the two he had unfortunately fallen for. And those other females hadn't shown signs of eventual objection to some offending essence within him.

In point of fact, it had been quite the contrary.

More than one of those females had given unmistakable signals of desiring a deeper involvement with him.

So go figure.

Cameron moved his shoulders against his bed of sofa cushions in a half shrug. His advice to himself was excellent; too bad he couldn't follow it.

How in hell did a mere man proceed in figuring out the mind of a woman?

Talk to his mother?

Cameron was swept by an impulse to do just that. He immediately quashed the impulse with a self-taunting, *Get real, Wolfe.*

He was pushing forty, for Pete's sake, long past the age to solicit maternal advice on the proper course to steer on the rocky road to love. Besides, although he felt certain the indomitable Maddy would proffer the advice, his mother would likely laugh herself silly first. So scratch that idea.

His brothers? Hmm... That idea had merit. If he was reading the signs correctly, they appeared to be having little difficulty with the opposite sex.

But, appearances were often deceptive, he mused. Of course, there was a way of ascertaining the answer. He could call, perhaps even seek advice from one, or all three, of his brothers.

Then again, perhaps not. Cameron grimaced. Not only would he tarnish his image as the older and wiser, if somewhat aloof, mentor to the younger trio, but knowing them they'd probably laugh even harder than their mother.

He was fresh out of ideas, overtired, half-asleep, and vulnerable.

Cameron groaned in protest as an image formed to tease and torment his weary mind.

Sandra. She of the sable hair and laughing dark eyes. She of the keen intellect and riposte. She of the cool demeanor and hot mouth. She of the sleek body and long, libido-enticing legs.

"Stop." His hoarse, whispered plea froze in the cold night air and echoed inside his head.

Please, stop, he repeated in silent supplication to his own consciousness.

He was getting punchy from lack of rest, he mused muzzily, encroaching sleep sending his thoughts drifting along another track.

He yawned, giving in to the heavy weight dragging down his eyelids.

How were his siblings faring in their relationships with their respective ladyloves?

Seven

A violent late-spring thunderstorm from the west pushed over the mountains of northeastern Pennsylvania.

Sergeant Royce Wolfe barely heard the rapid swish of the sweeping windshield wipers. Hands steady on the steering wheel, he scanned the road with alert, experienced eyes. He had gone off duty a short time ago, but he was a law-enforcement officer, on or off duty.

Lightning streaked the midnight sky, bathing the surrounding mountainous terrain in an eerie glow for a flashing second. Thunder roared overhead, shaking the earth below.

Memory stirred inside Royce's mind. It had

been just such a night as this, over a month ago, the first time he saw Megan.

There were differences. Important differences. A smile relieved the taut watchfulness of his ruggedly attractive features, eased the tension bunching his square jawline.

Oh, yeah. The differences were important. While maintaining his keen observation of the undulating road ahead, Royce gave memory free rein.

It had been storming that night, too, an early-spring storm, cold and sleety, the last gasp of an unrelenting winter.

He had first seen Megan Delaney slumped over the steering wheel of the sports car she had totalled running head-on into a highway guardrail.

Being off duty, but wanting to assist the patrolman who arrived on the scene minutes later, Royce had offered to follow the ambulance into town to secure a statement for the record from the accident victim after she regained consciousness.

That act of accommodation to a fellow Pennsylvania State Police officer had been Royce's undoing—and, eventually, the making of him.

Megan. His beautiful Megan, of the fiery hair, and the temperament to match.

She had hit that guardrail not entirely because she was driving too fast in inclement weather, as he had at first assumed. No, although she had been driving too fast, she had been in a state of rage and hysteria, tearing away from the scene of a near-rape in the parking lot of a restaurant located in the foothills, along a desolate country road.

Megan had understandably been left emotionally scarred and wary of men, much to Royce's distress, since he had experienced an immediate attraction to her.

A soft chuckle shimmered on the humid air in the closed vehicle, as Royce recalled the inner battle he had fought against his desire for the injured woman.

But all had ended well, as Megan had cast off fear to rush in, literally—again totaling a brand-new car—to assist him in the apprehension of her attacker.

And now he was driving through another storm after working the late shift. Only this time he was not headed home to his apartment, but to Megan, the home of his heart and soul.

Every light in the house appeared to be lit, Royce noted as he pulled into the driveway. A tender smile curved his lips. Megan's need to keep the house fully lit after dark when she was alone was one of the few lingering aftermaths of her ordeal.

He left the car and strode to the door, and as he jabbed his finger into the doorbell his stomach rumbled in anticipation of the snack-meal he knew she had ready and waiting for him.

Megan answered the door wearing a big smile and a skimpy, figure-revealing silk nightie.

"How did you know it was me?" he scolded in a soft growl, stepping inside and hauling her into his arms.

"I peeked out the window, Officer," Megan confessed, curling her arms around his neck. "Now, are you going to pick a fight or kiss me?"

"Dumb question." Royce flashed a grin and lowered his head to capture her mouth with his.

The snack she had waiting for him was destined to wait a little longer.

Scooping her up in his strong arms, Royce carried her unerringly into her bedroom, without so much as a minute slip of his lips against hers.

Megan was more than ready for him—she was way ahead of him. With a flick of each ankle, her satin mules went clattering across the room, and with a tug and a flip of her arms, her nightie sailed into the air. Then she went to work undressing him.

His blood running hot and eager, Royce trembled in response to her deft fingers, which found other, even more exciting employment after his clothes littered the floor near her slippers.

Their loving started slow and sweet, with teasing, suggestive murmurs and enticing all-over kisses and caresses. But by the time they could no longer bear the exquisite torture and merged into one, their loving was hot and fast and thoroughly satisfying.

Later, his senses sated, Royce sat alone at the kitchen table, wolfing down the sandwich snack she had prepared, appeasing a more mundane appetite.

"Royce..." Megan said, entering the room after having a shower, and now decorously covered by an ankle-length robe in a rich dark green velour.

"Hmm?" he murmured around a bite from the thick roast beef and cheese sandwich.

"Have you been discussing me with your mother?" she asked, taking the chair opposite him at the table, and snitching one of his potato chips to nibble on.

"Yes, just the other day," he said after swallowing. "I told her about you, and how I love you until it hurts." He raised tawny gold eyebrows. "Why?"

"Because I received this in the mail today." Megan drew a large square white envelope from the sideboard and laid it next to his plate.

Royce didn't need to open it. He knew what it was. He flashed a grin. "Mom sent you an invitation to Jake and Sarah's wedding?"

"Yes, obviously." She gave him an amused look. "Did you ask her to send it?"

"No." He shook his head.

Her expression sobered. "You don't want me to accompany you?"

"Get real, beautiful," he said, laughing. "You

didn't need an invitation. I was planning on taking you with me, anyway."

"Oh, I see." Though her voice was cool, her relief was visible. "And when were you planning to tell me?"

"Tonight. Tomorrow." He shrugged. "Plenty of time. It's still over two weeks until the wedding."

Shaking her head in despair of men in general, and him in particular, Megan placed the half-nibbled chip on her plate.

Royce noticed. But then, he noticed just about everything concerning Megan. And she had always joined him in the late snack.

"Aren't you hungry?"

"I thought I was." She frowned and placed a hand over her stomach. "But I've been feeling a little queasy every time I eat the last few days. I think I might have a touch of a stomach virus."

"Have you been to see Virginia Hawk?" he asked with quick concern, referring to the doctor who had treated Megan after the attack and the subsequent accident.

"No, of course not," Megan replied, dismissing the very idea with a flick of one hand. "I'm not sick. I'm not running so much as a low-grade fever. I feel certain that it's simply a spring virus."

"But suppose it isn't?" he persisted. "Suppose it's an aftereffect of the trauma you suffered, evolving into a stomach disorder?"

"Royce, I'm sure it is nothing of—"

"But you can't be sure." He rose to circle the table to her and draw her up into the warm protection of his embrace. "What if you're wrong, and it's something more than a virus? If you're ill, and can't travel to Sprucewood with me for the wedding, I won't go, either. I won't go anywhere without you, ever again."

"Oh, Royce." Megan's eyes were suspiciously misty; her voice was roughened by emotion. "I don't ever again want to go anywhere without you, either, but I'm sure you're worrying without reason." She sniffed and offered him a tremulous smile. "I'll be fine, you'll see, and as you pointed out a moment ago, it's still over two weeks until the wedding. Please don't worry."

"I can't help but worry about you," he murmured, stroking one long finger down her cheek, to the corner of her mouth. "I love you so much."

"I know, and I love you." Megan kissed the tip of the finger he drew along her lower lip. "That's why I didn't want you to know about this dratted virus."

"Will you promise me something?" he whispered, replacing his arousing finger with his even more arousing mouth. "Will you promise to see Doc Hawk if the symptoms haven't gone away within the next couple of days?"

"Yes, if you'll promise me something," she murmured against his teasing mouth.

"Anything. Name it." His tongue caressed her soft, parted lips.

"Promise you'll take me to bed within the next couple of minutes."

Laughing, Royce swept Megan up into his arms.

The second in the cluster of thunderstorms moving from west to east broke with a series of lightning cracks and resounding booms over Philadelphia shortly before six o'clock Monday morning.

The noise didn't wake Eric Wolfe; he had awakened some minutes before the storm hit. Propped up in the king-size bed in his apartment overlooking the Philadelphia Art Museum and the Schuylkill River, he had a panoramic view through the wide, west-facing plate-glass bedroom window of nature's violent display of breathtaking power.

But it wasn't violent or powerful enough to command Eric's exclusive attention. Every few seconds, his alert, expectant gaze sliced to the closed bathroom door.

It had been mere minutes, and yet the waiting was beginning to get to him.

Was she...or wasn't she?

When at last the door opened, he was caught unprepared, staring in wonder at a particularly long, seemingly horizontal streak of lightning.

"Eric."

The combined threads of trepidation and excitement woven through Tina's soft voice brought his head whipping around, his dark blue eyes probing hers.

Lord! How he loved this woman, this woman who had single-handedly healed the bitterness he had lived with after the death in the line of duty of his policeman father, thus freeing him to be a better, more effective undercover narcotics cop himself, this woman he had once suspected of having dealings with some low-life characters who were dealing in illegal substances.

But Tina Kranas had proved herself, her innocence, to his satisfaction long before she came to his defense by flying at the real guilty party—who happened to be her former husband—with a cast-iron frying pan.

"Well?" he prompted, then held his breath.

"It shows positive," she answered, holding aloft a home pregnancy strip. "It appears you are going to be a father."

"Hot damn!" Eric whooped, bolting from the bed and striding to her to catch her up in his arms. His immediate response chased the trepidation from Tina's eyes, leaving them shining with pleasure.

"I've gotta call Mom," he said, planting a quick kiss on her smiling mouth before releasing her to go to the phone on the bedside table.

"Now?" Tina laughed. "Eric, it's not even seven yet. You'll wake her."

"I know." He shot a grin at her, then continued to punch in the number. "I know, as well, that Mom would see me drawn and quartered if I didn't tell her at once."

The phone in his childhood home in the small town of Sprucewood, located some fifteen or so miles outside Philadelphia, was picked up on the third ring.

"Hello?" There was an underlying note in Maddy Wolfe's voice that only her four sons would have recognized and identified as fear of bad news. It was a note familiar to the families of most dedicated law-enforcement officers.

"It's me, Mom, and there's nothing wrong," Eric assured her at once, motioning Tina to his side and curling an arm around her waist. "In fact, it's very good news, news you've been waiting to hear."

"To use an over-used, trite phrase—" Maddy's voice had resumed its normal, wry tenor "—I'm all ears, son."

"Well, first I'd like your opinion on an idea I have." His eyes gleamed with a teasing light that was very familiar to Tina...and that would have been very familiar to the older woman, had she seen it.

"Get on with it, Eric." Now her voice held a warning that drew an appreciative chuckle from him.

"Right. Ah, how do you think Jake and Sarah might take to the idea of a double wedding?"

There was a brief pause, a breathless silence, and then: "Are you serious?"

"Oh, yeah," Eric said, tightening his arm possessively and protectively around Tina and gliding an adoring look over her glowing face. "Tina's pregnant, Mom. She just did the home test." Unable to contain the excitement bubbling inside him, he grinned again. "Metaphorically speaking, the rabbit died."

"You don't sound too despondent," Maddy observed, probing gently, hopefully.

"I'm over the moon," he said jubilantly. "We both are. It's no accident, you know. We were trying." His voice held laughter. "Trying hard."

"Before marriage?" A tiny note of censure there.

"Aw, Mom," he said, in the exact same tone he had used as a boy. "So what do you think—will Jake and Sarah go for it? We could kill two birds with one stone...so to speak."

"Or two Wolfes with one shotgun...so to speak," she retorted dryly.

It took a moment for the dawn to break in Eric's mind; Maddy waited with maternal patience.

"Sarah's pregnant!"

"Hmm..." she concurred in a murmur. "They told me just last night. I knew I had raised rambunctious sons. I just never realized quite how rambunctious.''

Eric roared. "Is Jake happy about it?" he asked when his laughter subsided.

"To quote your youngest brother exactly," she drawled, "'Is Elijah Blue?'"

Eric laughed again, then said, "I'll give Jake a call in a little while."

"You do that," Maddy replied. "And, Eric—"

"Yes, Mother?"

"Congratulations, son, and give my love to Tina."

"Thanks, Mom, I will."

Eric didn't replace the receiver after saying goodbye, but merely depressed the disconnect button, then moved his index finger to punch in the Sprucewood number registered to his younger brother, Jake. His intent was thwarted by Tina sliding her palm over the buttons.

"That can wait awhile," she said decisively. "At least until after breakfast."

"You're hungry?" Eric asked hopefully, somewhat surprised, since she'd been off her appetite the last week or so. At her nod, he dropped the receiver onto the cradle. "Good. I'll rustle up some eggs."

"No," she said, as he started to move, his encircling arm moving her along with him, toward the kitchen. "I'm not hungry for scrambled eggs."

He looked at her askance. "I hope you're not about to tell me you want pickles and ice cream."

"Don't be silly," Tina said. "No. What I want—must have—is chicken noodle soup."

"Chicken noodle soup!" Eric made a face. "At six-thirty in the morning?"

"*Eric,* please..." She batted her naturally long eyelashes exaggeratedly at him. "I'm eating for two now, you know. I need hearty sustenance."

He fought a grin, but it defeated him. "Okay, I give up," he agreed, releasing his hold on her and ushering her into the kitchen. "Chicken noodle soup it is."

"And toast bread."

"And toast." Silent laughter laced his voice.

"And a cinnamon bun."

Eric lost it; his laughter brightened the storm-dimmed room.

Thunder growled in the distance, rumbling a warning of the approach of the third storm in the clustered front moving rapidly from west to east.

A bemused smile tilting his lips, Jake Wolfe hung up the phone. He had been minutes away from leaving the split-level house he and Sarah had made settlement on two weeks ago, and into which he had moved the very next day, when the call came in from his brother Eric.

Imagine that, Jake mused, staring at the now silent instrument. Eric and Tina requesting they make the upcoming nuptials a double affair.

And Tina was also pregnant.

What a hoot! He couldn't wait to tell Sarah.

Sarah! Jake shot a glance at his watch, then shot down the three steps into the family room, then through the door connecting the house to the garage; if he didn't get his rump in gear, he'd be late.

He was supposed to pick up Sarah to deliver her to Sprucewood College in time to conduct her first class, and he had exactly five minutes to get there.

Fortunately, Sprucewood was a small town, and even more fortunately, the worst of the morning rush was over. Raindrops began pattering on the car roof as he turned onto Sarah's street.

She was waiting for him on the apartment's front steps, huddled beneath a small umbrella, the toe of one foot beating an impatient tattoo on the cement. She made a dash for the car as he glided to a stop alongside the curb.

"I was beginning to think you weren't coming, and that I'd be late to class," she gently scolded, sliding onto the seat beside him. "What kept you?"

"Wait till you hear," he said, breaking off for a moment to allow the laughter tickling his throat to escape. "You're gonna love it."

As usually happened, the rich, full sound of his laughter brought a delighted smile to her eyes and mouth. "I can't wait," she said in a teasing voice. "So, suppose you tell me."

"I had a phone call from Eric, that's what kept me," he began, pausing for another chuckle. "Damned if the clown doesn't want to get married with us."

Sarah blinked. Then she frowned her incomprehension. "What?"

"Do you remember I mentioned that Mom told me Eric had brought a young woman home to meet her, not just once, but twice?" he asked, then rushed on without giving her time to respond. "And that her name was Tina, and she was very nice, and that she baked lemon meringue pie almost as good as Mom's own?"

"Yes, of course I remember," Sarah answered when he finally paused to breathe. "How could I forget, when you made such a big deal out of it?"

"Knowing Eric, it was a big deal." Jake grinned. "Well, seems the ol' love bug's taken a big bite outta Eric's heart, and he and Tina wanted to know if you and I would consider a double wedding ceremony."

"Why, that's a wonderful idea!" Sarah exclaimed. "I hope you agreed."

"No." Jake gave a quick shake of his head.

"Why not?" Sarah frowned, and sent a quick glance to her watch.

"I wouldn't agree without talking to you first," he said. "You should know that."

"Thank you." Her smile was gentle, but fleeting. "I've got to go, or I'll be late." She groped for the release and swung the door open.

"But I didn't tell you the best part," he objected. "Eric and—"

She silenced him with a kiss, and then she slid across the seat and out of the car.

"It'll have to wait until lunchtime," she said, pressing the button to open the umbrella. "And if you don't get moving, you'll be late. Bye. Love you." She took off at a near-run along the campus walk."

"Sarah, slow down!" Jake called after her in sharp concern.

She flashed a grin at him over her shoulder, adjusting her pace to a brisk, striding gait.

Jake anxiously watched her until she entered the building. Then he set the car in motion to wend his way to the station.

After reporting in, he got behind the wheel of his black-and-white police cruiser and began his regular routine of patrol.

Jake loved being a cop, enjoyed waving to and exchanging friendly gibes with kids of incremental ages as he patrolled the area around the elementary, middle and high school. From there, his route took him around the outer boundaries of the college.

But even after seven months he still could not

drive the college perimeters without recalling the events of the previous autumn.

That was when Jake had first met, and been immediately attracted to, Sarah Cummings.

Now he could reflect gratefully on the incident, for it had inadvertently brought him and Sarah together. But at the time, the mystery of Sarah had nearly driven him to distraction.

The incident had involved the crime of car theft, or more precisely car-parts theft, undertaken by three upper-middle-class college students on a whim, just to see if they could get away with it.

And they might have, Jake conceded, had it not been for the threat posed by Sarah to the three of them, because she had accidentally overheard them discussing their nefarious activities, and his subsequent interest in her.

Oh, it had stumped him for a while, the glaring fact that she shied away from being seen in public with him, especially when he was in uniform.

But Jake had eventually worked it all out, then set about catching the young men with the goods— with Sarah's help, he admitted, smiling at the memory of her wielding a stout branch to knock a tire iron meant for his head out of the hand of the self-appointed leader of the three.

Savoring the warm memory of his beautiful Sarah rushing to his defense, Jake happily continued his patrol, stopping occasionally, chatting with friends and acquaintances, until it was time to meet Sarah for lunch.

She was waiting for him in their usual back booth in the off-campus hamburger joint where he had first spotted her seven months ago. She was wearing the same big round tortoiseshell glasses that gave her a wide-eyed, owlish appearance.

The sight of her softened and hardened Jake at one and the same time.

"Hi," he murmured, sliding onto the bench opposite her in the booth, slightly awed and amazed at the ever-deepening love he felt for her.

"Hi." Sarah returned his greeting, the glow in her eyes proof that she returned his love in equal measure.

"Got time to hear about Eric now?"

"I'm all yours for exactly fifty-five minutes," she said brightly.

"You better be—for fifty-five minutes, and forever," he growled.

"Eric?" She laughed and arched her eyebrows.

"Yeah." He grinned. "He and Tina are pregnant, just like you and me."

"I think it's wonderful."

"So do they." He laughed and shook his head. "And you really don't mind making it a double wedding?"

"Not at all. It'll be fun." Her eyes danced with amusement. "And your mother will love it."

"According to Eric, she already does." Jake

erupted in laughter as another consideration sprang to mind. "And I can't wait to hear what Cameron will have to say. Two weddings *and* two babies! He'll freak…"

Eight

Cameron woke to the sound of running water, both inside and outside the house. Frowning, he pried his eyes open to a slit and peered at the face of his watch. The position of the hands brought his eyes wide open.

Twelve-fourteen! He never slept so late—except on days when he didn't get to sleep until dawn. And this was, had been, one of those days, or nights, or whatever.

The sound of water running inside the house ceased abruptly. The running outside continued, but sounded faint and distant. But, as faint and distant as the sound was, it activated a sudden realization in the sleep-fogged depths of his mind.

The ice was melting, which could only mean that the capricious spring weather had once again turned seasonally mild. Which, in turn, meant that he and Sandra were no longer confined to the cabin.

Which also meant it was time, past time, to haul his carcass off the sofa.

Stifling a groan at a protest of his stiff and cramped muscles, aching from his six-foot-four-inch frame being confined to a six-foot area of space, Cameron levered himself into a sitting position.

Upright, and almost fully conscious, Cameron inhaled, and stifled another groan, this time in appreciation of the aroma of fresh coffee wafting from the kitchen, which explained the source of the previous sound of running water inside the house.

His nose twitched and his mouth watered as the aroma got stronger, seemed nearer.

"Good morning." Sandra's voice was utterly devoid of inflection, good, bad or indifferent.

But there wasn't a thing indifferent about the sensations that ripped through him when he glanced up at her. She appeared so feminine, so soft and sleek in her robe and slippers, that he longed to reach out and draw her into his arms, bear her down with him, onto the couch, and make love to her, with her, until they both forgot what had caused the friction between them.

Prudence cautioned him against fulfilling the longing; prudence, and the closed look of her.

"Good morning," he returned, wrapping his hands around the heated mug. "And thanks."

"You're welcome." She didn't smile; she turned away. "I'm poaching eggs. They'll be done in a few minutes...if you want some."

"Yes, I want some," he said to her retreating back, careful not to slosh the coffee as he stood up.

"Then come butter the toast."

Her tone—or rather the lack of it—didn't bode well for a comfortable, congenial meal, Cameron reflected dejectedly, trailing her into the kitchen.

His reflection proved correct.

Seated opposite her at the table, Cameron acknowledged that the three or so feet of space separating them was as good as a mile.

Sandra wasn't picky, or argumentative, or downright bitchy. What she was, in his view, was much worse. She was remote, withdrawn and—he shuddered at the thought—lost to him.

She deflected with a look, a frown, a raised eyebrow, every attempt he made, hapless as he knew it to be, to ease the tension between them.

He was beginning to feel desperate by the time he finished the two perfectly cooked poached eggs she had silently served him.

The very last thing Cameron needed at that point was the intrusive sound of his beeper.

So, of course, the way his luck had been running lately, that was exactly what he got.

Sandra briefly lost her rigidly controlled expression to a cynical smile.

Cameron had to quash an urgent impulse to hurl the blasted beeper through the window.

But the very fact that he had felt the impulse was both startling and edifying.

Cameron identified the root cause of his uncharacteristic feeling as he dutifully responded to the call of duty; in simple terms, Sandra had become more important to him than his life's work.

From the unreachable depths of her silent withdrawal, she monitored his every reluctant step to the kitchen wall phone. Then, as he reached for the receiver, she stood and walked out of the room.

"When you're finished on the phone, you can clear the table." Her remote voice floated back to him. "I'm going to dress."

Damn.

Fighting the desire to desert his post and go after her, Cameron punched in the designated number.

"Wolfe. What's up?" he snapped, the instant the receiver was lifted at the other end.

"It appears our quarry slipped through the net," Steve's familiar voice replied, in unfamiliar tones of heavy disgust.

"How?" Cameron literally growled the demand for a plausible answer.

"He's a cunning son of a bitch," Steve said.

"He kept moving in circles, then doubling back. Then he changed direction and made a run south. The local law lost him near the New Mexico state line. Seems friend Slim is heading home to Taos."

A conflicting wave combined of equal parts anger and relief washed over Cameron. Anger at the officers who had let Slim slip through their fingers, and relief at the realization that their carelessness had, in effect, freed him to pursue his personal agenda.

"Okay, Steve," he replied wearily, made tired by the inner conflict. "Keep me informed."

"Will do."

For long moments after the connection was severed, Cameron stood staring sightlessly at the instrument, examining possible approaches to take in bridging the widening chasm between him and Sandra.

How had it all started, anyway?

He shook his head, a frown knitting his brows, and glared at the innocent white instrument.

Oh, yeah, he had accused her, first of being childish, then of extreme militancy.

Dumb, Wolfe. Real dumb, because now he had to come up with a way to undo the damage.

As he turned from the phone, his glance collided with the kitchen table.

Telling himself that the first step in damage control had better start right there, he got busy cleaning up the breakfast dishes.

Some fifteen or so minutes later, Cameron found Sandra in the living room, staring out the window at the overcast but obviously milder day. He cleared his throat to draw her attention.

"More bad news?" she asked, not even bothering to turn and face him.

"No, just the opposite." Suddenly determined to have her look at him, he offered nothing more. His ploy worked; she turned to level a skeptical look at him.

The sight of her caused a strange and unfamiliar sensation inside him. For a moment, he simply stared at her, the look of her, feeling scared, deep in the pit of his stomach.

Except for Saturday evening, when they had both spruced up a bit for dinner, Sandra had dressed casually in old jeans and what looked like even older pullovers and shirts. She also had not bothered with makeup, except for a light application of protective moisturizer.

Now, the coolly composed woman facing him projected the image of a highly efficient professional lawyer—which, in fact, she was.

Though she was wearing jeans, they were neither old nor worn, but a slim-legged designer creation, with sharp, ironed-in creases. And, while she was wearing a shirt, it was silk, expensive, and tucked neatly into the belted jeans, the bottoms of which were tucked just as neatly into equally expensive black leather boots.

But that wasn't even the worst of it. Sandra's glowing, artifice-free appearance was gone, hidden behind a mask of expertly applied makeup.

She was breathtakingly beautiful, and appeared as removed from him, and the intimacy they had shared, as the sun appeared removed from the earth by the clouds.

"Let's not play silent games, Cameron." Her voice was as remote as her exquisite appearance. "If you have anything to say, say it."

Cameron tried a cajoling smile. "I thought, believed, we were both having a good time up until yesterday—playing games, I mean."

"That was then, and this is now." Not only did she not return his smile, her expression grew more severe. "And I'd appreciate it if you'd get on with it."

So much for cajolery, Cameron told himself derisively.

"Right," he said, shrugging in defeat. "From all indications, you are no longer in danger by remaining here in the cabin."

"The escaped criminal has been apprehended?"

"No." He shook his head. "It appears that Slim decided it was more to his advantage to make a run for it, instead of tracking me down to get even."

"But the manhunt is still on for him?"

"Of course."

"And you're free to go." Now she did smile,

but it had hopeless finality in it, and he despaired when he saw it. "Go ahead." She waved a hand. "Go join the hunt."

"Sandra—" he began, but that was as far as she allowed him to go.

"Get going," she insisted. "It's not only your job, it's what you want to do. So, go do it."

"They don't need me." He raked a hand through his hair in frustration. "Dammit! You know the only reason I felt I should remain here alone was that there was reason to believe he was tracking me. I don't want to leave here. I don't want to leave you."

"I think, in effect, you already have." She shrugged. "I believe we parted company yesterday."

"Sandra..." he began again, feeling like an idiot, standing in the middle of the room. "Can't we at least sit down...talk about it?"

She hesitated, a tiny frown marring the perfection of her face, giving him an assessing once-over. "I don't see how talking will—"

He interrupted her with a hoarse plea. "Please."

She sighed, then shrugged, then nodded—much to his fervent relief.

Springing into action, Cameron whipped around to yank the bunched-up comforter from the sofa.

Sandra chose to sit down in the chair farthest from his makeshift bed.

Cameron ground his teeth, but accepted her choice without a murmur…or a whimper.

"All right, we're seated," she said, pointing out the obvious. "Talk."

Talk.

Right.

Damn.

Cameron felt as tongue-tied as a teenager on a first date, and about as graceless. Nevertheless, desperate, he launched into speech.

"I don't suppose you'd allow me a few minutes to shave, shower and get into clean clothes?" he said, keenly aware of his grungy appearance in comparison to her perfection. "Or at least brush my teeth?"

She moved to get up.

"Okay, forget it," he said, motioning to her to remain where she was. "I'll do it later."

She sat back and crossed her legs, reminding him of the day, a mere two weeks ago, but seemingly a lifetime, when she had come to his office to inform him that she was taking a leave of absence from her work.

Only then, Sandra had been friendly.

Now, while she was not openly hostile, she wasn't exactly friendly, either.

"Cameron, I'm developing a headache waiting for you to begin talking," she said impatiently.

Nudged into speaking, he blurted out artlessly,

"I want to apologize. I'm sorry for accusing you of being childish and militant."

She smiled.

He winced at the derisive curve to her lips, lips that he longed to crush with his own—immediately after he scrubbed his teeth.

"Sandra, say something."

"What would you like me to say?" She raised her brows. "That I forgive you for saying what you so obviously believe?"

"I don't believe it." He gave a sharp shake of his head. "I was angry, and—"

She silenced him with a quick wave of her hand. "You were angry, and voicing the truth—according to Special Agent Cameron Wolfe."

"No! I—"

She again interrupted him. "But that doesn't matter. What matters is that it's clear we have no basis to continue this, er, relationship—" she grimaced "—for want of a better phrase."

"No basis?" Cameron laughed; he couldn't help it, despite the expanding feeling of dread inside him. "Sandra, we have spent over a week laughing, talking, loving and relating very well to each other."

"Yes," she readily agreed.

He began a hefty sigh of relief; she proceeded to steal his breath and quash his revived hope.

"But that was a time out of time," she continued, a faint, sad smile shadowing her lips. "It was an illusion, unrelated to reality, a game of 'Let's pretend.'" Then she sighed, and it held the sound not of relief, but of impending doom—his. "But life has a way of intruding, Cameron, shattering pretense and illusion with the ruthless blow of reality."

"Dammit, Sandra, that's ridiculous!" he exclaimed, springing up to go to her. "You and I—especially you and I, considering the work we do—deal in reality as a way of life." He performed his signature habit of spearing his long fingers into his sun-kissed hair. "Intrude? Hell, reality's there, a constant, in both our lives. And you know it."

"Yes, but—"

Now he would not allow her to finish. "But nothing. So we grabbed some time, time to relax, laugh, play, some time for ourselves, and for each other. Where's the illusion in that, the pretense?"

"It wasn't real, Cameron." She raised a hand to massage her temple. "It was fun and games. And you and I—especially you and I—know better than most that life is not fun and games. Reality is everyday, and the everyday Cameron and Sandra are two entirely different types, too different to coexist together every day."

"That's nuts!" He was forced to back up as she stood to face him squarely.

"No," she said sadly. "That's life."

The scared sensation in his stomach spread, permeating his being. "Sandra..." he began, afraid to ask, yet needing to know. "Are you saying that you don't want to continue exploring our relationship after we leave here?"

"What would be the point?" She shrugged, causing the silk to shimmer over her breasts, and the nerves to quiver throughout his body. "There is no genuine relationship to explore."

"No relationship?" He stared at her in disbelief and amazement, and was forced to fight an urgent impulse to grab her shoulders and shake her, or kiss her, or do something even more exciting— even if also reprehensible, under the circumstances. "You can't be serious."

"All right! There was a relationship...of sorts." Her composure, her even tone, revealed strain for the first time, encouraging Cameron for a moment. "But it was the stuff of kids playing house." She held up a hand when he would have objected. "There was no genuine communication, no mutual understanding."

"Uh-huh." Cameron heaved a tired sigh. "Square one. We're back to my rash and thoughtless charge of childishness and militant feminism."

"No!" she began, but then she echoed his weary sigh. "Yes, we're back to that—that, and the complete lack of understanding revealed by it."

"I told you I was angry."

"I know."

"And I was talking off the top of my head," he

went on, asking himself whether he should confess to the fear for her safety that had fired his anger.

"And I firmly believe you were voicing your mind and your convictions."

"Sandra, no—"

"And that's fine," she continued, as if he hadn't spoken. "You're entitled to them. The problem is, they're invalid, at least from my perspective. Which is a solid indication that we merely spent a week out of time, indulging our senses in our sensual sabbatical, while not learning a damn thing about each other."

Now Cameron was developing a headache. Very likely, he concluded, from beating his head against the brick wall of Sandra's obstinacy.

"You're wrong," he insisted, refusing to give up, out of a sickening fear of losing her completely. "I have never felt more connected to a woman. And I mean mentally, as well as physically." He succumbed to the need to reach out, touch the tip of his fingers to her smooth cheek. "I thought, believed, you felt the same."

"I did," she whispered. "But..." She shook her head, dislodging his hand, his fingertips. "I...I don't know." She again massaged her temple. "I need time to think. Time alone." She stepped back. "I need breathing space, and distance. I need to go home."

"You can't," he reminded her. "At least not

until we see what Whitfield is up to." He knew he had erred, and badly, even before he was finished.

She stiffened, and stepped away from him. "I'm a big girl now, and I can take care of myself. If I deem it necessary, I'll have a restraining order issued against Whitfield. But, for now, my headache's worse. I'm going to take a couple of aspirin and lie down."

"Sandra, wait," he pleaded when she turned and headed for the bedroom.

"If I fall asleep, I may well be in for the night," she said, as if he hadn't uttered a word.

"Sandra!"

"There is one more thing," she said, finally pausing in the archway to glance back at him.

"Yes?" he asked, with unabashed eagerness.

"I was listening to the radio this morning before you woke up. The weather service predicted that the temperature will continue to rise through this afternoon and tonight. By tomorrow morning, this ice will be gone." She hesitated briefly before adding, "And so will I."

Nine

Sandra was nearly finished packing her things by the time a beautiful spring dawn had bathed the landscape in tones of pearlized pink.

Unsurprisingly, after two nights of practically no sleep at all, she had fallen into a deep slumber mere minutes after swallowing two aspirin, then crawling into the too-empty bed. And she had slept straight through the rest of the afternoon and most of the night.

She had awoken rested and refreshed shortly before four a.m., her headache, if not her heartache, gone.

Finally, showered, dressed, and everything packed except for her makeup, Sandra stacked the stuff next to the bedroom door, then reluctantly left the room to face the by-then-bright sunlit day—and the sleeping Wolfe in the living room.

The living room was empty; the Wolfe was on the prowl in the kitchen. And the sight of him brought her up short in the doorway.

Barefoot, clad in faded jeans and a sweatshirt, both rumpled from being slept in—it was immediately obvious that he had slept, because he still looked groggy—his golden mane tousled, he looked totally disreputable and, to her admittedly biased eyes, absolutely delicious.

Although Sandra would have sworn her movements were noiseless, Cameron must have heard her—sensed her? smelled her?—for without so much as a glance over his shoulder, he muttered an invitation of sorts.

"Come have some coffee."

The weary sound of his voice undermined her determination and composure. There was a thread of near-defeat woven through his quiet tone that pierced her heart like a spear.

Defeat? Sandra asked herself, hovering uncertainly in the doorway. Cameron?

Get real.

Reacting to the mental gibe, she squared her shoulders and crossed the room to accept the steaming cup he turned to offer her.

"Thanks." Though her voice was steady, her

fingers were not; she hid the tremor by wrapping them around the warm cup.

"You're welcome," he murmured, turning back to attend to the pans on the stove. "I was just about ready to scramble some eggs. Do you want some?"

"Yes, please." Despairing at the crack in her voice, she raised the cup to her lips to sip the hot brew, in the hope of relieving the parched feel in her throat.

"Potatoes, too?" He didn't glance around, but busied himself with prodding the potatoes with a spatula.

"Yes." It was all so banal, Sandra had to will herself to keep from shouting her answer at him, merely to see if he'd respond in kind.

"Okay. You can make the toast."

Make the toast? she thought, rather wildly. She felt as if she were toast.

Nevertheless, she set her cup on the countertop and moved to comply.

Breakfast was less than scintillating. It appeared that, after a week of chattering nonstop to one another, they had both run dry of conversation.

Well…perhaps not completely dry.

"You're really set on leaving today," Cameron said, shoving his plate aside. "Aren't you?"

"Yes, I am." Sandra sighed, now wishing the conversational stream had remained dry. "I'm packed and ready to go."

"Uh-huh." His sigh echoed hers. "And nothing I can say will change your mind?"

"No." She shook her head, and blamed the abrupt motion for the sting in her eyes. "I told you yesterday, I need some thinking time, alone..." She tried to smile; it didn't work; she gave it up. "Without distractions."

"Then you admit that I distract you?" Cameron's voice held a note of hope.

"Yes, of course, you know you do," she said, then hastened to quash the expectancy that flared in his blue eyes, "But, distraction aside, I still need time." She actually felt his expression of deflation, yet she proceeded in her determination. "And I'm taking it."

The fire dimmed in his beautiful eyes, leaving them lackluster. His expression set into a mask of control. "Do you have any idea how much time you'll need?" His voice was devoid of emotion or inflection.

"No."

"I see." He sighed, and a tiny nonsmile curved his lips. "Were you planning to let me know when—or if—you've reached a decision?"

"Yes, of course, I—"

"That's the second time you've said that," he said, interrupting impatiently. "And there's no damned 'of course' about it." He expelled a short laugh that had more the sound of a snort. "I really thought, believed, that I knew you, understood you, but—''

Sandra interrupted him. ''That's exactly what I'm saying. We don't really know each other.''

''But we could,'' he said in a flat voice. ''If we wanted to make the effort.'' He pushed his chair back and stood up. ''I do.''

Struck by his implication that she was the one unwilling to make the effort, Sandra was swept by conflicting waves of anger and despair.

It was unfair, she cried in silent protest. He was being unfair, considering that it was he who had misread her.

''And, by your very silence, I must conclude that you don't want to make the effort.''

''And, naturally, your conclusions are always correct,'' she retorted, smarting anew at his previous assumptions and accusations as to her motives.

''Not hardly,'' he retorted cynically. ''At least, not where women are concerned.''

Now anger was gaining the upper hand. How dare he cast her in the mold of the woman who had dumped him? Sandra railed. And dumped him for monetary reasons, at that!

''You know practically nothing about women,'' she said, scraping her own chair backward and rising to challenge him, stare for stare. She even managed a credible curl to her upper lip. ''Other than their performance in bed.''

"That was below the belt, Sandra," he told her. "Literally, as well as figuratively."

Shamed by her hasty and ill-considered barb, Sandra felt honor-bound to concede. "I know, and anger is no excuse for dirty pool. I'm sorry."

"Yeah, so am I." He moved his shoulders in a tired-looking shrug, and began gathering the dishes and flatware. "I guess we'd better clean up. If you're going, I might as well leave, too." He turned away, then glanced back at her. "Would you allow me to use the bedroom and bath to shower and get my stuff together?"

"Yes, certainly." She circled the table to relieve him of the dishes in his hands. "You can use them now. I'll clean up in here, and in the living room."

"Thanks." With a fleeting half smile, he relinquished the dishes, then strode from the room.

Sandra stood still, staring after him long after he had disappeared from view.

Had she made the right decision? she asked herself, gnawing on her lower lip. Was she doing what was best for both of them by sticking to that decision?

She loved him so very much. And she was now hurting so very badly. Perhaps...

Sandra brought her thoughts to a dead stop. Everything had happened too soon. Their relationship had become too intimate, too hot, too intense, much too quickly. She needed time, they both needed time, to ponder, to reevaluate their respective feelings before continuing on together.

A breathing spell was needed at this juncture, she advised herself. Perhaps, after a week or two of some serious soul-searching, and rational, detached thinking… Who knew?

Sandra sighed as she went about the business of putting Barbara's getaway house in order.

One thing was certain. She hoped, prayed, that eventually she and Cameron could reach a mutually satisfying solution. Because she wasn't sure she could stand spending the rest of her life without him being a part of it. Whereas once she had enjoyed being alone, now, since being with him, a part of him, sharing both love and laughter with him, to be forever without him was unthinkable.

Hell, she missed him already.

The living room had been put to rights and Sandra was finishing up in the kitchen when Cameron exited the bedroom, loaded down with his own and her luggage.

"If you'll get me your keys, I'll stash this stuff in the cars."

"Okay." Leaving the kitchen, she skirted around him and started for the bedroom to collect her handbag. "But don't try to lug all of it yourself," she called back to him. "I'll do my share."

With them working together in silence, the chore was swiftly accomplished. Everything was stashed in their respective vehicles, except for their jackets.

Cameron tossed his onto one corner of the sofa. Sandra draped hers, along with her handbag, at the other end, fully aware of the symbolism of the distance separating the two garments.

"Is there any coffee left?" he asked, not looking at her as he walked around her, into the kitchen and directly to the coffeemaker on the countertop. "I'd like a cup before we leave."

"Yes, I saved it for you," she answered, devouring the look of him with her eyes as she trailed along after him, while trying to appear unaffected by the impact on her senses of the sight of him. "It's still hot."

"Good. Thanks." He glanced over his shoulder and offered her a real smile.

She gratefully accepted and returned his offering. "You're welcome."

She watched him hungrily while he poured out a cup of the dark liquid, quivering inside in response to the sheer masculine appeal of him. Attired in fresh jeans, a loose-knit white sweater and rugged boots, with his burnished hair gleaming from the shower and his face smooth from the razor, he was a sight to set any woman's heart aflutter.

Was she certifiably out of her mind in demanding that they part for a while, in denying herself the thrill and pleasure of his exciting company?

Possibly, but...

Sandra's thoughts fractured as, at that moment,

Cameron leaned forward, then went completely still, peering intently out the window above the sink overlooking the deck and the foothills beyond.

"Cameron, what—"

"Son of a—" His muttered curse cut across her voice as he suddenly set the cup on the countertop and strode to the back door.

Blinking in surprise and puzzlement, she watched him twist the lock, swing the door open and then stride out onto the deck.

Intrigued by his curious and abrupt action, she set her own cup on the table and followed him.

He was hunkered down in the center of the deck, staring intently at the floor.

"Cameron, what is it?" she asked, coming up beside him. "What's wrong?"

"That," he answered tersely, pointing at a muddy footprint on the floor. "And those," he added, indicating several other prints leading to and away from the window. "Seems we had a visitor during the night, or very early this morning."

A chill ran up Sandra's spine, and she shivered in reaction. "A visitor? Who?" she asked in a near-whisper, even though she feared she knew.

Cameron sliced a droll look at her. "That's the print of a cowboy boot." He got up to examine the other footprints. "And I'd say it was a safe bet it and the others were made by our friend Slim."

"But..." Sandra had to pause to wet her suddenly parched lips. "I thought the authorities were certain he had fled to the area around Taos, New Mexico,'' she said, glancing uneasily around her.

"A wily son of a bitch, is our Slim." His lips twisted in disgust. "Apparently he gave them the slip again." Pivoting, he crossed the deck to her, grasped her arm and hustled her to the door. "Let's get back inside," he ordered, literally shoving her through the doorway. "We're exposed here."

Her thoughts exactly, Sandra thought, clasping her arms around her body to contain a shudder.

Cameron headed straight for the wall phone, punched in a number, then stood, stiff and alert, staring out the window through narrowed, glittering eyes.

"It's Wolfe," she heard him say into the receiver. "And I think my tracker has found me."

Not waiting to hear any more, she walked into the living room and pulled on her jacket. She was doing up the buttons when he came into the room.

"What are you doing?"

"Getting ready," she answered, frowning at the authoritarian note in his voice. "We are leaving at once, aren't we?"

"No, Sandra," he said, moving around her to get to his own jacket. "You're not going anywhere. Not as long as he's skulking about out there."

"But then, why are you putting on your jacket?" she asked, then exclaimed, "Oh!" when he thrust a hand beneath the end sofa cushion and withdrew a holstered pistol. She took a step back. "I hate guns."

"So do I." A tired smile feathered his lips at the look of revulsion on her face. "I especially hate them when they're in the hands of criminals."

"You're going out there, looking for him." Sandra moistened her lips. "Aren't you?"

"Of course," he snapped, drawing the weapon from the holster. He tossed the harness onto the sofa, then raised his intent blue eyes to her. "It's my job."

"But...but..." she sputtered, watching him shrug into his jacket. "You can't go out there after him alone!" She reached out impulsively to grab his arm.

"Can't I?" He shook off her hand and moved away from her. "Watch me."

"Cameron, please," she pleaded, frantic with fear for him. "At least wait for backup."

Shaking his head, he walked into the kitchen and to the back door. "I won't take a chance on being pinned down in here. If there's going to be any more hunting done, then I'm going to do it."

She was right on his heels, her heart racing, her eyes wide and frightened. Dipping his head, he brushed a kiss across her parted lips, then opened the door.

"Lock this at once," he ordered, leveling a scorching, memorizing look on her face. "Stay inside, and away from the windows, until I return."

Obeying instinctively, Sandra locked the door the instant he closed it. Then she ran to the kitchen window, a shiver skittering up her spine as she watched Cameron swiftly cross the deck, descend the steps and follow the trail of boot prints into the wooded foothills.

The Lone Wolfe was on the hunt.

Crouched low, and moving fast, Cameron followed the boot tracks across the open area next to the house, then into the trees at the base of the foothills.

Even with the undergrowth, he had little difficulty discerning the erratic trail Slim had left. Moving slower, but at a steady pace, he followed the zigzag, circling path delineated by the indentations in the rain-softened earth from the distinctive slanted-heeled, pointy-toed cowboy boot.

It was tough going, and time-consuming, but after what Cameron judged to have been in actual measure approximately three-quarters of a mile, the tracks intersected a narrow, rutted roadway. There the boot tracks proceeded on a straight course, deeper into the woods, and to a small clearing, where a tree-scraped and battered van—likely stolen—was parked.

In the sylvan setting, all was quiet and serene; birds chittered and scolded each other in the treetops.

Cameron approached the vehicle with tense caution and bated breath. Stepping gingerly, so as not to dislodge a stone or crunch a twig, he moved up to the rear of the van, then along its closed side panels.

Pausing behind the passenger-side door, he drew a silent breath, leaned forward for a quick peek inside, then, finding the front seats empty, pulled back.

Preparing to move on the count of three, he tightened his grip on the gun, drew another, deeper breath, then counted—one, two, three, go!

His movements fast, sure, Cameron stepped forward, grasped the door handle with his left hand, pulled it open and burst into the front of the van, right arm extended to the rear, finger taut on the trigger.

The van was empty.

The pent-up breath whooshed out of him in a harsh exhalation. But, although the interior was devoid of life, there were clear signs of Slim's occupancy.

An open heavy-duty sleeping bag lay along one wall. Two six-packs of bottled beer, one empty, were set close to it, along with a crumpled potato chip bag, a package of cookies and a half-full milk container. Two plastic sandwich bags, both with the remnants of sandwiches inside, littered the floor.

Cameron drew a breath, and wrinkled his nose

at the strong smell of beer. The strength of the odor gave evidence of Slim's recent presence.

Unease unfurled in his stomach. Slim had been here, at least long enough to eat and swig some beer. And then he had left again, to go—

Sandra!

Stark fear clutching at his throat, Cameron scrambled back from the van, then circled around the front, to the driver's side. The mark of a boot heel was deep in the ground where Slim had stepped out. From there, the tracks led off, across the makeshift road and into the woods, back in the direction of the cabin.

"Goddamn."

Muttering the curse, along with several other inventive and profane utterances, Cameron took off at a watchful trot, following the trail of boot prints.

It led straight back to the cabin.

Standing at the edge of the tree line, yet concealed by the trees, his eyes crawling inch by inch, Cameron surveyed the terrain, and the situation. His gaze paused for long moments on the two vehicles, Sandra's compact and his own larger four-wheel, parked, his behind hers, in front of the cabin. There was not a shadow, not a hint of motion. All appeared peaceful, serene, in the warm midmorning spring sunlight.

There was not a sign of Slim—outside.

The short hairs at the back of Cameron's neck quivered as his gaze came to a halt on the cabin.

Although the clearing between the house and the trees was relatively short in distance, it was a decidedly far piece in time of exposure. He knew he'd be a sitting duck if he should leave the protective cover.

And yet, if Slim had somehow managed to gain entrance into the cabin, to Sandra...

Cameron stopped thinking and started moving.

He had traversed about three-quarters of the distance to the house, and was drawing even with the cars, when he caught a flicker of movement from the far side of his vehicle out of the corner of his eye.

He spun instinctively to face the possible danger. His sudden movement saved his life.

In what seemed like fast-forward action, Cameron saw Slim rise to his full height and fire off a shot from his hastily raised rifle.

The bullet missed Cameron's head by a fraction of an inch.

The sickening crack of the rifle shot halted Sandra in her tracks in the center of the living room, where she had been pacing since moments after Cameron had left the house. She had filled those moments by running into the bedroom to retrieve the pistol she had shoved to the back of the bedside table drawer, behind her paperback books.

The awful sound of gunfire had come from the front of the house.

Cameron!

Clutching the detested weapon in a trembling hand, Sandra dashed to the door, disengaged the lock and, unmindful of her own safety, yanked open the door and ran onto the porch.

The tableau that confronted her wide eyes sent her heartbeat into overdrive and her blood surging like ice water through her veins.

Cameron stood in the clearing near the cabin, exposed to the man standing on the far side of the large vehicle, caught in the cross hairs of the rifle nestled against his shoulder.

Sandra didn't pause to think or consider. Raising her arms and thrusting them out straight, she wrapped her left hand around her right on the butt of the handgun, took aim, held her breath and eased back the trigger.

She missed her target by a hair.

Still, her instinctive action saved the day, and her lover's life.

Zinging by as close as it did, the shot naturally distracted Slim for an instant. An instant was all Cameron required. Raising his own weapon, he took careful aim and fired.

He didn't miss. The bullet rocketed straight through Slim's right shoulder. The rifle fell to the ground. Slim followed it down. He didn't make it to the ground; he crumpled over the hood of the vehicle.

Across the short distance separating them, Sandra and Cameron stared at each other. He took two steps toward her, then stopped, slicing a look at Slim. The criminal groaned; Cameron steadied his aim on him.

At that moment, three cars, two with official emblems emblazoned on their white sides, tore, sirens wailing, up the private road. The sight of them broke the shock gripping Sandra.

She had almost killed a man!

The stark realization of how very close she had come, how very much she had wanted to take the life of another human being, made her feel physically ill.

Home. She had to go home.

The directive ringing in her head, a sob clawing at her throat, she lowered her still stiffly outstretched arms, turned and ran into the house.

Refusing to pause to think, to consider her actions or her reactions, she grabbed her jacket and dug in her handbag for car and house keys. Then, dropping the key to the cabin on the shoulder holster, she whirled and ran from the house, down the porch steps, and to her car.

"Sandra!"

Drawing in shuddering breaths, she ignored Cameron's call. Firing the engine, she turned the compact in a tight U-turn and drove down the road.

Sandra didn't so much as glance at the men standing along the side of the road, staring at her.

She didn't even glance in the rearview mirror for a backward look.

She had told Cameron she needed thinking time. Now, after being willing—no, determined—to destroy a life to preserve the life of the man she loved, she needed that time more than before.

She'd deal with it, Sandra knew. But she'd deal with it in her own time, in her own way.

At home.

Cameron knew where to find her.

Ten

Why hadn't they stayed in bed together?

The thought drifted into Cameron's mind as he stood in the open doorway to Sandra's apartment. A pang of regret clutched at his chest as his eyes noted the paleness of her cheeks, the dark smudges beneath her soft eyes.

Damn. What had he done to her?

"Hi, Annie Oakley," he said, his voice sounding strained to his own ears. "May I come in?"

A faint wisp of a smile touched her lips, and his heart, at his teasing gibe. Hope soared inside him when she nodded and stepped back, allowing him entrance.

"I missed you like hell this past week and a half," he confessed, gently closing the door behind him.

"But you didn't call, or stop by," Sandra said, motioning him into the living room.

"I was giving you the time you asked for," he said, absently taking in the clean, elegant, yet comfortable-looking decor of her home. "But I couldn't wait any longer," he admitted, offering her a coaxing smile. "I needed to see you."

"Oh, that's right, you're leaving for Pennsylvania soon." Her answering smile held acceptance. "For your brother's wedding. Jake, right?"

"Yes, but that isn't why I needed to see you." Cameron took a careful step, closing the distance between them. "I had to make certain you were all right." The evidence of her wan appearance convinced him she wasn't. "Are you having guilt fits about firing on Slim?"

"No." Sandra's voice held relieving conviction. "I read in the paper that he survived your shot."

"I planned it that way." Cameron frowned, deciding to clear up any misconceptions she might be harboring. "I don't get my kicks from killing, Sandra."

Her eyes flew wide. "I never believed you did!" she exclaimed. "Why did you think I had?"

"You hate guns."

"Yes, but..." Her voice faded, and she shrugged. "I knew what you did for a living."

He heaved a sigh. "I'm glad that's cleared up—it did have me concerned." He hazarded another step closer. "Now I'd like to clear up something else."

She didn't back away. She did arch her brows questioningly.

"It doesn't take a brick building to fall on me," he said, his tone rife with self-derision. "All it took was the sound of a gunshot."

She frowned. "I don't understand."

"Neither did I." He held his breath and took another step, bringing him to within two feet of her. "I mean, I didn't understand until then the reason you were so angry and impatient with me."

"And now you do?" She remained still.

"Hmm..." He nodded, and took a chance on touching her—just the tip of his fingers to the curve of her pale cheek; it felt like satin. Desire twisted inside him. He tamped it down, cautioning himself against screwing up.

Sandra shivered.

Encouraged, Cameron explained, "I now believe that you weren't angry because I accused you of being childish and bent out of shape about having your autonomy questioned. You were angry because I was so damn dense. I misunderstood your concern for me, my safety." He paused, then asked, "Right?" Then he held his breath.

"Yes." She smiled. "Now, will you tell me how the sound of a gunshot brought the revelation?"

The pent-up breath eased from his taut body. "Simple. You hate guns, and yet you not only handled one, but fired it with intent in defense of me."

"And I'd do it again."

Just five words, spoken with quiet conviction. Five beautiful words. Elation swept through Cameron, banishing his fear of her rejection. He took the final step necessary to sweep her into his embrace.

Sandra, his Sandra, the cool, professional, ofttimes militant lady lawyer, felt so fragile, so very delicate, lying passive against him. Cameron felt a powerful need to shelter her with his arms, protect her with his life, and adore her forever with his body.

He tightened his arms around her now trembling body, and buried his face in her scented sable hair.

Her arms curled tightly around his waist and, murmuring his name, she pressed her lips to the side of his neck.

"I love you." Cameron scoured his mind for stronger words, but there was no other way to say it. No way to dress it up, give it flourish. "Sandra, I love you."

"I love you back." She tilted her head to gaze into his eyes. "Cameron, I love you so much."

Although it was a short distance from the living room to Sandra's bedroom, it was much too far for two people, deeply in love, who had not seen each other, touched each other, kissed each other, for over a week.

As if by mutual, spoken consent, clothes were quickly discarded and they sank as one to the thickly piled springy carpet.

Mouths touched, teased, fused. Tongues tasted, dueled, plunged. Hands caressed, tormented, urged. Finally, finally, bodies angled, positioned, merged.

The coming together was glorious.

A spring storm raged overhead as Cameron cradled Sandra in his arms and carried her to bed.

Neither of them heard the storm—they were too involved in creating one of their own.

Their passion abated as the storm moved east. Exhausted, entwined in each other's arms, Cameron and Sandra fell headfirst into the sleep of utter satisfaction and contentment.

An increasingly persistent call of nature woke Sandra several hours later. Sighing in resignation, she slipped noiselessly from the bed and went into the bathroom.

Although her period was late by only a few

days, the nearly constant sensation of needing to seek relief, along with the extreme tenderness in her breasts, had convinced Sandra that she had conceived Cameron's baby.

At first, she had dismissed the idea as secret wishful thinking, reminding herself how careful Cameron had been to ensure protection.

Then she had had vivid recall of their encounters of the sensual kind while in the shower, when all thoughts and consideration of protection had been washed away by the flush of passion.

Now, experiencing her first twinge of nausea, Sandra knew without doubt that she was pregnant. Pleasure suffused her being, brought color to her cheeks and a sparkle of anticipation to her eyes.

Her baby.

Cameron's baby.

Their baby.

Nature's business taken care of, Sandra brushed her teeth, then hummed a lullaby while she luxuriated under a warm shower spray. Refreshed, excited by her secret, she sauntered into the bedroom, crawled back into bed and snuggled close to the warm body of her lover.

"Where were you?" Cameron growled in a loving tone, coiling one strong arm around her waist to draw her tightly to him. "I missed you."

"Good." Asking herself if she should tell him,

share her secret with him, she planted a kiss on his smooth, golden-hair-sprinkled chest.

He didn't give her time to tell him anything. Moving with the swiftness of the animal whose name he bore, he heaved himself up and over her.

"Good? I'll show you good," he purred.

And he did. She enjoyed every heated, open-mouthed kiss, every stroke of hand and tongue, every deep thrust of his taut body.

When it was over, and their shudders of ecstasy had slowly subsided, Sandra was spent, but exhilarated by the heady sensation of sheer feminine power.

Yes, she decided, she'd tell him. Forming the words in her head, she began, "Cam—"

"Wolves mate for life, you know," he said, raising his head to stare at her.

"Yes, I know," she said, the gleam in his blue eyes setting her pulses thundering.

"We've mated."

"Yes." A strange excitement robbed her voice of substance, making it sound whispery, barely there. "I...I know."

"Then, my sweet mate, I think you'll have to come with me to Pennsylvania." His voice held little more substance than hers. "Because I can't face the thought of being away from my mate for another week or so." The intent look in his eyes softened to one of entreaty. "Will you come with me, meet the rest of the Wolfe pack?"

"You just try to go anywhere without me," she said in a credible growl. Lifting her head, she caught his mouth in a long, hard, possessive kiss. "From now on, your Lone Wolfe days are over, Cameron Wolfe."

His laughter ringing joyously inside her head, Cameron returned her kiss with interest.

All together in one room, the Wolfe pack were more than a little overpowering.

Naturally, Sandra immediately took a liking to each and every one of them; how could she not? Though distinct and individual, each and every one of them was very much like Cameron. Tall, muscular, blond and blue-eyed, the four brothers presented a formidable, devastatingly handsome picture to the world in general—and four vastly different females in particular.

But there was one woman in the room who appeared neither impressed nor intimidated, Sandra noted with an inner smile.

Maddy Wolfe was decidedly the unopposed leader of this particular pack.

Sandra had liked Maddy from the moment Cameron proudly introduced his mother to her. Maddy was warm and welcoming, and had opened her home, and her arms, to Sandra, bestowing a brilliant smile and a quick hug on the younger woman. That had been two days ago.

At the time, Maddy had been alone in the house, which had afforded Sandra some time to get to know the other woman. It hadn't taken very long for Sandra to realize from whom Cameron had learned to be a many-faceted person, as well as a man.

That evening, Sandra had met Cameron's youngest brother, Jake, and his prospective bride, Sarah, a lovely young woman of keen intelligence and humor.

The following day, Eric had arrived, escorting his lady, Tina, who also was lovely, and intelligent, with a different, but obvious, sense of humor.

The day after that, Royce had appeared, with yet another lovely and intelligent woman in tow. Her name was Megan. She was flat-out gorgeous and intelligent, with a lively sense of humor.

Since it had turned out that, whenever they were confined together, the four brothers happily traded gibes, quips and dryly delivered insults, Sandra had decided that it was a good thing that their respective female companions all possessed a healthy sense of humor—seeing as how she couldn't imagine how they could survive otherwise.

Laughter, feminine and masculine, rang through the house. Through it all, Maddy's eyes danced with pleasure at the antics of her tall sons, and at the gentle ripostes of the younger women.

Being the only child of parents cool to emotional displays, Sandra soaked up the roisterous exchange of love and laughter like a dry sponge. She couldn't help but notice that Sarah, Tina and Megan were likewise basking in the warmth freely given by the Wolfes.

Sandra was glad she had agreed to come east with Cameron, for several reasons, the uppermost of them the whole new look and perception she received of him as he related with his family.

The Cameron she had come to know was shrewd and tough and passionate, with moments of tenderness and gentleness. The man she observed in his mother's home was the same, but with a larger, fuller personality. He was caretaker and caregiver, the son who had stepped forth to fill the gap when his strong father, Justin Wolfe, died in the line of duty.

Sandra already loved Cameron. Yet, though she would not have believed it possible, after she saw him in the role of loving son and supportive brother, the love she felt for him deepened, expanded, became all-encompassing.

Here was a man to hitch a life to.

Within two uproarious days, the assembled men and women were all chattering together like a bunch of magpies, as if they had all known each other for years.

Sandra was enjoying herself so much, she barely noticed the continuing off-and-on moments of queasiness in her stomach.

But when the nausea struck at quiet times, when she and Cameron were alone in the room they had taken in a motel just outside of town, it was a stinging reminder that she had not as yet shared her secret with him.

Although she no longer felt so much as a qualm concerning his reaction to her suspicion of pregnancy, she held off, waiting for the perfect moment to tell him he was going to be a father.

The Sunday before the wedding, they all gathered at Maddy's house for dinner. The men insisted on doing the cooking. The younger women insisted on helping. Maddy serenely directed the riotous proceedings.

It was great fun; Sandra enjoyed every minute of it, and happily raised her glass in a toast when Eric announced that he and Tina had decided to take the big step. Jake followed the announcement with one of his own, that he and Sarah were thrilled with Eric's suggestion to make it a double wedding.

After dinner, the men retired to the patio, ostensibly to discuss the new arrangements, but in reality to share a beer and rag each other.

It was late when Sandra and Cameron got back to their motel room. She was tired, but pleasantly so. He was amorous, but tenderly so.

Their loving was slow and gentle, sweet and endearing. When it was over, Cameron continued to stroke Sandra, loving her in a different way.

It was the perfect moment to share secrets. But, even as Sandra was again forming the words in her mind to tell him, Cameron confided two secrets of his own.

"It's going to be a triple wedding, you know," he said in an amusement-laced tone.

"Triple?" Sandra angled her head to stare up at him. "You mean Royce and Megan?"

"Yeah." He laughed. "He asked Jake and Eric if they'd mind while we were guzzling Mom's beer and lying to each other out on the patio after dinner."

Bemused, she laughed with him. "Does your mother know?"

He canted his head to give her a wry look. "Of course. Mom knows everything." He chuckled. "She also knows that all three of my future sisters-in-law are pregnant."

A thrill of sensation shot through Sandra. "All three of them?" she repeated, thinking the time had most definitely come for confession.

"Yes, and Mom's near delirious with excitement about it.'' He hesitated, stroking her hip. ''Er…Sandra?''

''I have something to discuss with you,''she said in a rush. ''I hope—'' that was as far as she got.

''I have something I want to ask you,'' he interrupted her to say in an attention-getting tone of urgency. He drew a breath, and then, staring intently into her eyes, quickly said, ''Sandra, you know I love you very much, don't you?''

''Yes, but…''

''Do you love me? Really love me?''

''Cameron, you know I do!'' she cried, made nervous by the intensity of his voice.

''Enough to marry me?'' he asked in a rush, then appeared to hold his breath.

Sandra went still for an instant. Then sheer joy burst through her, out of her.

''Yes! Oh, Cameron, yes, yes, yes!''

He exhaled, grinned, then laughed aloud. ''Oh, sweetheart, you can't imagine how scared I was to ask you, how scared I was you'd say no.''

Frowning, she levered herself up, unconcerned about her nakedness, to scowl at him. ''You, scared? It boggles the mind. Why would you even think I'd say no?''

''Well, honey, you're a professional, and all that.'' His smile was teasing. ''A feminist.''

She gave him a playful, but meaningful, punch on his bare shoulder.

He grabbed her and drew her mouth to his for a playful, but meaningful, kiss.

"We could make it a complete family affair," he slyly suggested. "I'm sure my brothers would be delighted with the idea."

She hesitated a moment longer, then drew a breath and took the plunge. "I suppose we might as well," she agreed. "Make it unanimous...in every aspect."

It took a frowning moment. Then Cameron's eyes flashed and widened.

"You're pregnant?"

"Well, I'm not absolutely certain yet...but I'm pretty certain."

"Sandra." He laughed. "Mom'll freak!"

"Yes, but what about you?" she asked, in a voice betraying uncertainty.

"Are you kidding?" He drew her to him, kissed her cheeks, her eyes, her nose, her mouth. "I'm already freaking. Oh, Sandra..." His voice got lost inside her mouth; it found a home in her heart.

Sandra placed a long-distance call early the next morning, to tell her parents the happy news.

There was not an unoccupied foot of space in the Sprucewood College campus chapel.

Resplendent in their bright spring finery, the female guests looked like blossoms strewn amid the more subdued shades of the gentlemen's suits and jackets.

Sunshine struck jewel tones of light through the stained-glass windows. A warm breeze wafted through the tilted panes.

Seated in the first pew, her eyes sparkling, her smile serene, Maddy turned her head to smile at the distinguished-looking couple seated opposite her across the aisle.

Sandra's parents, William and Lisa Bradley, had flown in from Paris just that morning. They were the only parents of the brides able to make the wedding.

Disappointed for the others, but happy for Sandra, Maddy nodded to the couple, then turned her gaze proudly upon her tall, stalwart, handsome blond sons.

Attired in navy blue suits, pristine white shirts and muted patterned neckties, the four brothers stood side by side in front of the small altar, facing but not seeing the assembled guests. All four pairs of gleaming blue eyes were fixed on the back of the chapel.

Jake looked nervous—but trying not to show it.

Eric looked too relaxed—a sure sign of nervousness.

Royce looked contained—another sure sign.

Cameron looked remote—a dead giveaway.

The Wolfe men were getting married—and were anxious about it.

A rustling murmur rippled through the chapel. An instant before she turned around, Maddy's eyes misted as she witnessed the blaze of love shining from the eyes of each one of her sons. A tear escaped her guard as she turned to look at the young women slowly pacing the distance along the aisle to the men.

Sarah was in the lead, her soft eyes riveted to Jake's.

Tina came second, her smile fixed on Eric.

Megan followed third, her face aglow for Royce.

Sandra was last, a picture of pure love for Cameron.

It was a beautiful quadruple wedding.

Every female cried; there were even tears in the eyes of some of the males.

The reception was more joyous and boisterous than the previous gatherings at Maddy's home. It was an absolute crush; there was only the tiniest space for dancing. No one seemed to mind.

Sandra loved every minute of it. But she wasn't sorry when, after a brief conference with his brothers, Cameron drew her aside to whisper, ''Watches have been synchronized. In precisely thirty seconds, Jake, Eric, Royce and I are going to grab our wives and break out of this joint.''

Sandra was breathless, and still laughing, long

after she had kissed, and Cameron had shaken hands with, her parents, and all the others had all hugged Maddy in turn, then, calling their good-byes, literally run to their separate cars.

After the four of them had given a final wave to one another, the four vehicles took off in different directions.

Cameron swept her into his arms the moment he shut the motel-room door. "You're so beautiful," he murmured. Then, in the exact same way he had the day he arrived at the cabin, he swung her around, singing, "Dance with me, I want my arms about you…" He broke off to declare, "I love you, my beautiful wife."

"And I love you, my handsome husband," Sandra vowed, smiling up at him through the tears of happiness welling in her shining eyes.

Cameron brushed his lips over hers. "Oh, my love, I'm so glad this Wolfe won't be alone anymore."

*   *   *   *   *

Turn the page for
a sneak preview of

Ryan Objects,

bestselling author Joan Hohl's
delightful contribution to

CARRIED AWAY,

the first Silhouette Romance
short-story collection,

also featuring *New York Times*
bestselling author Kasey Michaels.

This innovative family-theme duo is
on sale in April 2000.

And look for a brand-new
Joan Hohl Silhouette Desire novel,
available in late 2000.

Lingerie. Lindsey's Intimates. He should have known. But not just any lingerie. Oh, no, Ryan Callahan mused, noting the obvious quality of the merchandise.

Sauntering inside, his gaze made a slow sweep of the stock folded neatly on display tables, hanging on racks strategically positioned on the available floor space and against the walls.

Ryan was the sole male in the store, yet he didn't feel in the least uncomfortable or embarrassed. Strolling toward the sales counter, he studied the variety of garments on offer with a practiced eye. Having been a bachelor for twenty-six years, and being a healthy normal male not inclined toward celibacy, he had seen, touched, removed his share of alluring under things.

Maybe he was old-fashioned, he reflected, his gaze skimming over the more revealing pieces before settling for a moment on a rather demure, but, in his estimation, much more provocative nightgown and negligee ensemble displayed in a small separate section labeled For the Bride. The set was of cotton, fine but not see-through, white, flowing, tantalizing.

It occurred to him that the woman he'd come to see had at least one point in her favor. She had excellent taste…at least insofar as her merchandise went.

The thought made him recall his purpose in being there. He dismissed the stock and homed in on the counter.

A saleswoman was bagging a customer's dainty, transparent purchases. Ignoring the young customer, and the unmentionables, he evaluated the saleswoman.

Obviously not the owner, Ryan decided, taking a closer, appreciative look at the woman. Thirtysomething, he figured. About a foot shorter than his six-two, but every inch packed solid with feminine allure. Russet-shaded hair. Dark eyes, probably bittersweet chocolate brown, the kind that used to be called bedroom eyes. Delicate features. Creamy complexion.

Ryan experienced an unexpected and surprising

jolt of physical response—unexpected because a sexual reaction had been the last thing on his mind; surprising because it had been long months since he had felt a similar sensation.

Damn. He didn't have time for a dalliance, he told himself. He had a *mother* to contend with.

So where in the hell was the woman anyway? He didn't have all night. He had a dinner to attend.

Even as the grousing thought flitted through Ryan's mind, another clerk, older, more matronly in appearance, rounded the counter to take command of the register.

Ah-ha, the mother.

The older woman spoke to the other clerk. Thirty-something nodded and flashed a smile.

Oh, have mercy, Ryan thought, muscles clenching against a hunger unrelated to his empty stomach.

Thirty-something of the teeth-melting smile stepped to a door set in the wall a few feet behind the register. Ryan cut a quick, encompassing glance over her well-rounded form, clothed to advantage in a neat navy-blue pin-striped suit and tailored crisp-white shirt.

The clenching sensation continued as Ryan strode to the counter.

"May I help you, sir?" The older woman's voice was polite, pleasant, but unremarkable, not at all like the sultry, yet effervescent tones on his answering machine, which had brought him to this store.

"I hope so," Ryan said, frowning at the sudden certainty that this wasn't the woman he sought. "I'm looking for Mrs. Lindsey Dawson."

"I'm Lindsey Dawson," the younger woman said, as she turned from the door she had just opened.

She most definitely was, Ryan thought, feeling another jolt of response. He'd have recognized her voice anywhere.

"What can I do for you?" She smiled.

Ryan stifled a groan. In that instant, he could think of many things she could do for him, not the least of which was modeling that white negligee ensemble.

"We need to talk," he said in tones roughened by impatience and suppressed anger at himself for his stupid response to her, and, unreasonably at her for causing the response.

"We do?" Perfectly arched brows rose over dark brown eyes sparked by an inner amusement. "What about?"

"I'm Ryan Callahan," he said with blunt authority, as if that explained everything, which, of course, it did.

Her eyes widened, her smile dazzled, and her distinctive voice tantalized his senses. "Logan's father."

"Yes. Logan's father."

She glanced around, noting, as Ryan did, the curiosity on the older woman's face. "We can't talk here. We'd be in Betty's way," she said, smiling nicely at the woman. "I…er, was just leaving to go to dinner. Would you care to join me?"

That was a leading question, if he had ever heard one. His revitalized libido was signaling willingness to join her in the most basic of ways. Disgusted with his juvenile reaction to her, Ryan gave himself a mental shake. He was about to decline her invitation, but like quicksilver, changed his mind.

"Of course, if you have other plans…" she said as her voice trailed off.

"No." He shook his head, the decision made.

Minutes later, Ryan retraced the path back to his car, lecturing himself in time with his rapid steps. The woman was undoubtedly married, he reminded himself in an effort to quash the feeling of anticipation sizzling inside him. She was a mother. The mother of the woman now married to his son.

She didn't look old enough to be the mother of anybody's daughter-in-law. She certainly didn't look anything near what he had been expecting.

Damn.